# BEST
# WOMEN'S EROTICA
# OF THE YEAR

VOLUME FIVE

# BEST

## WOMEN'S EROTICA

## OF THE YEAR

VOLUME FIVE

# BEST
# WOMEN'S EROTICA
# OF THE YEAR

## VOLUME FIVE

*Edited by*

RACHEL KRAMER BUSSEL

**CLEIS**
PRESS

Published in the United States by Cleis Press, an imprint of Start Midnight, LLC, 221 River Street, 9th Floor, Hoboken, NJ 07030.

Cover design: Allyson Fields
Cover photograph: iStock
Text design: Frank Wiedemann
First Edition.
10 9 8 7 6 5 4 3 2 1

Trade paper ISBN: 978-1-62778-290-6
E-book ISBN: 978-1-62778-503-7

Brief quotations in "Outlaws," by Angel Leigh McCoy, from *You* by Anonymous (Bantam Books, 1975).

# CONTENTS

# CONTENTS

# INTRODUCTION:
# TOTALLY OUTRAGEOUS
# IN EVERY WAY

If you're ready for some outrageous sex, you've come to the right place. For *Best Women's Erotica of the Year, Volume 5,* I asked authors to get as wild and over-the-top as they could. The hot fantasies and incredibly arousing tales they delivered achieved those ends in ways that went far beyond my expectations.

We start out with a business negotiation that takes a turn I imagine isn't an everyday occurrence in your office (though lucky you if it is!) in "Terms," by Sierra Simone, before turning to a special kind of dirty talk in "Just Inappropriate," by Alexa J. Day. Then Sabrina Sol brings us a spin on the Oval Office that's totally steamy in "At the Pleasure of the President."

The twist in the futuristic "Outlaws," by Angel Leigh McCoy, offers a striking take on the power of the written word and the need for intimate human contact, while "Nymph and Satyr," by Justine Elyot, will likely have you wanting to visit an art museum very soon.

When you call a phone sex line, who's the woman working on the other end? What are her fantasies, dreams, and desires? These are some of the questions best-selling author Balli Kaur Jaswal explores in "After Midnight" (and if you haven't read her novel, *Erotic Stories for Punjabi Widows,* it's a fabulous story). For a sweet and definitely dirty spin on workplace lust, "Frosting," by Kathleen Delaney-Adams, takes us on a lesbian sex fest in a cupcake bakery that will have you licking your lips.

In Lee Minxton's "Dirty Girls Always Go to Heaven," Laney shows Erik what happens to "boys who tease" (spoiler alert: a very hot activity that's a popular sexual fantasy).

Those with a mermaid fetish or who are curious about how mermaids get it on will adore the beautifully written "If the Ocean," by Loretta Black. Then Emerald gives us "Something New" as a couple turns from monogamy to a different way of expressing themselves sexually. Travel back in time to "The Summer of 1669" in Jayne Renault's story of forbidden love and desire.

In Anna Mia Hansen's moving "Broken Thing Fixed," Sigrid helps Bjorn, while helping herself as well, while in "One Interpretation," by Stella Harris, a professor gets an unexpected visitor who turns her approach to teaching, and sex, on its head.

In A. Zimmerman's kinky "Peripheral Voyeurism," Claire attends a BDSM party with Ryan and pushes herself and her obedience. An exhibitionist discovers the thrill of showing off, naked, in "Dancing with Myself," by Quinn LeStrange.

Anyone who's ever been through the agony and the ecstasy of moving will appreciate the sexy thrill that's uncovered in "Vintage Treasures," by Angora Shade.

In "Sheer Pleasure," by A. Z. Louise, "enby princex" Billie discovers the scintillating allure of a certain type of sexy clothing that changes everything.

In "The First Moment I Saw You," prolific romance novelist Caridad Piñeiro puts a very hot spin on instant attraction.

Popular erotic romance novelist CD Reiss gives us "The King's Return," in which an estranged couple discovers that the power of BDSM still binds them—with a twist.

To round out this collection, we've upped the ante on the outrageousness, with a ripped-from-real-life tale from award-winning porn star and director Joanna Angel, "One Last Gang Bang," and another portrait of a specific subculture, the world of aerialists, in the lesbian public sex extravaganza "Spin," by Lauren Emily.

As I hope I've made clear, there are many ways to be outrageous on display here, sometimes literally, sometimes with more nuanced approaches. All of these stories, though, have characters who are anything but prim and demure. They sometimes have to overcome hurdles, internal and external, to pursuing sexual pleasure, but when they do, they find themselves relishing the kind of bliss they crave.

I hope you enjoy these stories as much as I did. Please keep in touch by emailing me at bweoftheyear@gmail.com to share your favorites and what you'd like to see in future volumes, and visit bweoftheyear.com to learn more about the series.

Rachel Kramer Bussel
Atlantic City, New Jersey

# TERMS

## Sierra Simone

The sound of turning pages filled the room like a symphony.

Sarah Markham leaned back against her desk with undisguised satisfaction, arms folded across her chest. She'd made sure to have the men sit as she stood, made sure the offices were empty, made sure to dress for the occasion in her favorite dress and the shoes she liked to think of as her War Heels.

Jake looked up at her. "These terms are outrageous," he said.

"Nevertheless, they are the terms," Sarah answered.

She uncrossed her arms to straighten her hem in a display of cool nonchalance, and she didn't miss how the eyes of the three men in front of her went to the crisp line of fabric against her stockinged legs. How they went still at the flash of pale thigh. Any other time, it would have infuriated her; this was her office, her goddamn company, three years of the hardest work of her fucking life, and she would have respect. She tolerated nothing less from her inferiors, clients, and competitors.

Tonight was different. Tonight, these three men could look all they liked. Tonight she had them exactly where she wanted them.

She would get her respect, but first she'd get her revenge.

Both Marq and Brady looked just as unhappy flipping through the deal memo as Jake, but they had the good sense not to challenge her just yet. Jake had always been the impetuous one, the one full of temper and impatience, but Marq was the CFO of their company and dealt solely in practicalities and pragmatics, as did Brady, their COO. They both now gazed at her with distinct wariness as Jake tossed the memo on the coffee table in front of their armchairs.

"We can't do this," said the CEO. His voice was flat and edged with cold fury. "You know we can't. The shareholders wouldn't allow it. Being bought and stripped off for parts would be better."

"Hmm," Sarah said, pretending to take this under consideration for the first time. Marq's wariness seemed to sharpen into suspicion as he watched her straighten and walk around her desk. She opened a drawer and removed another sheaf of papers.

"I do have another offer," she said. "However, it is very unconventional, so I understand if you'd rather just leave."

But they wouldn't leave, Sarah knew, and they didn't. Jake's face was no less furious when she passed out the new memos, but she could see the desperation behind the fury. Their company was failing, and hers was thriving. They had a bankruptcy lawyer on retainer, and they'd knocked on every door there was that wasn't hers . . . and they were out of any options that left them both the company and their pride.

So they'd surrendered their pride and come to her, just as she'd known they would. And she would have a lot more than their pride by the time they were finished.

She had to admit to herself that it was more thrilling than she'd dreamed to watch their expressions as they read the new memo. She nearly laughed when Brady looked up at her with stunned incredulity, and then his eyes dipped back down to her hemline.

They had always liked the way she looked, even when she was an intern working for them, and it had been so exciting to feel their eyes on her back then.

It was even better now.

"This is harassment," Jake said. She was gratified to see his hands were shaking. "Blackmail."

"Yes," she said.

"It's wrong, Sarah."

She thought about this for a minute. "Yes," she agreed.

That had rather been the point, after all. To be wrong.

Jake struggled for words, but Marq didn't. "This is legally unenforceable," he pointed out. "We can sign every single page and renege on every single one of your demands, because no court is going to support this. No lawyer would even try."

"You're right," Sarah concurred. "But if you look carefully, you'll notice I only need your signature on the thirty-day non-compete. That means you are not allowed to take any definitive or permanent action with the company until the non-compete expires, and at the end of that period, I'll purchase your company with all the conditions you see listed below."

Their eyes flicked back down, and she knew they couldn't believe what they were reading. The conditions were unbelievably good—like nothing they'd get anywhere else. They'd retain almost full control of the company and they'd be shielded from the usual slate of cost-cutting and downsizing measures.

Sarah wasn't heartless. The employees of Jake's company had never been her intended victims, and she'd like to do right by them.

"Of course," Sarah added slowly, "I'll only choose to purchase if you meet those 'legally unenforceable' demands."

Jake's hands were clenched tightly around the paper, a tightness echoed by his mouth and eyes. Christ, he was handsome when he was angry. "You're not fighting fair," he said.

Their eyes met across the room. "Well, I learned from the best," said Sarah.

He looked away first.

"Let's get one thing clear," she said, looking at each of them. "If you don't take my deal and declare bankruptcy instead, you will all be fine. You have more than enough money and prospects, and it may be embarrassing, but that's the worst it will be. There's no reason to agree to my deal out of fear."

"What about anger?" Jake muttered.

Sarah smiled, and it was the smile of a woman used to the sight of seas parting in front of her—seas that she'd parted herself. "Yes," she said, heat gathering low in her belly as she thought about an angry Jake underneath her . . . or above her . . . or tied up and glaring from her bed. "I'll take your anger."

"So you're saying we have a choice," Marq clarified.

"A real choice," she said, not wanting any confusion on their part. "You can leave right now. In fact, you can leave any time during the thirty days without any repercussions."

"But then you won't buy the company," Marq replied.

Sarah inclined her head in agreement. "Precisely so."

Jake made a derisive noise. "You know very well that we can't walk away from a deal like this."

"Oh, but you can. I won't punish you for choosing to walk away. So if you take it, take it because you want to and you want what I'm offering."

Brady—who'd always been the slightly puppyish one, the blond-haired, blue-eyed, overgrown frat boy—blinked at her. "And this deal? Is it really what's written down here?"

"Yes," she answered simply.

Pink bloomed high on his fair cheeks, and for the first time, the men looked at each other, and also for the first time, she could see them actually considering it. Thinking about what it would mean.

They seemed to share some kind of wordless communication, and when Jake looked back at her, there was both hunger and fury in the clench of his jaw and the shine of his eyes.

"We'll do it."

"Sign the papers," she said softly. She'd never take Jake Costa at his word again, and he seemed to realize this because there was a touch of guilt to the way he broke their stare to reach for a pen to sign the memo.

"Thirty days," Brady read aloud. "We belong to you for thirty days."

Sarah picked at a pleat of her dress. "*Belong* is not the word I'd use. You'll be available to me both here in my office and at home to satisfy me within certain reasonable parameters of time, but otherwise your movements and actions will be fully yours."

Brady shifted in his seat, and Sarah was interested to note the heat crawling up his neck. She felt heat everywhere too, between her legs and at the tips of her breasts and, strangest of all, deep in her chest near her heart. Perhaps everyone felt that way when they finally got what they wanted. There couldn't be any other reason that she could discern.

"Do you want . . . all three of us at once?" Brady asked, his voice coming out a bit strangled. "The memo is unclear."

"Sometimes I'll only want one of you to service me. Sometimes I'll want all three." She couldn't help the smile that curved across her mouth then, and she didn't know if it was because the future was now filled with the promise of sex and power, or because this future was currently torturing the three men in front of her with a delicious mix of lust and discomfort. "If you'll recall," she added, "I've been with you all at the same time before. It was—"

"—three years ago," Jake cut in. He gave her a look that intensified the burning near her heart. "I haven't forgotten, Sarah. None of us have."

They'd certainly seemed to do a good job of pretending to forget then, Sarah thought bitterly. But she'd turned that pain into anger, and then turned that anger into the drive to build her own firm, and this was the only outlet for all that hurt and fury that she would allow herself.

Thirty days. Three men at her fingertips, available with hands and mouths and cocks whenever she wanted. She'd fuck them right out of her system and then go back to building her empire.

The men shared one final look, but it was a foregone conclusion. Even sitting, it was easy to see that their cocks had gone heavy and thick, that their pupils had blown out into huge pools of lust, and they couldn't stop shifting—Brady crossing and uncrossing his legs, and Marq bouncing a foot in what looked like eager anticipation, and Jake's left fist clenching and unclenching on his knee.

With some rustling and scratching and fluttering, the papers were signed and set on the table. Jake stood up and walked to where she leaned against her desk; even in her War Heels, he towered over her. She gazed up at him in frank appreciation—the broad shoulders and strong neck, the cut jaw and perfectly straight nose. The usual rash of dark stubble and hair that was rumpled from his frustration and desperation. He had olive skin, dark hair, and dark eyes—eyes that were flashing now in a combination of temper and lust that made Sarah's pulse race.

"So you've got us now," he said. "What are you planning to do to us?" He leaned forward, a hand on either side of her hips, his thigh slipping between her own to part her legs. His mouth dropped to her ear, breath and lips and the faintest brush of stubble tickling her flesh. "And *why* are you doing it, Sarah, my lovely? Why all this?"

He asked it so only she could hear, but she didn't answer quietly. "You know why, Jake. You goddamn know very well why."

He froze at that and she straightened up, forcing him to take a step back, and she leveled a look at Brady and Marq. "Last chance," she told them. "This is your last chance to walk away completely before it ever even begins."

"No, I'm ready to start," Marq said in a deep voice. He unfolded himself from the chair and walked over to her and Jake. He was as meticulously groomed as Jake was rough—his hair closely cut, his face clean shaven, the collar of his shirt a blinding line of snow against his dark brown skin. Brady joined him.

"Me too," Brady echoed. "I'm ready."

She allowed herself the unabashed pleasure of taking them in, these tall and handsome men now exactly where and how she wanted them. They were hers now, and god, she needed them. Her body had been aching for release for so long that she'd almost forgotten what release felt like—but building a kingdom from the ground up had taken all her time, leaving nothing but the occasional fuck from whichever hookup app was the most convenient. But they never were satisfying—not satisfying the way that night had been three years ago. The night she'd never been able to truly hate or regret.

Not really.

Just as she could never really hate or regret knowing any of the men in front of her.

"Good," she said, the burning in her chest so hot she felt like she might catch fire. She needed to get control of the situation—and of herself most of all.

She parted her legs in a deliberate movement that had all of the men going very still—the kind of stillness one associates with deadly animals and birds of prey. "Brady," she said quietly. "On your knees."

Brady hesitated, but when Sarah pulled up her hem to reveal her bare pussy, a shudder passed through his entire body and he fell to his knees.

"That's right," she said as he slid his large hands around her to cup her bottom. "Just like that . . . *fuck*. Fuck yes."

His surprisingly soft lips brushed against her exposed, swollen clit, and now it was her turn to shudder. She hadn't had this in how long? Months at least, and even then, it hadn't been *this,* the dual pleasure of having a willing mouth service her pussy while the men around her loomed with hungry expressions and ready erections, promising even more.

And then Brady's tongue breached her seam, and her head dropped back even as her hand wove through his thick blond hair to hold him more tightly to her.

"Oh god, that feels so good. Lick me. Eat me."

Jake growled next to her, and she opened her eyes to see him close and furious . . . and jealous.

She found she rather liked the idea of him being jealous.

"Do you want to taste me?" she asked.

His voice was rough and needy when he spoke. "I want to fuck you."

"When I say you can," she said, and he scowled.

"You're so sexy when you're unhappy," she purred, running her fingers over his torso, enjoying the feel of the firm muscles underneath. "It's honestly not much incentive for me to keep you otherwise."

His head ducked when her fingers reached his belt, and when she finally palmed the hardness there, his breathing gave a sharp jerk and started coming in uneven gasps. She laughed at the pain on his face when she pulled her hand away.

God, the next month was going to be fun.

"All of you undress," she said. "I want to see you."

Brady scrambled to it, boyish and clumsy and seemingly just excited about the possibilities being naked would afford, and Marq undressed as he did everything—with care and deliberation. But

Jake—Jake undressed with barely restrained rage, obviously furious at being directed to do something so humiliating, ripping off his tie and toeing off his shoes in jerky, powerful movements that had Sarah's body responding immediately. She liked his power, his volatility. She liked that temper, that barely contained strength. She wanted it underneath her, moving between her thighs as she rode him, and she wanted that proud heart beating fast under her palm.

If she hadn't killed any such ideas inside herself three years ago, she might have believed she was in love with him. She might have believed she was in love with all of them, in different ways.

Soon, the three men stood before her in nothing but muscles and gleaming skin, the malest parts of them standing at attention, rigid and swollen and tight. She almost had to catch her breath because the men were so beautiful, so sleek and strong and so very, very hers.

She parted her legs again as a signal to Brady, and, good boy that he was, he knew what she wanted, and soon he was under the skirt of her dress giving her the relief she craved. "At night," she said, struggling to keep her voice steady through the onslaught of sensation Brady was giving her, "I'll expect help undressing. You may start now."

Marq got there first, reaching behind her neck and pulling her thick fall of hair to one side, careful not to snag any in her zipper as he tugged it down her back. They lifted the dress above her head, and soon she was only in stockings, heels, and a delicate lace bra that did nothing to hide the hard points of her nipples.

Unable to resist the pulled furls and their ceaseless ache for touch, she cupped her breasts, and then was surprised and pleased to feel Jake yank her hands away and replace them with his own—as if he were even jealous of her touching herself. "These are mine," he said on a groan, as their weight settled in his hands. "*You* are mine."

Her chest seared at the same time as her temper flared. "No, *you* are mine. Check the papers again, Costa."

His eyes burned into hers, and at that moment, Brady slid a finger inside her, working her from the inside as he returned his mouth to her clit. Sarah grabbed on to Jake's arms for balance, her knees going weak, and Marq pressed in with kisses and nips along her neck.

When the orgasm came, it ripped through her like a storm, and still her eyes never left Jake's. Still he stared at her, like he could *make* her his if only he tried hard enough. There was something extremely compelling about that. Something that made her chest clench again.

She rode out the orgasm clinging to Jake and with Marq's mouth trailing kisses all over her shoulders and arms. When she finally finished, Jake surged forward, ready to fuck her. It had been like that three years ago too—what had started as her taking notes in a late-running executive evening had turned into a frantic, fumbling conflagration. And Jake had been the spark, the bellows, the everything that fanned each moment into flames.

He still was, but this time she was in control. She put a hand on his chest to hold him back. "Marq," she said. "There are condoms in the upper desk drawer."

She didn't have to tell him twice—he got to the drawer and back as quickly as he could move, and she was waiting for him, squirming in anticipation as he rolled on the condom and moved between her legs.

"Sarah," Jake growled from beside her. His impatience thrilled her.

"Only when I say you can," she reminded him as Marq rubbed the slick, wide head of himself against her wet opening and she shivered.

"I want to come again," she told Marq.

Marq's face pinched in concentration as he eased himself inside, pushing inch by thick inch until he was completely buried. Brady, his mouth still wet from her, stood next to them, one big hand lazily working along his length as he watched his business partner stretch her cunt.

But Jake didn't touch himself or her. He stood completely still, every muscle etched in frustration, his dark eyes full of some emotion she couldn't name. He watched as Marq fucked her hard against the desk, as Marq reached between them and rubbed her clit, as she came with a low moan and Marq followed her, pumping his release into the condom as he stopped moving and stared down where they were joined.

When he pulled out, Jake grabbed her wrist, and there was a hectic hunger in his face. "Say it, Sarah," he pleaded. "Let me fuck you."

Sated now, and deeply pleasured, she felt indulgent. There had been times when she imagined torturing him for hours—days even—keeping his cock hard and ready for her but not allowing him the privilege of her pussy until he'd begged and groveled. But there would be time yet for begging and groveling—she wanted to feel all that passion and pride underneath her *now*.

"Put on a condom," she said. "Then lie on the floor and wait for me."

It earned her a frown—Jake was a man who fucked on his feet, not on his back—but the delicious struggle between his ego and his need didn't last long. And it was easy to see why: his cock was so hard that it had gone a dark red, the crown fat and shiny and wet, and he couldn't even roll on the condom without hissing at his own touch. And his body was clenched so tight with restrained desire that even after he stretched out along her rug, his belly was ridged with hard, tense muscles.

After stopping to whisper instructions to Brady and Marq, Sarah eased off the desk and walked over to the man who three years ago had given her a night of wickedness and then broken her heart. She stood over him, pressing a stockinged foot against his cock, which wrung a groan out of him, and then moved it up his muscled abdomen to his chest. She liked the way it looked and felt, her small foot framed by all that broad strength, her small foot keeping him pinned helplessly to the floor while his cock ached and bobbed at her nearness.

Would she have always wanted this? Even if Jake and the others hadn't treated her so indifferently, so coldly, after that night? Maybe she would have always eventually grown to crave the sight of a man trembling with fury and lust and defeat in front of her. And maybe it didn't matter.

"Get down here," Jake said in a harsh voice, reaching to yank her down on top of him, and she let him, because she wanted to feel his strength, his desperate need.

He hauled her against his chest, his hands threading through her hair and pulling her face close to his, taking her mouth in a kiss unlike any other she'd ever had. *Mine,* his mouth said, and *mine,* hers said back, not with words but with nips and silky, tangling tongues and quick, hungry breaths. She liked that battle, she liked the fight in him, and she liked it even more knowing that she would win. She would make this proud man hers—for the next month, at least.

"Why are you doing this?" he asked again, breaking their kiss and raking a fierce gaze over her.

"Because I want you," she said honestly. "Because I wanted you three years ago and you didn't want me, and I vowed that one day I'd change that."

His eyes searched hers. "We always wanted you, Sarah. *I* always wanted you. But we didn't know how . . . It was the first time the three of us had been with a woman together, and we didn't know how to be around each other after that, much less you. When you left . . ." His voice broke off. "When you left, I knew I'd ruined something important. I knew I'd fucked up in a way I'd regret forever."

Her breath caught. She'd honestly never thought about *them,* never considered that they'd crossed some personal Rubicons of their own that night. But it had all happened so fast, too fast, and there'd been no time for anything but finally touching and tasting and grabbing hold of the desire that had stalked the four of them since she started working there.

"I'm sorry," Jake admitted, and she heard the words echoed by Brady and Marq. "I'm sorry."

She didn't answer. She couldn't, and maybe she didn't need to, at least not with her voice. She gave Jake a lingering bite on that full lower lip of his and then pushed herself onto the thick, latex-sheathed pole behind her.

Jake's back arched off the ground at the hot swallow of her cunt, and Sarah's back arched too, her fingertips digging into the warmth of his chest, and this was a new Rubicon, right here, right now. Not forgiveness, maybe, but it wasn't only revenge anymore either. With Jake as a steed of taut lust underneath her, and Marq at her side, kissing along her neck and fondling her full, aching breasts, and Brady behind her, a bottle of something from her drawer in hand—something better than forgiveness or revenge ignited between them.

Something right.

Jake's large hands were gentling her thighs and hips as Brady began opening her ass with his fingers. She felt so *full,* so pampered, and when Brady pushed the slick, blunt head of his cock against her rear entrance, she felt no fear because these men were hers and they'd never hurt her.

Brady's legs tangled over Jake's behind her, and then, with the same stretch and bite of pain she'd felt three years ago, she was cradling both of them inside her body. "Make me come," she mumbled, shivering, sweating. "Make me come so hard I scream."

It didn't take long. She slumped forward onto Jake's naked chest as he and Brady found a rhythm that suited them, and she knew they wouldn't last long either, not with how tight and hot and slick it was. Not with her squirming in agonized sensation between them and Marq fucking his fist as he bent over to kiss her everywhere. As the orgasm started so deep in her body that she was sure she'd break apart, Marq let go with a low grunt, hot stripes of his release painting her hips and the hair-dusted thighs of his friends.

Sarah wailed against Jake's chest as the first wave took her, her vision crowding with static and her blood pounding in her ears. She writhed between the two men, unable to bear it. It was too much, too much, and she felt like a leaf, fluttering wildly on the wind, helpless and out of control.

The men did their best to soothe her, to hold her close and reassure her, but soon they came too—Brady with a series of fast thrusts and a low moan, and Jake with strong arms crushing her to his chest as he muttered a string of rough curses, his hips rolling up into her the entire time.

And then it was done. They were spent, sweaty and clammy and lax, and they stayed for a moment that way, the three men cradling Sarah between them, dropping slow kisses along her back and neck and shoulders, until she could think clearly again.

She lifted her head to meet Jake's eyes, and what she saw there made her chest burn like it never had before.

"Let's go home," he said in a low, graveled voice, and the men helped Sarah to her feet after cleaning up, and they dressed her, as tenderly and carefully as any attendants. And then they went home, where they had more than a night waiting for them. They had a month.

And what a month it would be.

# JUST INAPPROPRIATE

Alexa J. Day

Watching him undress usually distracts me. It's soothing, this part of our evening ritual. He silently empties his pockets and slides his belt free of the loops. I steal glances at his face in the mirror when I'm not studying the movement of his shoulders and back under that plain white shirt.

Everything has its own place on the dresser. The worn leather wallet first, followed by an untidy mound of change. His keys form a pyramid next to them. The metal catch of his watchband snaps in the stillness, and he shakes it off his wrist before he sets it on top of the wallet. I think the watch face even points the same direction every night.

I completed my part of the ritual when I stepped out of my shoes and hoisted myself onto the mattress. It probably doesn't seem high up off the floor to him. People still ask if he played basketball here in the years before he joined the faculty. He does have that look about him. Long fingers and big, broad palms. The lean strength of him. Wavy brown hair and quick blue eyes.

We'll sit here for a little while, still mostly dressed on top of the navy-blue comforter, and we'll talk about today's unfinished business or the book on his nightstand. I'm surprised by how much I enjoy this winding down of the day. By the time he turns out the light and reaches for me, I feel like the two of us are a mated pair, alone together in the world. We'll abandon our daylight selves and fall into each other, suddenly restless and ravenous.

That's how it usually works. Tonight, something's in the way.

The mattress dips beneath his weight as he sits on the edge to take off his shoes, and the pressure of unspoken words becomes more than I can stand.

"That couple tonight."

He looks over his shoulder at me, his ankle on his knee. "What couple?"

I wish I could let this go. "Older couple. Preppie clothes. Over by the bar."

"Oh. Those two." He drops his socks right next to the hamper before joining me on the bed. "Looking at us."

"Yeah." I ease over next to him, my hip against his. "You know them?"

"No. You?"

"No." The nervous sound I make almost passes for laughter. "So if we don't know them, there's really only one reason they were staring at us like that."

I expect him to suggest another reason. He's an eternal optimist, but not a clueless one, and if he didn't know there was an elephant in every room we entered, we wouldn't still be together. He knows this college town better than I do, though. Maybe they're parents of students, or they're alumni, or they're interested in something other than my being a black woman sharing a tiny table in a darkened bar with a white man. I can still be wrong about all this.

I've never brought this up during the evening ritual, and it feels blasphemous. I'm about to apologize for saying anything at all when he turns to me.

"Have you considered that they think you're too young for me?"

His voice is firm, as it might be for a confident but misinformed student. If he weren't smiling at me right now, his tone would give me a flashback to law school, which still has the power to haunt me after all these years. My face grows warm, just as it did then when easy answers deserted me under the scrutiny of my class-mates and a stern professor.

"Honestly," he says, "that was the only thing I used to think when people stared at us."

"They think I'm too young for you."

He settles back onto the pillows and nods.

His comfort in the brief silence stirs my curiosity. "Is that . . . something you think about?"

"That you're too young for me?" He grins at his own joke, no doubt waiting for me to protest that we are the same age.

"A younger girl across the table. On your arm."

In his bed.

His laughter is a rich, rolling wave. "I like this job. So no."

"Not like that." I shift over onto my hip. His eyes slide over to me. "I'm not asking if you think about doing anything. I'm asking if you think about it generally."

"You want to know if I fantasize about younger girls."

"Not illegal. Just inappropriate." I can't believe how easily he's guided me from casual racism to the content of his fantasies. "The thought doesn't excite you?"

Something darker waits back there, hidden away from me behind his placid eyes. I've been trying to get to his secret stash of fantasies for months, the closely guarded hoard of desires that he uses to gratify his powerful mind when he's not in bed with me.

He already knows everything I want. The dirty things I like to hear were just another language for him, something to practice and repeat until he achieved mastery of it, until even his thoughts were possessed by words no longer foreign.

I want a chance to become fluent in his language, but first I must hear him speak it.

His smile is almost innocent. "Not even a little."

It's a badly constructed lie, but it's served us both well. I am no longer thinking about that couple who stared at us, and soon we're talking about that stupid reality show we're supposedly too smart to watch.

I think I love him. It's too soon to say I love him.

Before long, we've finished debating the relative merits of the two Chinese restaurants nearest his apartment and he shifts on the bed to rest his head on my shoulder. I stroke his hair. My fingertips slide over the firm waves, shot through with silver. His chest rises and falls on a deep breath.

"It does excite me."

"What does?"

The bed creaks underneath him until he's sitting up again, looking down at me. Not a trace of a grin to lighten his expression this time.

The weight of his confession rests on my chest. "I see."

"You know I—"

I press my fingertips to his lips. "Don't. Don't be decent. Tell me."

He gazes up at the ceiling, his long fingers laced on his flat stomach, and his eyes drift shut. He'll drop into that fantasy soon enough.

Not soon enough for me.

"That couple tonight." I feel like a hypnotist or something, weaving a seductive suggestion. "Let's say you're right."

His mouth curves into a wicked grin, and dark lashes flutter on his cheek.

"They think that girl you're with is too young."

"She is. Way too young."

I want to see the girl across the table, and I'm surprised when my thoughts produce someone who looks like Alice in Wonderland. A wide-eyed blonde, someone as far removed from me as this behavior would have been from mine when I was her age.

"How does it feel, robbing the cradle?"

"Scandalous. They don't like it. But as long as she wants it, they can't stop me."

I stretch my legs out alongside his. He reaches for me. His big palm slides over the curves of my calf and thigh before it settles behind my knee.

"And she wants it?"

"Oh yes. Very much."

I see all of it now. The awestruck girl across the table from him. A disapproving couple who can't stop my professor boyfriend from fucking her. My pulse quickens.

"They wonder what you're doing with a girl that young."

"They know what I'm doing with her." Illicit desire darkens his voice. "They know."

"How did this start? I know she didn't seduce you."

"No. No, she didn't."

"Tell me about the first time you kissed her." I bite back the suggestions that bloom in my imagination. This world and this girl belong to him. I'm a visitor in the darkened corner of his mind, my hands squeezed between my thighs.

"She's in my office. I'm the only one in the department with hours on Friday afternoon. We're alone up here. We're on the same side of the desk so I can see her notes."

She's not just a girl. She's a student. Ever present but forbidden.

And yet here she is with him in that narrow, paper-strewn space. His sleeves rolled up over his forearms. Her hands trembling on his chest even as she reaches up to meet his kiss. And they're alone. He wouldn't even have to shut the door.

"She's had boys before, guys her age." His warm voice curls around me as I watch her touch her lips to his. "She wants more. She doesn't know what yet. Something they can't give her because they don't know how."

"But you can." I link my fingers with his. "You know what she wants."

I know it, too. She wants more than the hot, rhythmic grunting of a mindless partner, pawing at her with sticky hands and growling demands for baseless adulation. I know she wants more than that because I've had more than that. This girl's longing is nameless but real enough to burn.

"Her tongue. She holds it at the back of her mouth when she kisses." The pressure of his hand on mine increases. "Her lips. Tight together. Like she's holding something in her mouth and doesn't want it to escape."

"Tight around your cock, too." It's the first thing in my mind, and I can't stop it from spinning out into speech.

He sighs. "She's hungry. Greedy. After that first time, she can't get enough. God. She'll go all night."

He falls silent again, this fantasy gliding to a stop. My mouth is open to encourage him when he opens his eyes. His arms wind around me, and I see myself reflected in his gaze. Not the world-weary attorney ready to take command.

A youthful girl, her smooth brown face uncreased and open. Starving for something she's never tasted.

I'm not young like that. I was never young like that.

When he slides the tip of his tongue over my lips, I open for him. But just enough.

His arms tighten around me as his tongue teases me. I will my hands to rest on his shoulders when everything in me wants more. His broad back, the long column of his neck.

But this youthful stranger he sees in me, she doesn't know about all that. She doesn't yet understand that she can take as much pleasure from him as he will seek from her.

He works his thigh between mine. "Open for me. Arms around me."

My skirt rides up as I comply with a slowness that makes us both ache. His mouth is working behind my ear, the heat of his breath setting me aflame. I rock my mound against his thigh. Friction rises between the soft fabric that separates us.

"Good girl." He kisses me again. He's more assertive now, all but challenging me. Coyly, I flick my tongue at his from the back of my mouth.

He pulls away, grinning triumphantly. Finally. All the lingering glances, the subtle exchange of warmth and attention, the spark of curiosity just bright enough to lead this girl into his forbidden embrace. Into this fantasy where no one can stop him but her.

I turn into his palm when he caresses my face. His thumb strokes my lips, and soon he's easing it gradually over the swollen flesh into my mouth. I take his wrist in both hands and watch his eyes darken with hunger as I slide my tongue back over the pad of his thumb.

Damn if I don't feel it now myself. Young. Wanting so much to please this man. Wanting everything he can give me. Wanting it all now.

Smiling around his thumb, I tug playfully at his shirt. He unfolds himself from me to undress. I get off the bed to follow suit.

This won't be the first time I've stripped for him. I usually stand close enough to tease him, my thighs and my ass not quite close enough for him to touch or to bite.

Tonight, the young, timid girl inside me reaches to turn out the light.

"Don't. Let me see you."

I withdraw my hand, glance at him over my shoulder. The shadow of this forbidden desire has changed him. He's unfamiliar now, in his nakedness, although I've seen him like this uncounted times. Giving in to this temptation has made him seem stronger. Powerful.

"That's right," he whispers. "Let me see you."

The sound of his voice reaches into my very center, and I need to obey. I face him when I pull my top off over my head. The last time I did it so slowly was a lifetime ago. I feel him watching me, his fantasy undressing for him. I fumble with the skirt before I push it over my hips. He strokes his erection and sighs as I reach behind my back for my bra hooks.

My panties are sticking to my overheated flesh when I peel them off. His breath catches as I step out of them. He easily closes the distance between us and bends for another kiss.

I part my lips just a little more than before, and his tongue pushes boldly into me. His hands smooth my hair. When I slide my arms around his bare shoulders, he pulls me to him, trapping his hard-on between us.

My whimper into his mouth is genuine.

"You taste sweet." His fingertips trace my spine, raising goose bumps on my arms. "Do you like this?"

"Very much."

"Want more? Tell me."

"I want more." He kisses me obligingly. His big hands cup my ass, and I rub my breasts wantonly against him as if I've never felt his coarse hair on my nipples before.

My mask slips for a second when his palm engulfs the back of my head. I kiss him hard, eagerly claiming him. He moans into my mouth.

He lets me kiss him like that, enjoying the sudden wellspring of desire, before he takes my hands loosely in his. I let him lower me to my knees, where I brace my hands against his thighs. The head of his cock bobs before me, and I look up at him as I wet my lips. The sight of him, gazing hungrily down at the young girl he's seduced, melts something inside me. I trace the head of his cock with my tongue. Once. Again. Then I wrap my lips around him, tightly.

He sighs. I take hold of his shaft with both hands and squeeze. He moans, pushes his hips toward me.

Here on my knees I can feel myself embody this young girl more than ever. His cock in my mouth, filling it. His body straining above me. On any other night, he'd fuck my mouth greedily, taking everything I offered him. Now, with this girl, he's forced to call on exquisite patience. He must control himself because she can't yet control him. I can practically hear his teeth grinding.

I let him ease back into my mouth, lifting my tongue beneath him, like I've never taken so much. His head nudges the roof of my mouth.

I moan around him. I try to adopt an uncertainty I have never felt with him. He answers me.

"You're so good, baby." He rocks into me and back again. "So good."

I swirl my tongue over and around him, slowly, hesitantly, as if I don't know the way.

"Relax." He pushes his cock deeper into my mouth. I back off a little and he puts his hand on my head. "That's it. Take it all."

I let my mouth go slack. I want to show him how well I follow his instructions, how ready I am to be introduced to more of his dark desires. He's slowly pumping himself into my mouth, reminding me that he'll be the one to decide when I'm ready for the next level. I moan around his shaft again and look up at him, worshipfully, a young girl eager to please. Above me, he is a man transformed. I want to encourage him, to see more of the seducer hiding behind my safe, reliable boyfriend.

As if he's heard my thoughts, he withdraws from my mouth. "Come here."

I climb up onto the bed, and he follows, angling himself on top of me. His long fingers sweep up my thigh for my clit. The surge of pleasure makes me moan.

"Yes." My voice cracks in my throat.

"You ready for me, sweetheart?" His fingers push into me where I'm so very wet for him. He edges my legs apart with his thighs. "Make room for me."

I remember my first time, how my legs seemed impossibly far apart, how strange it was to feel warm skin between my thighs. His cock eases over my lips, and I gasp as he enters me. My nails dig into his shoulders. So much. How much more?

I remember this feeling, too. Full. Stretching to take him. Like this was what I was meant to do. To claim him inside me. I remember finally understanding why people threw everything away for this depth of sensation.

"More," I sigh.

His body is all but vibrating with the need to fuck me harder than this. I feel him aching to take me the way he usually does. The head of his cock brushes over the most sensitive parts of my core. I lurch up into him and he knows he's home.

"Yeah," he whispers. "Just like that. Take it all."

I offer myself up, lifting to push myself onto him. He pushes into me to the hilt and withdraws.

"That's right, sweetheart." He pistons into me. Smoothly. Slowly.

"Please," I whisper.

His cock stills inside me. His lips and tongue caress my throat. "Please what?"

"Please, I want it all. Please."

He closes his teeth on my earlobe, and it feels too good for me to feign a girl's surprise. He grinds himself into me and then slams his cock home. The things he says—sweet, reassuring things—make me so slick and hot for him. And when I finally come for him, my climax deep and intense, he meets my gaze, his pupils gone a fathomless black, before he subjects me to a merciless pounding.

When it's done, he reaches over me and turns out the light before gathering me into his arms. The universe is just the two of us again, sweating and panting, our hearts slowing into their normal paces.

In the dark, he whispers into my hair. "Thank you."

I reach for his thigh, familiar again as we let reality overtake us. "Thank you for letting me share it."

His throaty laughter warms me again, and I smile, unseen, in his embrace.

I think I love him. It's too soon to say I love him.

# AT THE PLEASURE
# OF THE PRESIDENT

Sabrina Sol

The first time he'd touched her, *really* touched her, she'd flinched.

More from the shock of it all than anything else. Because you didn't flinch when you wanted to be touched again.

And, God help her, she desperately wanted that.

As if he could read her mind, Jack looked up from his phone and caught Olivia staring at him. She should've looked away, but he held her gaze with such intensity that she couldn't move. Heat crawled up the back of her neck and traveled to her face. Arousal spread everywhere else.

"Is there anything else you need?" a voice asked in the background.

*I need him,* the voice in her head answered.

"President Vargas?"

Reluctantly, she tore her eyes away from Jack's and turned toward Alicia, her chief of staff.

"No, thank you. I've kept you way too late as it is. Go back to your hotel room and get a good night's sleep. What time are we meeting in the lobby again?"

Alicia stood up from the couch and gathered her things. "Six. We want to get back to town by seven when the polls open."

Olivia nodded. She couldn't believe the election was only hours away now. To say the road to get to this point had been difficult would be a ridiculous understatement. It all seemed so surreal that she, the daughter of Mexican immigrants, was running for her second term as president. Needless to say, she'd been criticized and analyzed on everything from her foreign policy to her shade of lipstick. But she'd survived.

What she hadn't overcome yet was this silly new attraction to Jack.

When they'd first met eight years ago, she'd been married to David. Then, after David had died, she'd been the leader of the free world.

America's first female president couldn't have crushes. Or urges. Her first term had been all about proving herself capable. Her second term—if she had a second term after tomorrow's results— would be about getting things done. There was no time for long looks or butterflies in her stomach. Especially not because of him.

Not that Jack had ever given her a reason to think there were flying insects in his organs because of her either. He'd always maintained a professional distance. He was friendly, but not too friendly. He only hugged her or held her hand when the occasion called for it—like at David's funeral. That's not to say he lived as a monk. There were whispers among the staff and an occasional article in a gossip magazine. But it was never a topic of discussion between them. That would've been too personal. They were colleagues. Nothing more.

Until North Carolina.

It was the last of the rallies in the state. She'd been walking down the stairs at the back of the ballroom stage when her ankle twisted on the last step and she literally fell into his arms. He was all hard chest and biceps, and it took her a few seconds to regain her balance because she was too busy enjoying the physical contact. The rest of her team had already turned the corner and hadn't yet noticed they weren't behind them.

"I got you," he'd said. But his sultry tone hinted there was something more underneath the words.

"I know," she'd replied without thinking.

He'd smiled at that before his expression changed. He searched her eyes and then her lips before dropping to where her breasts were crushed against his torso. And then the hands that held her waist squeezed tighter.

Over the last two weeks, something had definitely changed between them. At least, it had changed for her. When he sat next to her in meetings, she couldn't concentrate on anything but his cologne and trying to identify the spice behind the alluring scent of it. Of him. When he passed her papers or even a cup of coffee, she swore his fingers lingered on hers seconds more than necessary.

"Jack, are you coming?" Alicia's voice brought her back to the present again.

He cast a quick look at Olivia and then answered, "Yeah. I'm just responding to a few emails. You go on ahead. I'll see you in the morning."

Her heart rate quickened at the thought of being alone with him if even for just a few minutes. Maybe that was the point of him staying behind? Nervous energy made her jump to her feet and follow Alicia to the foyer of the hotel suite.

"*Gracias, mi amiga.* Whatever happens, I'll always be grateful to you," she said as she leaned in to give the other woman a quick hug.

Alicia smiled when they broke apart and grabbed her hands. "You're welcome, President . . . Olivia. It's been my pleasure to be a part of your team, and I'm looking forward to continuing to serve another four years."

She squeezed her friend's hands in appreciation. "You're sweet to be so optimistic. But we both know what the polls are saying. America doesn't seem to want a single woman for president."

"I thought you never listened to polls? Besides, you've been a single woman for the past two years and the country is thriving. You are going to win tomorrow. I can feel it."

They hugged again before Olivia unlocked the door to let her out. Her security detail immediately came to attention.

"Everything okay, Madam President?" the lead agent asked.

"Yes, everything is fine. Ms. Chavez is just retiring for the evening."

That put them at ease. Olivia closed the door and locked it. Then she took a deep breath before going back to Jack.

He still sat on the sofa in the suite's small living room typing away on his laptop. He really *was* responding to emails.

Heat flushed her cheeks again, but not from lust this time. Why on earth had she thought he'd made an excuse to be alone with her? Embarrassment brought her wild heart to a stop. Jack Walker hadn't been flirting with her these past two weeks. She had simply misinterpreted the extra attention. They'd both been in campaign mode and, of course, it had drawn them closer. He probably thought that now that she was a widow she'd needed the extra hand-holding.

For such a smart woman, she'd been pretty dumb.

*Eres tonta.*

Olivia busied herself with tidying up the sitting area after Jack insisted he didn't need her help with the emails. Ten minutes later, it was his turn to head to the door.

"Do you think you'll get any sleep tonight?" he asked as she reached to undo the chain.

That made her stop. She shrugged. "Probably not. But I guess I should try. What about you?"

"Same." He smiled and took a step closer.

Olivia willed the butterflies to settle down. "Well, no matter what happens, I feel good about the campaign we ran."

"Me too." Another smile. Another step.

They were almost touching now. She tried to control her breathing. And her heart.

*Stop it, Olivia. You're not some silly schoolgirl. Say good night and send him away.*

"Well, like I told Alicia, whatever happens, I'll always be grateful."

She closed the distance between them to give him a quick hug as well. But when she tried to pull away after a second, he wouldn't let her go.

"Whatever happens . . ." he repeated.

Desire overwhelmed her, and she had to grip his arms to steady herself. Oxygen must have stopped flowing to her brain because that could be the only reason why she did what she did next. Olivia lifted her head and kissed Jack's left cheek.

His raised eyebrows told her she had surprised him. But it was her turn to be surprised when he returned the kiss . . . on her mouth.

The election, the world, the universe were all forgotten. The only things Olivia could focus on were Jack's lips on hers. They were soft and warm and dotted with trickles of the champagne they'd toasted with earlier. And they didn't just reawaken her slumbering libido—they brought it back to life.

The kiss only lasted a few seconds. Yet she knew instantly she wanted another.

Jack, on the other hand, didn't look like he knew anything. He took a step back and dragged a hand through his salt-and-pepper hair. He shook his head and stared at the ground. "Damn it. I'm so sorry, Olivia. I shouldn't have done that."

His regret cooled her desire a few degrees, but she refused to be embarrassed this time. "Don't apologize. I kissed you back, didn't I?"

His head shot back up to look at her.

"So what do we do now?"

Hundreds of answers ran through Olivia's head. He probably expected her to tell him that they should forget about what had happened. That they should go on pretending they both didn't want something more from each other. Because any earlier doubts of their mutual attraction had been erased with that kiss.

That emboldened her.

"Tomorrow could change so many things," she said as she met his eyes. "My fate—my future—rests in everyone else's hands but mine. Tonight, for once, I'd like to make my own choices."

Jack took her hand. "And what do you choose?"

She smiled and stepped closer to him. "You. For one night. Let's forget who we are and what we do. For tonight only, I'm just Olivia."

He nodded in understanding. "And I'm just Jack—a man who would do anything to kiss you again."

Instinctively, she licked her lips. That was all the permission he needed. Jack pulled her toward him, letting go of her hand to cup her face. Their mouths fused together once again. But this time, the kiss wasn't timid or unsure. It was frantic.

Frenzied.

A moan escaped her, allowing Jack's tongue to seek entry and dance with hers. Lust flared from deep within her core. Olivia grabbed the lapels of his suit jacket, desperate to be closer to him. In return, he pressed his body against hers, his need evident even through the layers of their clothes.

"I want you, Olivia," he groaned as he moved to nip her jaw.

"Yes," she sighed. "I want you too. So bad."

Jack stopped and lifted his head to meet her eyes. "Are you sure? If someone found out . . ."

She already knew what he was going to say so she pressed her finger against his lips. She didn't want to think about repercussions or consequences. She didn't want to think at all.

Olivia only wanted to feel.

"My choice, remember?" she said.

He nodded and grabbed her hand. She led them to her bedroom in the hotel suite, stopping just inside the doorway. He began kissing her again, softly and hesitantly. As if he knew just how scared she was despite her words.

It wasn't that she'd never had sex before, obviously. She and David had been married for nearly sixteen years. But they'd stopped sleeping together, literally and figuratively, for five of them even before he got sick. To his credit, he'd refrained from his extracurricular activities as soon as she was elected. Or at least he'd been more discreet about it. And she'd been way too busy—and way too paranoid—to even think about having sex with another man while she was still married.

Olivia wasn't just having a dry spell: she was having a dry era.

That's why she was responding so intensely to Jack's touch. At least, that's what she was telling herself as his deeper kisses made her nipples strain against her bra and liquid desire pool between her thighs.

"I want to touch you," she admitted when he let her take a breath.

Jake studied her face for a moment before reaching out to caress her cheek with his thumb. "Do you know how fucking sexy you are?"

"No," she said truthfully. Sexy wasn't exactly a word she'd ever used to describe herself. Especially not during a debate or in an interview with *The Washington Post*. Not that she purposefully tried to hide her femininity. It was just better for everyone if her, um, assets weren't a distraction. During her first year in office, she accidentally wore a sleeveless dress during the annual Easter Egg Roll on the White House lawn. Fox News basically accused her of being a stripper. Since then her wardrobe consisted of sensible pantsuits, skirts that fell on or below the knee, and mother-of-the-bride evening gowns.

He didn't laugh at her admission. Instead, he looked at her earnestly and said, "Well, you are."

That's when it hit her. In that moment, Jack wasn't thinking of her as the president. She was a woman he wanted to have sex with. And that thrilled her more than anything had in a very long time.

Olivia stepped back. Slowly and deliberately, she began to undress. First she unzipped her navy-blue skirt and let it fall to the ground. Next came her crème-colored silk blouse and nude stockings. He stopped her before she could slide out of her full slip and bra.

"Let me help you," he said, his eyes dark with desire.

He hooked his fingers in both straps and pulled them off her shoulders. She gasped as he lowered his head and swiped his tongue over the curve of her cleavage. Hands cupped both breasts, kneading and caressing them and eliciting throaty moans she never knew she could utter. With one deft move, he yanked everything down and caught one taut nipple with his mouth.

"Jack!" she cried out.

He continued sucking and licking as his hands moved to her backside. She was quickly spinning out of control. And she didn't care one bit.

"Do you know how many times I've dreamt about doing this?" he said after a few minutes.

When she shook her head, he answered his own question. "Thousands."

That admission startled her. "Really?"

Jack crooked an eyebrow. "Yes, really. You're beautiful, Olivia. And not just your body. Your mind, your spirit, your fierceness. I swear every time you give a speech, I get a hard-on."

That made her laugh, and then she kissed him for all of his lovely words that made her feel so good. So desired.

"Well, you're pretty amazing too. But I don't think it's fair that you're still wearing clothes."

"Then take them off me."

Olivia went to work doing just that. His red tie, suit jacket, and white shirt were gone in seconds. She couldn't help but run both of her hands down his hard, bare chest, reveling in its solidness. He sighed and threw his head back. "That feels so good."

"And what about this?" she asked before licking one of his nipples.

Jack swore to God and every other deity. Knowing that she did that to him only revved up her need even more. She wanted to do it again. And again. And again.

But as she began to mark a trail with her tongue down to his navel, he stopped her and brought her back up to face him. "As much as I would fucking love for you to suck me off, tonight is all about your pleasure."

When she opened her mouth to protest, he silenced her with another searing kiss. As their tongues reacquainted themselves, he guided her toward the bed. Olivia sat on the edge and watched with anticipation as he undid his belt. He took his wallet from his pants pocket and revealed a wrapped condom. Although she wanted to ask, she kept quiet and waited patiently until he was fully naked in front of her. His cock was thick and long—a beautiful sight to behold indeed.

"Lie down," he said.

Olivia gladly obeyed, thinking he would be inside her soon. But Jack had other plans.

With both hands he opened her to him. First he kissed the inside of each thigh. It was sweet torture that only escalated her desire. He blew a slow breath over her heated sex as she clutched at the comforter for dear life. She knew she was about to fall—so, so hard. Olivia propped herself on her elbows to get a better view of what he was doing, but as soon as Jack's tongue slid over her tight clit, she collapsed in ecstasy. "*Dios mio,*" she said on a strangled groan.

Her thighs trembled every time his hair brushed against them. It was almost too much. Almost. And when he sank his tongue deep inside her, Olivia squeezed her eyes and prepared for an eruption of seismic proportions.

"I'm going to come already. I'm coming, I'm coming."

Each desperate pant increased in volume, and she knew her orgasm wouldn't arrive quietly. But a scream would send a team of agents barreling through the door, and she couldn't have that.

So she covered her mouth with her own hand just as the explosion ripped from her body.

She was still reeling from tiny aftershocks when she realized Jack was on top of her. Then he was slowly sinking into her slick heat inch by inch. Pain tempered with pleasure passed through her body as it stretched to let him in.

"Are you okay?" he whispered over her face.

Olivia was more than okay. She was in heaven. "Yes," she whispered back.

He kissed her as he pulled out and pushed back inside. "It's going to be quick because I can't wait any longer and you're so fucking tight," he said gruffly. "But I promise the next time I'll make it last."

She nodded and lifted her hips up so he could penetrate her fully. It was the most amazing feeling in the world. That is, until he started thrusting into her rough and fast.

"Yes, like that. Harder. Don't stop," she said in between gasps.

They rocked and rolled in unison, their bodies slapping together in an erotic rhythm. He kissed her one more time before moving to his knees. With one leg hooked over his arm, he was able to reach the spot deep inside that spurred a second release from out of nowhere.

Her body arched. Her toes curled.

"That's it. Come with me, Olivia," Jack grunted before stilling on top of her as his own orgasm hit.

It took several minutes before either of them could talk. Gratification rolled through her veins like a new addictive drug, and she doubted she would be able to walk anytime soon. Jack eventually moved and pulled her to his chest.

"I knew it would be amazing," he said, caressing her arm with his fingers.

"Thank you." It was the only thing she could think to say.

He twisted to his side so he could face her. "What for?"

"For making me believe that I deserve pleasure like this."

"Of course you deserve it. I should be thanking you for letting me give it to you."

She smiled. "Well, then, you're most welcome."

Jack left sometime after one in the morning. As promised, their round two had been more drawn out and he'd been as attentive as before. Sleep came easily as Olivia was both physically and mentally exhausted. It took her two snoozes on her phone's alarm before she dragged herself into the shower. The hot water woke her up fully, as did the memories of Jack's kisses. She smiled even as she washed away his scent because she knew the images of what they'd done together would live forever in her mind.

Her hair and makeup team arrived just after five, and for an hour she was preoccupied with getting ready for what would be a very, very long day. She arrived on time to the hotel lobby and was quickly greeted by Alicia and a cup of coffee.

"You look refreshed," she said with a big smile.

Olivia choked on her first sip. "I do?"

Alicia nodded fervently. Olivia thought about it for a second and realized there was no harm is being a little truthful. "Well, I guess I do feel a little rejuvenated in a way."

"I'm so glad," Alicia said, looking at her phone. "The cars are right outside. We're just waiting for the vice president and his staff."

Olivia took a gulp of her coffee just as a rumble of voices approached. Alicia glanced up and announced, "Right on time. Good morning, Mr. Vice President."

Jack offered them both a wide smile. "Yes, it's a very good morning indeed."

Alicia beamed and threw up her arms. "I'm loving the positive vibes from you both. It's a good sign. Now, let's go vote for you two, shall we?"

Olivia and Jack exchanged sly smiles as they headed to the hotel's double doors.

"After you, Madam President," he said, and held them open for her.

"Thank you, Vice President Walker. You're so kind," she said.

He shrugged as she walked by. "You know me. It's always my pleasure to be of service to you any way I can."

"Oh, I do know," she said under her breath.

She immediately began planning the next time she could call on Jack for his special type of secret service.

# OUTLAWS

Angel Leigh McCoy

I ached for fulfillment in an age where robots diddled me with more expertise than I did myself. Day in and day out, in and out, I poked and prodded, rubbed and rodded with every possible attachment, gizmo, and hybrid vegetable I could find. Like Icarus, I hooked myself up to my mechanical wings and tried to fly. I spent thousands of globals, charged to my credit account, for the latest technology—get off in style, get off with the turn of a dial, water-proof, shockproof, new and improved, satisfaction guaranteed or your money back—but no matter how many orifices I filled, and filled to bursting, I couldn't satisfy that one elusive hole that yearned the most. It had opened up inside me, yawning wide and slavering with a hunger I didn't understand. It ate at me from the inside out like a greedy ulcer, hidden deep in my psyche where even a Hyper-Dildo™ couldn't reach.

Then, *he* came out of nowhere and inserted himself into my pursuit of happiness.

It happened in the Women's Spa on Level 30; I was relaxing in a Jacuzzi. The warm water enfolded my naked body and rocked me. Eyes closed, I let my mind drift and tried to suck an ocean of healing into that chasm in my soul.

"I want to fuck you," he announced, close, too close, too male. I blinked open my eyes and focused on him. He had gotten into the tub, unnoticed—brown, curly hair, brown eyes—trusting eyes—masculine mouth, sculpted neck, broad shoulders, smooth chest, flat stomach, dark pubis, erection. Erection. His penis looked angry, purple-faced in the rippling underwater, and pointed an unfamiliar accusation at me.

I had seen pictures of cocks before, flaccid examples in college textbooks: disease samplings, warped constructions, and symptoms of sexual deviance. Curious, I had studied the fleshy acorns with their oozing sores and, through the course of my education, had developed a natural aversion to the male sex organ. I had never seen one up close and personal, certainly hadn't expected to see one in the Women's Spa. This penis, the one swimming beneath the surface of the water, stared at me with its one eye, voluptuous and healthy.

Long ago, centuries ago, women had let men put cocks inside them. Though I knew the history, I had somehow, until that moment, missed the connection between erection, arousal, and the fat dildos with which I pleasured myself. My pussy took notice.

Tearing my eyes from the engorged member, I glanced around for other spa patrons, but they had all left. I was alone with a fucker. A crazy fucker, no doubt, who might touch me, or worse, get me arrested for conspiracy to touch and be touched. I glared at him. He was early twenties and handsome, not like the elderly sex offenders pictured on the evening news or the ones caricatured in the psychology textbooks.

The man spoke again, his tone gentle. "You believe them when they say you mustn't."

"Are you insane?"

"No. I feel you—your need. It's like mine. I've been waiting for you. I want to fuck you. Please." His voice had a soft depth, not the least bit threatening, sincere. He took my hand so gently I didn't think to react, and he pulled it down into the water, down to his erection. The shock, oh the shock, the cock electric and blue burning. Flesh to flesh, skin to skin, forbidden touching.

I yanked my hand back. Fighting the thick water, I fled from him and climbed out of the tub in a rush of splash and drip.

His gaze pursued me across the tiled room and into the dryer tunnel. I felt it as acutely as if he were still touching me with his hands. Just inside the dryer tunnel, I stepped onto the conveyor belt. It slowed my flight, moving me along at its leisurely pace.

When I glanced back to see his streaming, wet-shiny body rising up out of the Jacuzzi, my inner walls clenched.

Blast after blast of warm air assaulted me. The drying winds tugged at my hair, invaded my space. From below, they thrust up between my legs and groped at my cunt. From above, they pushed down on me and tweaked my nipples.

*The nerve of him!* I considered reporting him; it would have served him right. What he'd done was criminal. Men did not belong in the women's baths, and they should never show their bodies.

I wanted solitude. At my locker, I punched numbers into the keypad and removed my belongings. My robe provided a soft shell of protection against the erections of the world, but offered no comfort to my disturbed mind and crotch. I hurried to the exit, murmuring apologies to the strangers I skirted.

I had never appreciated the privacy of the complex's transport system as much as I did that afternoon. The car moved like a solitary corpuscle through the building's veins. I huddled, ruffled, in a corner of the ascending Bubble and clutched my robe around myself. I watched the red-on-black display count off the levels, *32, 33, 34, 35 . . .*

Softly, I chanted to myself, "59, 59, 59, 59," anxious for the shelter of my suite. The correct digits appeared, and the Bubble slid sideways, 59A, 59B, 59C, 59D, 59E . . . through the horizontal shaft to my apartment. The doors opened directly onto my living room. After I'd stepped across the threshold, the doors closed with a vacuum suck. I relaxed. I was safe again, at least physically.

In my mind, I heard, "I want to fuck you," in that masculine, natural voice. "I want to fuck you . . . fuck you . . . fuck you." My pussy throbbed.

Men lived in their quarter, and we women lived in ours. Thus, the government kept us separated and safe from the venereal bacteria that had killed hundreds of thousands. Marriage and love had become outdated concepts. We made babies in the clinic, not in the bedroom.

And we never saw them without clothes—except in schoolbooks.

He'd been naked, his skin clear and shining with water, his cock an eager . . .

"No," I denied aloud and went about my business. Nothing, however, distracted me enough. He haunted me with his lewd and unacceptable, not to mention illegal, request.

I tried to console myself on the Stroke-57. I straddled it and sat down on the positioning nub. The small probe slid easily into my moist cavity. I spread my nether lips around the mechanical mouth, fingers parting my pussy. I brushed my clit; electricity ran up my spine and seized my heart. I gasped.

The machine sensed me and began its foreplay. As the stroke bed came to life, I leaned forward onto the angled bench, rested my cheek on the soft pillow, and closed my eyes. I wrapped my arms around it and held on.

He'd been muscular, his hand enormous when it had wrapped around my wrist.

The vibrations shook my tits.

Warm. His touch—and his eyes. He'd had tears in them. And his lips had parted with wanting . . . me.

The mouth undulated between my labia and licked with jellied pressure across my clit.

Hot. His cock had radiated heat through its skin, healthy skin stretched over the hard proof of his arousal.

He wanted to fuck me.

The probe thickened to my preset proportions. It pistoned, increasing its depth and speed.

When I came, it was upon his cock that my pussy clenched, and I threw my head back and lifted my breasts up, offering them to his gaze and . . .

The Stroke-57 clunked to a halt and was still between my legs. The probe receded.

I told my best friend Mikeila about the man in the spa.

"He did what?" she cried in horror. "What did you do?"

"I walked away."

"Good." Mikeila shook her head. "Stupid fucker. I can't believe the nerve. He's lucky his ass isn't in jail right now."

"His cock was hard."

Mikeila grimaced in disgust. "You poor thing." She folded her hands in sympathy. "Did you tell the attendant?"

I shook my head and lied, "He didn't touch me." Then, to justify the guilty secret, I added, "I don't even know who he was."

"The world's going to shit," Mikeila grumbled. "Fuckers everywhere. I was watching this show on the vid last night. They were interviewing sex offenders—people convicted of everything from holding hands to . . . fucking. They want a revival of the *old days*. Can you imagine? They've forgotten . . . the crimes of passion, the teenage mothers, the population explosion, rapes, suicides, disease, incest, crack babies, and fanatics who bred their own followers. I mean, come on! Let's get some perspective, people. With today's technology, they don't need to be sticking their . . ."

My mind wandered, as it often did when Mikeila was on a roll, drifting back to how that cock had felt against my hand, hard wood wrapped in the richest silk. I remembered its heat and how it had twitched, like a living thing. The word "delicious" came to mind.

"No, no, no," I murmured, denying, denying, denying.

Mikeila asked, "What do you mean 'no'?"

"Sorry. I just . . . Can we talk about something else? It was so . . ."

"Crude?"

"Yeah."

"Primitive?"

"Yeah." I lowered my eyes. "If I see him again, I'll report him."

Days later, he found me at the Millennium Café. A book suddenly appeared on the table beside my espresso, held in a strong, masculine hand.

"Read it," he whispered. "It'll get you wet."

I glanced at the book. *You*, the title read simply. *By Anonymous.*

He turned and walked toward the exit. His black jumpsuit gave him a neat, tight look, rippling tension. He stopped in the doorway and shifted sideways to let someone pass. The rotation slid his crotch across my view. The leg of his pants had a bulge, a thickness that shared the confining space with his thigh. Because I knew what was in there, I felt intimate with him.

Lifting my gaze, I caught his attention on me. Heat put flames to my cheeks. In those dark eyes, I saw amusement, but he wasn't laughing at me. He was enjoying me.

A waiter approached, and I covered the book with my hand.

"Can I get you anything else?" the server asked.

"No. Thank you."

When I looked back toward the door, *he* was gone.

Once in the privacy of my suite, I tried to decide how to dispose of the book. I could have tossed it in the incinerator or flushed it page-by-page down the toilet. I could have buried it among the food scraps in the communal composter. I could have wiped it clean of my fingerprints and left it lying where the police would find it.

I did none of those things. Instead, I picked it up and opened it to the first page.

*Just a peek,* I thought. Maybe it wasn't what I imagined. Maybe . . .

*I want to fuck you,* the handwritten inscription said. He had signed it, *Émile.*

I tossed the book down and paced. Émile. He had a name. He had a face. He had a—glorious—cock, and he wanted to fuck me with it. I chewed a fingernail until it bled.

I didn't read the book. Nor did I throw it away. It hid like a criminal in the back of my closet, behind the box of old photos and the forgotten shoes. I watched for him, in crowds, at the spa, in the café. I came to assume he had given up on me or been arrested.

Then, one day, he approached me in the open-air plaza.

I was seated on a concrete bench beneath an imported gingko tree. I had come for the sunshine. He had come for me. He loomed, casting the shadow of his body over me. The sun's jeweled light put a halo around his head and obscured his features.

He greeted me with, "Mark Twain once said, 'Of the delights of this world man cares most for sexual intercourse, yet he has left it out of his heaven.'"

"Who?" I squinted up at him.

"Mark Twain. Samuel Clemens? One of the greatest literary minds of the early twentieth century. They've banned his works, of course." He sat down beside me.

I couldn't have been more aware of his nearness. My heartbeat accelerated, my energy expanding to vibrate beyond the confines of my skin.

Émile spoke with quiet assurance. "They've imprisoned us in our own bodies."

"We've evolved," I replied, rote.

When he laughed, it drew an unbidden smile to my lips. "That's what the Darwinists say to control us. They pet us with words that soothe our egos and make us believe we've risen above our animal lessers to become more angelic, more godlike. In our near-divinity, we're conceived in test tubes." He grinned crookedly. "Only the best genes allowed, mind you, handpicked by our leaders."

His grin faded, and he returned to seriousness. "We become addicted to their dogma because it tells us we're special. They teach us that our physical and emotional urges are evil and marry us to masturbation. So we lock ourselves in our one-person homes and play with ourselves in solitude. We are the priests and nuns of Holy Loneliness."

"What are you talking about?"

"In the meantime, the legislators are fucking their secretaries."

"I don't believe that."

He smiled. "Don't you see? Separating us from one another, all of us, makes us meek. If we can't touch one another, we'll never rise up against injustice." His fingers brushed my hand, and I instinctively pulled it away. "See what I mean?" he said. "Why can't I touch you?"

"Because . . ." I tried to justify my government's laws, my reaction, myself, ". . . the temptation to do more . . ." My voice faltered. His eyes had the softness of copper and the strength of walnut. I cleared my throat and continued. "It'll put us back in the Dark Ages; we'll have war, social disturbance, disease . . ."

He interrupted. "Sex, lust, exploration, creativity, art, poetry, closeness, sharing. Love."

"No."

"Yes." Émile looked me square in the eyes.

We breathed a sigh together.

Finally, he stood. "Read the book."

"I threw it away."

"Read the book." He gently touched my forehead. Anyone who'd seen the gesture would have assumed it was an accident, he did it so carefully. I knew better. My virgin skin tingled where he'd left his mark.

I went home and read the book.

The language in it had the flavor of antiquity which allowed me, at first, to distance myself from its content. He'd been right, though: it made me wet. I could only read a chapter at a time, sometimes less, before I had to ease my distracting clit with an orgasm. I had never read anything like it. Contemporary erotica involved men or women with a machine—never two people *together*.

I approached the story from an analytical viewpoint, despite my regular masturbation breaks. I examined its social and interpersonal implications. I pondered the health issues and moral factors. I judged the characters, because I didn't want to understand them. The title, *You,* implied something that tickled the back of my brain. The hole inside me, the one I couldn't fill, ached. Eventually, I forgot to think and began to feel. The characters, Russell and Leslie, established a hot residence in my soul. I knew their bodies as well as I knew my own. I knew their hearts. They fucked inside me. They licked each other, they sucked each other, and I learned a new verb for their sensual communion: they *made love.*

By the time I finished the book, I had lived a vicarious life that felt alien to what I knew and had believed. The touching described in the book cracked my foundation and made the entire structure of my world unstable.

Émile had underlined a passage at the end. It read, *That is the view from where I am. From what I am. I do not know where you are, or what you have become beyond our last time together. But if these truths are your truth, as they are mine—but only then—then come, my love, and let us love.*

I cried.

Once introduced to my bloodstream, this new venereal virus spread, changing how I viewed the world. A storm churned within me, a tumult I couldn't fathom. My machines began to disgust me. Their parts no longer fit me; their patented functions no longer fulfilled me. I took to masturbating on my own, more satisfied with the flesh-on-flesh of my fingers than the mechanical lick of a self-lubricating, multispeed, variable-pressure tongue.

I was angry that my worldview had irrevocably changed. I broke dials and threw dildos against the wall, shattering plastic, bouncing rubber, and denting metal, none of which eased the torrent. I walked numerous emotional paths and left much debris in my wake. Anger, denial, disgust, self-loathing, fear, depression, confusion, intellectualization, guilt, loneliness . . . and, finally, acceptance.

I made the book my bed companion. In my fantasies, Émile became Russell and I was Leslie. Together, we *spent a lifetime unlocking secret portals of passion—and enjoyed together all the enduring pleasures of love and lust . . .*

Then, one day, my intercom buzzed. I threw on my blue silk robe and pushed a button on the console. "Who is it?"

"I'm here," he said simply.

I took so long to respond that, by the time I did, I was afraid he'd gone. My hand shook as I punched in the code that would allow him entrance to my sanctum.

The Bubble doors opened, and he stepped inside. Behind him, the vacuum suck of the closing doors sealed us in together.

His presence imbalanced me, and I began to tremble. He said nothing aloud, but his brown, hungry eyes spoke volumes. I came alive, my soul electric, my nerves on fire.

Carefully, like a trainer with an untamed animal, he came toward me. His hands reached for the belt of my robe and pulled it free.

The robe opened to reveal my nakedness. I couldn't look at him, but I could hear his breathing and smell his spicy warmth. My heart fluttered like a trapped bird. My breath betrayed me. It expressed my fear and my thrill. It quickened with my body.

He exhaled audibly.

At the edge of my vision, I saw his hands approaching my shoulders, and I tensed—instinct, anticipation. The touch came gently, unilaterally warm and caressing, pushing the draped silk away. My robe fell down my arms to the floor; his hands followed it all the way to my fingertips. I was naked to him.

Slowly, he knelt before me and wrapped his arms around my hips. He pressed his cheek to my belly and hugged me, a sensation I hadn't had since childhood. I swallowed, panted; tears welled in my eyes. His lips burned against my belly. He kissed downward to the curls of my mound, rubbing his face in them, and then his tongue penetrated the slit there.

It touched my clit.

I looked down, surprised and ready to shove him away. My hands rose and fingers twitched, but I didn't touch him.

He flicked his tongue against the tender nub, overcoming fear with pleasure. I let out a soft sob and closed my eyes. My soul reeled.

He moaned a deeper harmony.

That moment, more than any other, marked a change in me. The intimacy brought my world into sharp focus. My past turned black and white while my present sparked with all the colors of the rainbow. I was alive, and the universe welcomed me. I widened my stance at his guidance. His tongue lapped in the swollen grasp of my labia, stroking across the nucleus of my sex. With delirious, pulsing thrusts, he stabbed the slick organ between my nether-lips and purloined my clit, claiming it as his own. Moisture gathered and ran down my quivering thighs.

I touched him then. Tentatively. I laid my shaking hands on his head. Whisper-soft, his hair flowed through my fingers. My thumb brushed an ear, skin to skin, touch sensation building connections between us. The irreverence of it, my wicked, personal rebellion, thrilled me in ways I had never expected. A sense of revolution rose up inside me, felt good and right, and condensed all the questions, so many questions all boiled down into one simple truth: *Why not?*

My orgasm showered me with sparks. I fell, from grace, to earth.

Émile caught me. He had awakened my soul with his book and with his tongue. He carried me to the bed and laid me down upon it. He didn't say a word—for which I was grateful. No congratulations and no preaching about my prior sin of ignorance. He knew that he had converted me, knew beyond all doubt; the time had passed for words and come for action.

He undressed. I watched his clothes fall away, obsessed with the blush on his neck and the butter-mint flesh of his nipples. The incline of his stomach drew my eyes downward, narrow waist and stream of hair, both naturally pointing south. He removed his pants and reacquainted my eyes with his erection. This time, no light-refracting water distorted the image. The thick wand pointed at me, but I felt no accusation, only a yearning that I shared. He stood over me, me the priestess laid out on the dais of my past, he the slave of my choices, at my mercy. He wrapped his hand around his veined shaft and stroked himself once, for me, so I could see how tame it was, then he laid it across my trembling lips. It smelled of burning wood and morning rain, of gingko and man.

I tentatively rubbed my lips against skin unbelievably soft and forgot to worry that I didn't know what to do or that I shouldn't, or that I wouldn't. I wallowed in sensuality and welcomed the way he held his cock's globed head against my lips.

I touched my tongue to it, exploring.

He gave no pressure, made no demand. His gaze never left my face, his own expression one of wonder and . . . lust.

I opened my mouth and suckled the rosy plum, as Leslie had done, and to my delight, Émile—just like Russell—whimpered. I felt greed birth inside me; I wanted to please. The sounds he made, the susurrations of pleasure, fed my heat, making me hunger for more. I would have given up the world for just one more of his earthy moans.

He withdrew, and I watched him slide a primitive sheath over his cock. The thought that I had hurt him or offended him clutched my heart, but he murmured a quiet comfort and came to lie on top of me. He pushed my legs apart and settled between them. His weight, so reassuring and physical, pressed me into the mattress. Émile, *my Émile,* as I had come to think of him, brought his face near mine, letting me smell my own juices on him.

I felt an overwhelming need to fall into him and tumble through his veins, to touch his every hidden corner and become a permanent part of him. Heat, so sexual and real, transmitted lust between our bodies. From chest to thigh, he fit himself to me; I marveled at the perfection of it. His shaft slid through the velvet-wet lips of my vulva.

With slow pressure, he breached me. His cock cut a torrid trail straight through my wilderness. It pushed aside my clinging walls and forced its way deep. Only one word could describe it: "Alive." That solid pillar of flesh lived.

Émile rubbed his lips across my chin and licked at my mouth. I tasted him and tasted myself.

His cock jerked inside me, and my own muscles responded with a squeeze that made him gasp. His hips pulsed in slow, short strokes.

From some primal source, I responded to the evolving choreography, following and leading, creating an ecstatic dance greater than either of us could have managed alone. I couldn't take my eyes off his face, entranced by the expressions of lust and elation moving across features already grown dear, seen through the fog of my own passion.

The machines hadn't taken pleasure in me. They hadn't murmured my name. They didn't shiver when I scratched at them or falter in their rhythm when I touched the right nerve. They lacked heat, meaning, and life.

My body expanded toward release, tension building along my spine and stealing my breath. Émile's lust and mine mixed, heat rising into the promise of ecstasy. I remembered how Russell and Leslie had loved each other, but even their cherished words hadn't prepared me for the strength of this or the feeling of completion. It filled my hole. He filled my hole.

I came again with a rush that rolled me. It turned me head over heels and threatened to drown me in its bubbling wave. I held my breath as long as I could, then gasped for air, sucking in the mist of our passion. I cried out for Émile, and he joined me. His cock pulsed and bucked inside my cunt.

I thought the convulsions would never end; I hoped. Slowly, however, the aftershocks dissipated, and Émile fell heavy upon me.

We vibrated. Sweat glued our bodies together. He held me in his strong arms, the thunder of his heartbeat against my breast. Our kisses grew tender and adoring, thankful, and we exalted each other with caresses. For me, the world had acquired dimensions I'd never even known I'd missed. *How could I have known?*

Society frowned on us, judged us, and threatened punishment for our transgressions against its human-fabricated, human-fallible laws.

It couldn't comprehend that Émile and I pursued truth in each other's arms.

I learned to pity the fat old men who manipulated legislation for their own greedy purposes, who kept people apart with closed minds and locked hearts, who denied the endless possibilities of love. Even more, I pitied those innocents molded from birth by prejudice instilled generations earlier, those birds pinioned by false teachings and inherited beliefs.

Outlaws, my Émile and I fled through the underground. We moved to a wilderness colony of fuckers like ourselves. We built our home and called it Ibiza, beyond the horizon in a place where we were free to hold hands in public, to sleep in each other's arms, to kiss good morning, and to *make love*. Two by two, others joined us, left the cities and came in search of human fulfillment, of diversity and understanding. We, the people; we, the fuckers . . .

# NYMPH AND SATYR

Justine Elyot

It takes about half a minute for me to realize that I'm looking directly at a woman's breast. And that other polished marble curve is supposed to be an ass. When I step back, it all becomes clear. This harmonious jumble of twists and bends, rising from the lawn like a giant stone vine, is a couple, fucking.

"It's very erotic, no?"

An exhibition guide, bored on a slow summer afternoon, comes to stand beside me.

"Once you see what it is," I reply. Our brief interaction at the till in the visitor center has revealed my nationality, and she hasn't even attempted to engage me in my schoolgirl French.

"You prefer a more traditional style? Perhaps over here . . ."

Behind the next hedge, a man of bronze is leaning over, his muscular buttocks and upper thighs straining in their pose. The guide leads me around him until I see the woman crouched beneath him, her breast in his hand, her legs parted to admit his substantial erection.

The urgency of his expression, the rapture of hers, the sense of their bodies fluid in motion despite their stillness is exciting, moving even.

"It makes you wonder about the meaning of the word *inanimate*."

I am thinking out loud, but the guide enthusiastically agrees.

"Yes, yes, there is so much life, so much movement, so much spirit," she says.

"You can feel their passion."

"I could see that." Her smile is a little knowing and I blush, suddenly awkward. "I wish I could have photographed your face—your reaction."

"You're a photographer?"

"Yes, I love to work here because I am inspired a lot by our visitors. The expressions, the reactions I see—they're fascinating to me. Sometimes shock, even disgust. And then, many times, arousal."

My British reserve kicks in, and I begin to size up escape routes from this peculiarly intimate conversation.

"That's really interesting. But I didn't realize . . . er . . . are all the sculptures here so . . . sexual?"

She laughs.

"You didn't know?"

"I should've read the reviews on TripAdvisor." My laugh is more self-conscious than hers.

"There is a museum in the town if you prefer. It's free with your ticket."

"Oh, no, I don't have a problem with it." I don't want to come over all "No sex please, we're British." For some reason I don't want her to think that of me. I try a nonchalant Gallic shrug but suspect it doesn't quite come off. "It's just unexpected, that's all. But I like it here. So peaceful."

"Ah, yes, it is. I will leave you to enjoy your peace."

"Oh, I didn't mean . . . ."

She smiles, as if to say "no offense taken," and walks back to the baby chateau that houses the main collection. I watch her hips in their well-fitted pencil skirt, the swish of her hair around her neck and shoulders.

*Chic,* I think wistfully. Or enviously. Both, perhaps.

I turn back to the sculpture, and my wistful envy grows stronger. Why didn't Andrew and I ever have sex like that? Except we did, back in our student days. Glorious, joyous, gymnastic sex all over campus, once on the top deck of an empty bus, once on the banks of a river.

When did it become so . . . quotidian?

I smile to myself, thinking that at first it was quotidian in the strict meaning of the word, the one the French use: daily. But then it became the English version—mundane, an everyday chore.

*Give us this day our daily shag.* In the early flush of our now-dead love, Andrew and I made up an alternative version of the Lord's Prayer. We felt so daring, both of us lapsed Catholics. I remember the transgressive thrill of it, the sly glance toward the window to make sure we weren't about to be struck down by a retributive thunderbolt, then I snort, remembering the last line: *Deliver us from anal.*

I haven't thought about that in years.

The chain of images and remembrances this sets off is only broken when somebody speaks, close to my shoulder. A male voice, deep but soft with a touch of pleasant hoarseness, in French. In my confusion I only catch snippets of what he says—*"je me demande . . ." "utilisé . . ." "modèle . . ."*

"I'm sorry," I stammer mechanically, twisting my neck to take him in.

Tall, very broad shouldered, silvering hair, elegant suit.

"Oh, English?" he says. "Excuse me."

I'm strangely flattered to be taken for a Frenchwoman—and a bit surprised, to be honest, given that I'm wearing the standard middle-aged-Englishwoman-in-summer uniform of a flowery dress, light cardigan, and flat sandals.

"No, no, it's okay, I can speak French," I tell him, in French, forgetting that I don't really want to talk to anyone, that I'm here to find solace and pleasure in my own company.

"It's not necessary. I'm not French anyway," he replies in a deliciously accented English.

"Oh, you're not?"

"Italian," he replies, with a transfixing smile.

I notice then how very dark his eyes are—black, almost. Along with his prominent nose, they give that smile an ironic, somewhat devilish appearance. And yet the effect is magnetically charming, to the extent that my pulse speeds up and something flip-flops low down in my stomach.

"I was saying," he continues, "that I wonder if the artist used human models to pose for this."

"God, I hope not, for their sake," I say with a laugh. "Imagine holding that position for hours on end. I doubt it's even possible."

"I don't know," he says, softly, playfully, and I feel a blush creep along my hairline, knowing that he's watching my face. "It might be fun to try it."

*Oh my god, am I actually being chatted up in a sculpture garden?*
An embarrassed giggle slips out of me before I can check it.

"Oh god," is all I can think of to say. Or rather, gasp.

"You don't think so?"

"I . . . don't know. I suppose it would be nice to be immortalized."

"Yes, to have that moment of complete communion, always. These moments aren't so frequent in life, and they disappear so quickly. Especially as we grow older."

He sighs, gives me a sadder version of the ironic smile.

I am pierced. I have the strongest, maddest urge to put my arms around his neck, rest my cheek on his shoulder, draw him close and closer, bring some warmth into my arctic circle.

I think it must be the sun.

"Yes, well . . . I . . . ought to . . . sorry . . ."

The danger sets me into flight. I smile, a grimace of apology, and begin to back away across the lawn.

"What did I say?" he asks, gesturing.

"I'm sorry," I repeat. "I'm just . . ."

I make it to the next hedge and pick up pace, fleeing through the stone and marble and bronze bodies in their varying stages of foreplay and coitus.

Beyond the sleek, sculpture-dotted lawns there is woodland, comparative wilderness, and I plunge into it with relief. I enjoy the brush of the cool, long grasses against my itchy legs. Shade, dappled or deep, casts itself over my overheated body and works to dispel the panicked excitement that drove me here.

I find a glade and spread myself beneath a friendly-looking lime tree, flattening the grass into my shape. My breath slows and steadies; I feel my limbs sink into the earth as if weighted with stones.

*In for five . . . hold for five . . . out for five.*

Shafts of warmth and light cross me diagonally, and I enjoy the feeling until it gets too hot and I take off my cardigan. I tilt my hat down over my eyes, let the sun move over my skin like a lover.

A lover.

That heavy, erotic summer day feeling gets underneath my hide and burrows into me. I feel phantom tongues on my nipples, invisible fingers stroking my tender inner thighs. My skin puckers as a breeze sighs across it. The breeze is a human touch, preparing me for what is to come.

I want his weight, his substance on top of me. I want his tongue in my mouth, his fingers tight around my wrists, his knees jamming my legs apart. I want to feel him hard and thick, pushing through my tight passage until it is filled with him. I want to yield, utterly, to sensation and pleasure. I want to enter a place where self-consciousness is overcome by desire.

I want to feel again.

My dress is up around my waist, my fingers inside my knickers now. I know I am wet, but I moan a little as my fingertips gather the evidence. My clit is slick and fat, fit to burst.

I cup a breast with my other hand, rubbing at a nipple. The linen of my dress and the cup of my padded bra add layers that are both frustrating and arousing. Considering this, I remove my hand from my knickers and try to stimulate myself through the thin, silky material. It's easier this way to imagine that the hands belong to someone else.

But oh, I wish they did, and that they were bigger, stronger, less hesitant, more purposeful.

And I wish they belonged to that man.

I think of his face, the way he smiled, the quickening of interest down in the depths of his eyes. Did I imagine it? I want to breathe him in, the gorgeous scent of him, something expensive mixed with something primally masculine.

"Ohhh," I moan, my pleasure heightening as I imagine his eyes on me, watching me. "Why did you run away from him?"

"Yes, why?"

I let out a little scream and sit up, snatching my fingers away from my knickers as if they have caught fire.

I can't speak, can't even gibber. There is no acceptable reaction to this scenario, because this scenario is beyond the normal limits of human embarrassment.

He is standing there, smiling, holding on to an overhanging

branch and leaning toward me. His unruffled elegance contrasts strongly with my rumpled, red-faced panic.

"No, I'm sorry," he says, chuckling softly. "Lie down again. I didn't mean to disturb you."

I don't lie back down.

"How long have you been standing there?" I ask in pained accusation.

"I'm not sure. You made such a charming picture, I couldn't look away."

"Yes, well." I reach for my bag, preparing to lurch to my feet and take flight for a second time. "I don't usually . . . I don't know what came over me . . ."

"Ah, no, no." He lets go of the branch and moves closer to me, tutting.

I realize with a kind of fascinated dread that I won't be able to get up or run away now. I'm rooted here, held in place by that same strong magnetism he exerted on me by the sculpture.

"You can't run away from me again," he reproves me, squatting in front of me. His expression is serious, and I feel obscurely guilty for even thinking of it. "You don't even want to, do you?"

"I . . ."

He runs a fingertip along my brow, unplastering the sweat-soaked hairs that have flattened themselves to it.

I shiver, and we both know that it can't possibly be anything to do with the cold.

"A man and a woman," he whispers, then corrects himself. "A *beautiful* woman—"

"Oh, I'm not beautiful," I interrupt reflexively.

He puts a finger to my lips, his eyes darkening into severity.

Goose bumps.

"I've heard you Englishwomen won't accept a compliment," he scolds. "But I will give you no choice. Do you understand me?"

I nod.

"Do you?"

"Yes," I mutter grudgingly.

"Now," he says, his voice dropping lower, softer. "Don't say anything more, until you want me to stop."

He shifts forward onto his knees and slides a hand to the back of my neck. His palm is hot, but dry, which can't be said for my skin. He bends toward me until his forehead rests against mine, our noses brushing.

"I want to kiss you," he breathes.

He waits a second, for the *stop* that doesn't come.

That second shimmers between us, a heat-hazed Rubicon. Like the metaphorical river, my pussy gushes and bursts its banks, dewing my thighs with its heady scent. My body warps, metal in a furnace, bending to the will of our desire. I am fluid. I am ready.

The second passes. He takes my hand, fits his lips to mine, exerts a gentle pressure, and lets it grow until I push back and it's a kiss, oh, a kiss, I remember now how good they could feel.

Mouth to mouth, we hold tight to each other. I cling to him through the storm that sweeps through me, needing his solid strength to keep me upright. His hands wander into the dip of my shoulder blades, the curve of my spine, lightly at first, then with increasing purpose.

Any defenses I might have had have dissolved now, mingling with the particles of humidity in the air that envelops us.

*It doesn't make sense,* I think confusedly, *to seek more heat in this weather.*

And yet it does. Nothing has ever made more sense than to open myself to him, offer my breasts to his caress, feel my nipples tingle and harden beneath it.

He eases me back down into the grass, pushing up my skirts, his mouth still hungry on mine, his hand hungrier as it glides up my thigh. I hook my leg around his hip, signaling my wanton desire.

His hot breath floods my mouth, mixed with a low growl of lust.

My fingers scrabble and pluck at his shirt buttons. Inside the damp linen, they find dewy skin. My palms imprint themselves on it, greedy and grabbing. I run my fingertips over hard little nipples. I pinch them; he grunts then bites down on my lower lip.

His teeth graze rather than incise, but the gesture fills me with wild excitement. I arch my back, bucking up against him, grinding my mound into his responsive hardness. He wedges a hand in between, fingers sliding inside my knickers, finding my steamy heat and plunging into it.

"*Puttanella mia, come sei bagnata,*" he croons, lifting his mouth from mine only for the duration of the words.

I'm not sure what they mean, but I don't care, and I hiss a long and heartfelt, "*Si,*" in return. The Italian lesson I'm already getting is good enough for me.

He explores what he finds between my thighs, tracing the outline of my swollen clit with skilled delicacy. My hips speak for me, begging for more, harder. He understands that language.

The pleasure is dizzying and it takes me a moment to remember what I meant to do. Ah, yes. My hands move to his belt buckle. He grabs them with the hand that isn't at work inside my knickers, places them gently but firmly out of range.

"*Aspetta,*" he admonishes, and I understand, but all the same he follows up with, "Too fast, let me give it to you first."

"But I want you now," I plead. "I want you inside me."

His resolve is overwhelmed. He rears up, pulling his fingers out of me, and unbuckles the belt with a snap. I watch with fascination as he unzips, unveiling what he has in store for me.

It's enough to make the driest mouth water, but that mouth

dries again when my brain gives a shape to the blot of anxiety lurking behind all the blind lust.

"Oh! I don't suppose you have . . . ?" I raise my head a little, resting on my elbows, hoping my awkward flush will complete the sentence for me.

He smiles enigmatically, reaches for his jacket, takes a wallet from the inner pocket, and from that . . . yes . . . the sun glints off the corner of a foil square.

"You are in a hurry," he teases. "I like to take my time."

"Yes, but . . . you know . . ." I look around the glade in illustration. "Not the most private of places, is it? Someone might come."

He laughs, his eyes wicked.

"Ah, yes, I think so," he says, tearing the foil with sharp teeth.

"Please," I urge, bucking against him.

"You'll get what you want," he promises, sheathing up. His trousers are around his knees now, his shirt undone, with incipient grass stains at the elbows. Even so, he manages to retain a certain elegance. He is, I sense, a man who commands a lot of respect in the world.

He reestablishes himself between my knees, pushes me back down with a hand on my chest, fixes his lips to mine, and yanks my knickers aside. These simultaneous actions are followed just as quickly by his swift plunge inside me.

I am so wet that my pussy offers barely anything in the way of resistance, but I feel that good stretch, a yielding of muscles stiff from disuse, and I moan at how perfectly he fills me.

"Mm, that's good?" he asks in an intense whisper. "You feel good. You feel tight."

"I want to keep it," I whisper back, contracting my muscles around him as if forbidding him to ever withdraw. We kiss, hard and starving, basking in the connection, trying everything we can to deepen it. If I could get him any farther in, I would, but he is as big and thick and hard as any man will ever be in me, and it's glorious.

The moment lasts precisely as long as we can stand it to. I try a shimmy, as far as I can with his satisfying weight pinning me to the ground. He reads my signal, braces himself, pulls slowly out, maddens me by holding himself with just his tip hovering around my taut vagina.

I try to force him in, pushing the backs of his thighs with my heels, lifting my bottom, but he has full control. He seizes my wrists, holds them down above my head, kisses my neck.

"Ask me nicely," he suggests, and his slight struggle with the pronunciation renders the words ten times sexier. *Askame. Nizerly.*

"*Per favore,*" I sigh, hoping my bad accent has the same effect on him.

Apparently it does.

He penetrates with sturdy strokes, but the rhythm isn't frantic. It isn't the right kind of day for that. He keeps it slow, makes me feel every inch of him as he eases back and forth. He releases my wrists and there is kissing, stroking, lots of sighing into each other's throats. I am wet all over, inside and out. Pools gather in the small of my back, between my breasts, the backs of my knees, the crack of my buttocks. It all seems to combine with the swirling gush within me, showing him that he can do anything he wants to me.

He grabs me suddenly and rolls me over with a laugh of relish, so that I sit astride him. I bend low, offering my breasts to his eager mouth. Wisps of dry grass are clinging to my bottom and thighs and he brushes them aside, very vigorously, almost spanking them away.

"Mm," I encourage, kissing his neck, licking the tender spot below his earlobe, moving down until I can feel his pulse, mad against my tongue. He smacks me harder. "God yes."

He grabs my stinging bumcheeks, one in each hand, and squeezes hard. I straighten my spine, cup my breasts, play with them, watching his eyes upon me. He makes me grind against him, controlling my movements, working me hard until I am ready to collapse back onto his chest.

There is a flash of light somewhere away in the trees to our right and I wonder vaguely if a storm is coming, but before I can look toward the spot he has rolled me over again and has my legs up over his shoulders, pounding into me now, his mouth open as he pants, his eyes drilling into mine. *Watch what I'm doing to you,* they say, *and don't you dare try to deny you want it.*

I shut my eyes, obscurely afraid of admitting the depth of my desire for him, but he won't have it.

"*Guardami,* look, look at me," he commands, his palm firm against my cheek. I try to hide my face in it, but he won't have it. Defeated, I raise my eyes to his.

Deliberately, making sure I don't miss a moment, he licks the tips of his fingers and places them between my lower lips. He rubs in time with his thrusts, spreading my legs wider, watching my face, waiting for the right signs.

"Tell me when," he says, but I'm already perilously close, skimming the edge, his face blurring until he is nothing but a pair of giant black vortices pulling me into them.

I hope my jagged cry tells him what he needs to know, along with the sudden tightening of my grip on his shoulder. I hope he can feel the tremor in my belly and the spasm around his cock. I hope he can interpret the way my voice is rising and gaining in volume.

"Yes, yes." His teeth are gritted. "Oh, *siiii, si, si, si, si.*"

He pounds into me, flattening me into the grass, his neck flushed dark red, his chest shining so that the short dark hairs look painted on, his eyes rolling up into his head.

My orgasm seems to go on and on. When it finally ends, he collapses on top of me, crushing me, kissing me, cradling me.

"Incredible," he whispers into my ear.

"Mmm," I agree, still far away from the power of speech. It is out there somewhere with the sunbeams, in the heat haze we have woven around our bodies.

We lie like that until it becomes uncomfortable. I twitch beneath him; he releases me and sits up, looking down at me.

"Don't look at me," I mumble into the ground. "I'm literally a hot mess."

"I like it," he says, stroking my hair. "You look like a woman after making love. What is bad about that?"

I cringe a little at "making love," but reflect that it is probably a translation thing. Or he is simply being gallant.

"Nothing," I say, turning to face him again. "God. That was . . . uncharacteristic. I mean, impulsive. Not like me at all."

He laughs, bends to kiss the tip of my nose.

"Perhaps you don't know yourself very well," he says.

"What, you think I'm really the kind of woman who . . . does this . . . with strangers all the time?"

"I think you're really a very sensual person," he says, shaking his head. "It's not a bad thing. For me, it's a very good thing."

"Well, yeah," I say with a self-conscious little laugh.

"No, don't do that," he says, leaning over me on one elbow, his brow sternly gathered. "Don't go back to that. Let's be honest. We saw each other, we wanted each other, we took each other. It's simple and it's good."

"Like the people in the sculptures."

"Like them, yes."

My phone beeps in my bag.

"God, what time is it?" I sit up, plucking dried husks from my hair.

"I don't know." He deals with the condom, buttons up his shirt, tucks himself back into his trousers, reaches again into the inner pocket of his jacket. This time he brings out a card. "I'm here until Friday," he says. "If you want to be that person you don't think you are again—call me."

"Oh. Thanks." I stand up, let my skirts fall back down, dust myself off.

"And I hope you will," he adds, hooking me against him for a last long, scorching kiss.

I'm still reeling a bit when he leaves.

*It'll be the heat,* I tell myself, watching his broad back and the creases in his linen jacket until they disappear in the tangle of trunks and branches.

I brush my hair, freshen my face, spritz myself with body spray, and head for the reception desk.

"Ah." The exhibition guide greets me from behind the desk like an old friend. Her smile tells me what I wanted to know.

"When do you finish work?" I ask her.

"In fact, I finished ten minutes ago. You are the last visitor to leave."

I nod, holding her gaze.

"So . . . is there a bar near here where I can buy you a drink? I'd like to find out some more about your work. I wonder if you got any inspiration this afternoon?"

Twin patches of red appear on her cheeks.

*Busted,* I think.

"Sure," she says. "There's a little place a half kilometer away from here."

"Good," I say, watching her gather her belongings together, her dainty hands, her glossy hair, the swell of her buttocks as she leans over to switch off the till. "I don't think I've ever been thirstier in my whole life."

# AFTER MIDNIGHT

Balli Kaur Jaswal

The girls on the TV ads for After Midnight Chat Line are shown
by components: red lips speaking into the phone; long fingers
clutching the sheets; milky smooth thighs parting slowly. A silky
voiceover assures the customer that if he calls the number now,
those same parts will be waiting for him. For Rika's first shift, she
dresses for the role—lipstick, kohl-rimmed eyes, a lacy lingerie set
that she bought on discount. She puts the phone on speaker mode
and lies sprawled across her bed, running the tips of her fingers
along her inner thighs as the first call comes through.

"What's your name?" she purrs. The caller tells her he wants to
fuck her. "Tell me how," she persists. He is going to fuck her. He
is fucking her now. "You listen to me, bitch, I'm fucking you," he
commands, but there are no further instructions. He grunts and
gasps, and then hangs up.

*She's waiting to talk to you . . .* A flash of fine print at the
bottom of the television screen explains the charges per minute.
Special requests for specific girls are dealt with by the operator.
Rika pictures the operator as a brusque woman sternly holding

back thirsty men. She likes to think it's a woman looking out for their interests, instead of the man who hired her over the phone, who asked her to moan and pant and talk dirty so he could see if she had what it took. Rika tries not to dwell on such wishes because they only make reality harder to accept. Take that first caller, for example. Rika wanted to sound the way the women in the ads looked—coy and seductive, as if she could draw him into a realm where they were lovers. But his hasty and urgent commands made it clear that this was a transaction, and it only went one way.

Many of the other calls are like that. At the end of her inaugural shift, Rika drinks a warm glass of water with lemon slices to soothe her voice. The cheap bra's underwire is popping out and digging into her skin. She decides to save her makeup for occasions when she leaves the house.

Before working for the phone sex line, Rika danced in a bar. In a glittering sari and bridal jewelry, she swayed her hips and cast demure smiles at rheumy-eyed men perched like crows along a wire. *I'm yours, I'm not yours.* This was the tension that made customers return. The girls divided their shifts between dancing onstage and mingling with customers to encourage them to buy more drinks. The men were easy to please—all it took was a giggle or a toss of her hair. Management had strict rules against touching since the last police raid, but Rika and the other girls found that brushing the rustling fabric of their saris against a man's fingers made those same fingers reach into their wallets.

Cell phones weren't allowed during working hours. At the start of each shift, the dancers surrendered their phones to a big Ziploc bag. The men didn't like seeing them on their phones because that broke the fantasy of these girls existing just for them. The illuminated screens were entire other worlds where these men didn't belong. After closing one night, Rika and the other girls went to retrieve their phones and found the bag empty and one of the girls missing. She had sneaked away from the bar at some point and gotten into the manager's office. The drawers on his desk were flung open, but when she couldn't find any cash, she took their phones instead. Because the manager didn't lose anything, he shrugged about the losses and told them he didn't want to hear any complaints.

Rika and the other girls had to pay for their own replacement phones the next day. On the registration form, Rika put herself down as *Miss* although the other girls put themselves down as *Mrs.*, choosing the names of the bar patrons or Bollywood actors as their husbands. The man at the counter glanced at the *Miss* on Rika's form and looked as if he was going to ask if she was sure. She stared back, challenging him.

The phone calls started that night. Unknown numbers, different men. Rika couldn't block them. They wanted to know if she was interested in making friends, and when she hung up, they called again, undeterred. Sometimes it seemed as if she was answering the phone in the middle of a conversation, where the men were already in the throes of passion and just needed Rika's voice to finish the act. After three continuous nights of this, Rika marched back to the shop. "You sold my number, didn't you?" she asked the man at the counter.

He shrugged, not bothering to deny it. Rika imagined slapping him hard across the face. He would bring a palm to his stinging cheek and regard her with newfound respect. This kind of thing only happened in movies though. In real life, Rika sensed the heat of anger from other men working in the shop—how dare she? Her father and her brothers were like this. If she spoke up against one, the others would emerge from shadowy corners of the household to silence her. This was what drove her to leave, to take her first chance to escape. The city gleamed with possibilities at first, but after the exhilaration of new beginnings wore off, Rika found herself still contending with sneering, leering men.

The calls continued. Rika began leaving her phone off at night after her evenings at the bar. She shared a cramped bedsit with three other dancers. Clothes spilled out of gaping suitcases; there was no space for a chest of drawers. Power outages were common in their part of Delhi. One night, when the lights blinked and vanished with a sigh, it was during Rika's turn to charge her phone from the only working wall plug that all the roommates shared. Her battery was only at twelve percent. Rika couldn't turn her phone off because she needed the alarm to wake her up for her next shift. But when she left it on, a man called over and over again until her battery was nearly flat. Finally, she picked up. "Listen you bastard," she hissed. "What the hell do you want?"

There was a pause, which lengthened into a long silence. The phone sounded a warning—five percent. Rika continued. "You want me to moan and whimper the minute I hear your voice? Go to hell."

The man's breathing became heavier, and Rika realized she was turning him on. Her phone bleeped again. She also noticed that this excited her. She reached into her pants and slipped her fingers in, surprised at how wet she was. "You want me to spread my legs and brush against your cock? I won't do that. I'm not interested." But she pictured it as she talked, and her fingers worked faster. "I'm not going to let you suck on my tits," she said, gasping between words. The phone bleeped a final warning and then shut off just as she came.

After the third police raid on the nightclub in as many weeks, Rika thought about that call. She had seen the advertisements for the After Midnight Chat Line and wondered if she could be one of the girls on the other end. The girls on the ads intrigued Rika. Even though she knew they were just acting, she was mesmerized by the way their chests heaved and their bright red mouths rounded with the vowels of desire.

It's a paycheck, and this is the most important thing. Rika doesn't know the exact source of her disappointment after each call, but it's the same hollowness that haunted her when she first realized that the independent city life she craved was just a fantasy. Here, like anywhere, men are in charge.

One night, while Rika is settling in and getting ready for her shift, there is a knock on the apartment door. It is her roommate Vani. Vani is a lanky dancer with streaks of red henna dye in her long, wavy hair. She is one of the most popular girls at the bar because of the way she croons along with the songs from classic Hindi movies, her pitch matching the singers' perfectly. The men sing back to her, off-key and riotous, convinced they are heroes.

"I thought you were going to be out for the evening," Rika says as Vani breezes past her.

"I've had enough," Vani says. "The police come around looking for bribes all the time. They're threatening to shut the place down for a week now. I can't go that long without pay."

"A week?" Rika asks. Vani will lose half her month's rent in that time.

"At least a week, they said. I just walked out of there tonight. The managers told us to stop attracting the wrong kinds of men, because that's why the police keep targeting the bar. As if we're the problem!"

Rika knows the management's blaming tactics well. The first time the bar was raided, they rounded up the girls and scolded them for luring low-class clientele, arousing the authorities' suspicion that it was a brothel. "If you behaved better, we wouldn't have this problem," the manager barked, pacing like a sergeant. Show less skin, show more skin—the problem was the same. They were expected to be the kind of women the men wanted to touch but could only admire. They were supposed to look like brides but dance like lovers.

"What are you going to do now?" Rika asks.

Vani locks eyes with her. "What have you been doing?"

Rika bites her lip. She hasn't told her roommates much about her new job, only that she is working remotely. She supposes they figured out quickly enough that it isn't a telemarketing job.

"I talk to men on the phone," Rika says. "It's like what we do at the pub—create an illusion for them." *But I want to be in the illusion too,* she refrains from confiding, because of what Vani might think of her. "They hang up too quickly," Rika says. "It's just a transaction for them. At the pub, at least they stayed around—on the phone, it's easy to end things at the press of a button."

As Vani keeps a curious gaze on Rika, she feels self-conscious. Rika isn't close to the other girls in the apartment, preferring to keep to herself. "Let me do one call," Vani says. "I just want to try it out." Rika obliges her because she doesn't know what else to do. She doesn't want any conflict with her roommates.

Vani makes herself comfortable on Rika's bed. At midnight, the phone rings. She picks up and answers breathily. "Hello," she says. A smile spreads across her face. "Oh, I remember you. Sure, what do you want me to do?" A giggle. "That's very naughty. I'll do it just for you though." Vani is rubbing her thighs together, and her free hand is roaming over her own body.

"Tell me something," Vani whispers into the phone. "Do you miss me when we're not talking? Do you think of me?" A pause while she closes her eyes and listens to the response. Rika watches with interest. The men don't usually have much more to say to her.

Vani continues. "Did you have a hard day today, baby? I know, you work so hard, don't you? You work so hard for me. I've been here just thinking about what you do for me. Come here and take my clothes off, darling. I'm so ready for you. I've been waiting all day."

Rika could only hear the caller's voice as a murmur on the phone, but he is talking now, saying things that make Vani react with excitement.

"Mmm," she moans. "Oh, I need you. Yes, yes. You're making me so wet. Don't go just yet. Wait. Wait." She gasps and groans, writhing around on Rika's bed, her eyes squeezed shut. When the call finally ends, Vani's cheeks are flushed. She opens her eyes and hands the phone back to Rika.

"Make him forget he's a customer," Vani advises, wiping the sheen of sweat from her brow.

"I've tried that," Rika says. "They're not interested in me like that." They must hear her disillusionment—the dull edges of her voice, the flatness of her moans. Vani threw herself into the experience, but Rika is unable to create a convincing fantasy.

But then Rika thinks about the caller she scolded during the blackout. Who was he, that she was so aroused when she scolded him? Probably the man in the cell phone shop who had sold her number or the manager at the phone sex line who wanted her picture. He was the man who came to the bar and smashed a glass on the floor once and complained Rika had an attitude problem because she wouldn't kiss him. He was the manager who made her sweep up the glass, who didn't want to hear her side of the story. He is the police, the catcallers on the street. She is so helpless with rage sometimes that she can feel the heat of it simmering beneath her skin.

"Try it," Vani says. "Close your eyes and think about your lover. Doesn't matter that he doesn't exist. Why do you think we all used actors' surnames when we registered those replacement phones?" *Why didn't you?* She doesn't ask, but the question hangs between them and remains unanswered.

The phone screen lights up, signaling a new call, so Vani slips out of the room. Rika answers with the same breathy greeting that Vani used, and she smiles as if the caller's voice genuinely brings her joy. "Has it been a long day?" Her voice drips with honey.

"A very long day, baby," the caller replies. He has one of those gravelly voices that will either descend into deep groans or rise to whimpers at the peak of his ecstasy.

"I can help you relax, then," Rika says. "Do you want a massage?"

"Yeah," he says.

"I'll give you a good massage," she murmurs. "I'll give myself a massage too, okay, baby?"

"Okay," he says. His voice perks up a little bit. This is turning him on. Rika tries to get into the fantasy as well. She pictures him tall, with broad shoulders and a kind smile, but the image doesn't remain long. "Let me start with a back rub for you." She lets out a soft moan to indicate that she is touching herself as well. "Does that feel good?"

"You sound good," he says. "Do that again. Do that while I put my cock into your mouth."

Rika moans. The sound comes from deep within, edging her into the realm of fantasy. Her thin pallet with threadbare sheets is now a sprawling four-poster bed, covered in royal-silk sheets and plump pillows. She is lying back, her arms spread wide like wings as the man lowers his face between her legs. His tongue tickles and teases her while she writhes with pleasure. Over the phone, she can hear his breathing getting heavier.

"What are you doing now?" he whispers.

"I'm letting you get on top of me," Rika says. But in her mind, she is raising her hips to let him taste her. The room around her dissolves farther into the vast, luxurious space of her fantasies. Deeper and deeper he goes, until he disappears and she is only aware of her delicious wetness. It doesn't matter what the man looks like because he is irrelevant. He is only there to keep that electricity fizzing through her nerves. Outside, the constant puttering and shrieking of traffic gives way to a silence in which Rika can only hear her quickening heartbeat. She slips a hand into her pants and her fingertips circle her clit, making new pulses of pleasure with each round. She moans into the phone as if she's enjoying the caller's commands, but her own teasing is all she really feels. Her slick fingers work faster, stroking and pressing, bringing her to a climax that she expresses in a loud, unapologetic gasp that echoes down the phone line. The caller grunts his own finish a few seconds later.

Rika doesn't even hear what she says to him after that, but she knows it keeps him going. For the rest of her shift, she calls to mind all the men who have expected her servitude and silence. One by one, they line up in the room she has constructed. They kneel politely before her, and on her command, they give her what she is owed. Men use the tips of their tongues to make her gasp and cry out. Their lips savor the heat between her legs. When has Rika ever felt such control over her own pleasure? She tries to think of a scene in her real life that compares to this fantasy, but none measures up. Every time she has been approached or touched by a man, she's felt like a conquest. Now here are all the men, obliging her as if it is their duty.

Rika is reluctant to open her eyes once the call is over. She murmurs her good-byes to the caller, who lets out a satisfied grunt and then hangs up. Her eyes flutter open and she fully expects to be thrown back to reality, but something has changed. She is in her room again, but that fresh excitement from her first days in the city has returned. It glimmers at the edges of her vision and brings a note of joy to her voice that the next caller believes is reserved just for him.

# FROSTING

Kathleen Delaney-Adams

Perched gracefully on the corner of Michigan Avenue and Oak Street, Beloved Cupcake Wedding Boutique was unparalleled in femininity. Its pale-pink brick exterior with whimsical scalloped edging and flowering window baskets exuded all things girly girl and served as a magnet to the squealing brides who crossed its glamorous threshold. The inner sanctum was posh and elegant, offering velvet couches in varying shades of pink and red and vibrant displays of sugary confections. A large window offered clients a view of the kitchens, where busy worker bees bustled about around the clock, applying the perfect finishing touches to an endless round of wedding cakes and cupcakes. Beloved Cupcake was *the* destination for indulged and indulgent brides-to-be who desired a pampering and romantic pre-wedding experience.

Decadence and opulence oozed out of the very walls as the three young women on the schedule for the day scurried about the kitchens. It was a beautiful Monday morning in late August, and all was in preparation to open the shop before the arrival of their very important first client of the day.

Estelle's razor-sharp heels heralded her entrance as she clicked briskly along Magnificent Mile and opened the door to the shop. The owner and proprietress, she was dressed to the nines in an austere blouse and tight black pencil skirt, her hair pulled back from her face severely in a French knot, with nary a stray wisp of hair in sight.

Estelle was everything Beloved Cupcake was not. Haughty, rigid to the point of uptight, crisp, and businesslike. Her shopgirls adored and feared her in equal measures, and thus would do anything she asked of them. She was a fair employer and a patient teacher. If she were emotionally remote and distant, none could fault her for that in light of her artistic flair and expertise. She was second to none in the bakery profession, and working for her was an honor in high demand.

Estelle was already firing off instructions the moment she crossed the threshold, and her tone brooked no argument. Their first client of the day was the esteemed Ms. Olivia Donahue, a woman with formidable money and clout, and a wedding designer whose word would carry great weight in the bridal community and beyond. To say Estelle needed this contract was an understatement, and her anxiety threatened to undermine even *her* cool exterior.

To her shopgirls, Estelle appeared calm and in control, which soothed their own nerves as they pulled the cakes from the ovens and prepared to start on the frostings. They would offer their visitor an array of textures and tastes, designed to entice her to sign on with Estelle's team exclusively to provide the cakes and dessert arrangements for Ms. Donahue's vast clientele.

Ms. Donahue arrived alone and promptly at her appointment time. She was dressed impeccably in winter-white trousers and a faux-mink wrap. Her posture was ramrod straight, and her perfectly coiffed updo had appealing strands of gray mixed in with warm chestnut. Her regal features lent an aura of untouchability, an aura she took pains to cultivate and maintain. She had a reputation for severity and looked every inch as if it were well earned. She was also stunning and no doubt knew it. She glanced disdainfully about the lobby before perching primly on the edge of one of the velvet couches.

Estelle crossed to her in long strides, extending her hand and a polished smile.

"Ms. Donahue. We are thrilled."

Ms. Donahue nodded briefly and accepted the cup of tea one of Estelle's staff hurried to offer.

"Shall we get started?" Estelle queried. "I'm sure you have a busy schedule. I think you will enjoy the portfolio I've put together."

As she reached for the leather binder to move it closer to Ms. Donahue, she felt a hand on her thigh. She raised her eyes and met Ms. Donahue's direct and piercing gaze.

"Yes?" She paused.

Ms. Donahue's hand remained on her leg in a firm grip, a grip too familiar and possessive for Estelle's comfort. She fought the urge to shift her leg away. Afraid the gesture would appear impolite to the guest she desired to impress, she remained still.

Ms. Donahue's voice was cultured and strong.

"I prefer to learn a bit about someone's character before I deign to do business with them."

"I see." Estelle remained outwardly cool, although her heart pounded at the other woman's touch. "What did you have in mind?"

A quick flash of amusement crossed Ms. Donahue's face. That brief crack in her frosty demeanor made her all the more attractive, and Estelle found herself inexplicably flushed with heat.

"Come, dear. I merely want to observe you and your girls for a while. Watch your interactions, ascertain how you conduct your-selves."

"Of course." Estelle stood, smoothing her skirt along her thighs and ignoring her fluttering stomach. She felt her poise slipping away and fought the sudden waves of hunger coursing through her. This would not do. She was a consummate professional and refused to let this woman unnerve her, however suddenly attracted, and acutely aware of that attraction, she might find herself.

"Follow me." Estelle was happily unaware that her profes-sional veneer stretched thinly over unmasked desire—a fact that did not, however, go unnoticed by Ms. Donahue.

Accustomed to being observed, Estelle nonetheless found herself greatly distracted by the other woman's presence. She worked dili-gently with her staff for several long moments to complete that morning's order for a bridal shower, all the while aware of Ms. Donahue's proximity. She tried in vain to concentrate on the swirls of coral frosting she was mixing, flustered by the obviousness of Ms. Donahue's intense eyes steadily focused on her. She could not know that her firm ass swayed with her every movement, show-cased deliciously by her tight skirt, and that just a hint of lace along the top of her stockings peeked out each time she bent at the waist to reach for a bowl or spatula. They were visions in femi-ninity and sexuality, enjoyed tremendously by Estelle's would-be client.

As Estelle leaned across the counter for a wooden spoon, she felt the press of another body against hers. Insistent. Demanding. She froze and tried to turn. She was stopped by a pair of hands gripping her waist and held firmly in place against the counter.

"A moment, dear." Ms. Donahue's voice was low and calm in her ear, her lips brushing lightly across Estelle's hair. Warmth spread beneath Estelle's skin, a surge of liquid heat infusing her to her core.

"My staff . . ." It was all she could think to stammer by way of protest.

"Ahh, now, now. I believe they are here to learn. Let's not make this difficult. I see no need to send them away."

With her back to her captor, Estelle could not see the smooth smile of anticipation on Ms. Donahue's face, but it was implied in her voice. Estelle's heart thudded with fear and lust, an internal debate. She had not the time, nor the mental acumen, to struggle with her warring emotions before Ms. Donahue's strong hand on her back bent her neatly at the waist.

Unable to resist, Estelle yielded, surprising both herself and her client.

"Yes," Ms. Donahue purred. "Good. Good girl."

Estelle bristled, offended by the diminutive word. The thought flashed across her mind that she should be angry; how dare this stranger presume to touch her and boss her about in this way, and in front of her employees?

Estelle found she could not rustle up any resistance, however— she was too intrigued and aroused. She found herself whispering, "Yes, yes," when she felt Ms. Donahue's cool, deft hands slip beneath her skirt. The older woman raised it slowly upward along Estelle's thighs and over her ass. Ms. Donahue murmured quiet approval over the swath of ivory lace that barely covered Estelle's tight and fetching bottom. Her hands caressed Estelle's skin, lightly as a breath, molding her ass and hips, feeding on her flesh, taking her fill.

Estelle was dimly aware that all activity in the kitchen had ceased as her girls watched the scene unfolding before them, too shocked to continue their preparations or to consider protesting. She felt fevered and frightened, a trembling of limbs and heart and mind, a racing in her blood. The thought of refusing to surrender slipped from her mind entirely. It wasn't simply a matter of the business contract anymore. It had become bigger and deeper than that. An age-old yearning to let herself go completely, to give up her need for control, stealthily entered her bloodstream. Estelle felt as if she had waited half her lifetime to have this woman's hands on her. Helpless, powerless to stop what she both feared and longed for, she succumbed, panting and immobilized. Through the fog of her lust, she felt so clearly all she had denied herself for years. There was such relief in giving over, giving in. Such heady joy in allowing herself to have all she desired. And there was nothing she desired more in this moment than granting Ms. Donahue full access to herself.

The room held its collective breath as Ms. Donahue dropped to her knees in one fluid motion that managed to look effortless and commanding. She gripped Estelle's thighs in both hands for support and traced her tongue along the edge of Estelle's back seam. Estelle felt warm, wet sweetness running up her calf and thigh, a slow, delicious shudder racking her body. She moaned when Ms. Donahue reached the top of the seam and continued licking along the edge of lace at the top of her thigh. A cry escaped her mouth as that sweet tongue began exploring her lace panty, moving between her legs, lapping at the bit of fabric that covered her already saturated pussy.

Estelle nearly wept when Ms. Donahue stopped abruptly and stood. She was left bereft and hungry, her hips rocking slightly of their own accord.

"I did not tell you to move." Ms. Donahue's voice was a hiss. A well-modulated hiss, but a hiss nonetheless. Estelle chilled and attempted to hold her consumed body still.

Adept fingers slid between Estelle's lace and her skin. Ms. Donahue slipped the panties down Estelle's thighs, letting them drop to her ankles and leaving them there. With the well-positioned toe of her snakeskin slingbacks, she forced Estelle's legs farther apart. Estelle felt the lace fabric around her ankles strain and then tear as her legs spread open. Her slick and exposed cunt heated all the more despite the cool air she could now feel on it. She had never felt so exposed, so vulnerable, her fierce reserve torn from her as easily as her thong had been. She had never, to be sure, felt such fear and longing, conflicting emotions that forced her to question all she believed of herself.

She had never felt so hot for someone, for some*thing* in all of her life.

Her arousal was a palpable scent that filled the room, mingling with the smell of sugar, wafting in the sweet faces of her no-older-than-twenty staff. Their innocence rapidly abandoning them, they stood in a huddle, watching with reactions that moved between aghast to curious to their own heated and newly developing passions. Adele, a pretty blonde sorority girl, turned toward Stephanie and ran her fingers across her perky little tits, smiling as Stephanie's nipples became erect and strained against the fabric of the camisole she wore. Maria saw her coworkers fondling each other and moved quickly to join in the fun, slipping her hand beneath Stephanie's ruffled apron to touch her very wet pussy. They writhed and moaned in a corner of the kitchen, grabbing at each other, grappling with camis and cotton panties and warm, pliant skin, exploring newly blossoming tastes, much to Ms. Donahue's delight. She had not bargained on a group scene but found the thought most delicious and decided then and there she would allow them their bit of play for now. She had all she desired spread out before her on the counter.

Estelle was delectable indeed, her swollen pussy open and inviting, her tits smashed beneath her, her breath ragged and gasping. Ms. Donahue scooped up a handful of Crisco shortening from the open tin on the counter and shoved her hand deep inside Estelle's cunt, a hard, fast thrust that caused Estelle to scream before she could stop herself. Ms. Donahue punch-fucked her with an adept frenzy, pumping in and out while Estelle rocked on her fist, unable to control her crazed need. Jackhammer thrust followed thrust, Estelle so wet and open she was sure Ms. Donahue was inside her to her elbow. She was unaware that she was weeping, feeling nothing save the fiery ache in her cunt. This abandon was unprecedented, yet her control slid away from her easily and with but a moment's hesitation. She gave in completely and fully, surrendering herself over to Ms. Donahue, demand met and answered. She came suddenly and with a violence she did not know she possessed.

It was over as abruptly as it began. She sagged against the counter, spent and grateful she had something to hold her upright on her stilettos. She fought to regain her breath, her speech, although she was unsure if she intended to thank Ms. Donahue profusely or let loose a string of profanity. She had her professional reputation, after all, not to mention her personal dignity. Both, she feared, were all but lost in the face of this . . . this ravaging hunger . . . these ripening passions.

Just as she thought she should rouse up a bit of a protest, if only to save face, she felt Ms. Donahue wipe more shortening along the entrance to her asshole before sliding a long, elegant finger inside.

Ms. Donahue was almost gentle as she rode Estelle's ass with first one, then two fingers, with well-crafted, almost lazy finger-fucking. Estelle could not bear the pace, the slowness, her own need still ricocheting through her. She writhed and moaned and trembled, attempting to force Ms. Donahue's fingers in deeper. When she felt her tongue lapping at the crease of her pussy, she opened her legs as far as she was able and began to beg.

"Please. God, please, no, no, please. More. More. I need it."

She moved and rocked, Ms. Donahue's tongue and fingers

keeping rhythm. She thought she would explode, crying, "Yes, YES!" as she began to come.

Ms. Donahue stepped back, withdrawing all touch, all pleasure, just as Estelle was cresting, about to break open. She froze, cried out in frustration, and collapsed back on the counter sobbing. Broken. Aching.

Ms. Donahue selected a towel from the rack and daintily wiped her hands. She removed a compact from the purse that still hung from the crook of her elbow and carefully applied a fresh layer of soft red lipstick. Only then did she turn once more toward the group of women who were now still, watching wide-eyed, anticipation on their fresh faces.

"Dears." She smiled. "I know you can do better than that. I came to be wooed. Please, a demonstration of your abilities."

Ahh, youth. So eager to please. After mere seconds of hesitation, the women moved swiftly, removing their camis, granting Ms. Donahue sweet visual access to their lithe, full bodies and round, creamy breasts. She sighed with great satisfaction as Maria used a spatula to smear coral frosting across Adele's full, heavy tits before lapping if off with her tongue, quick little licks that caused Adele to squirm and whimper. Stephanie knelt and began to lick and probe at Adele's pussy with her tongue and fingers, attempting to imitate Ms. Donahue's own expertise. It was so sweet, so inept, Ms. Donahue would have laughed had Stephanie not begun touching her own pussy. Mmm, now *that* was yummy, and Ms. Donahue felt her own cunt growing steamy again. For several long moments, she enjoyed the girls' sexual antics and floundering, flowering bodies. She would not have missed the ecstasy on Adele's face when she came splashing onto the hands and mouths of her friends, shouting jubilantly. That might very well have sealed the deal, she decided.

She turned away from the girls in time to observe an exhausted, barely recovered Estelle push herself back up on her feet. Estelle was still trembling, but she lifted her eyes bravely to meet Ms. Donahue's haughty stare. She knew she must look a fright, torn panties around her ankles, thighs sticky with juice, limbs shaking. Ms. Donahue, on the other hand, appeared competent and completely un-mussed. Was it simply and irrevocably terrible that Estelle ached only to be used by her all over again?

Ms. Donahue smiled stiffly. "I will consider Beloved Cupcake to be sure. I have one more bakery to visit this afternoon. I will be in touch. Good day."

She turned and moved swiftly and gracefully out the door, leaving behind the faint scent of Chanel.

Estelle stared after her, nearly whining out loud. An eternity seemed to pass before she remembered her staff, her shop, her bridal shower order. She looked over her shoulder at the three disheveled women now gawking at her in embarrassment.

She hastily retucked her blouse, smoothing her skirt back over her thighs, and kicked the remains of her lace thong under a table. Patting her hair to check its status, she sighed.

"I'm sure we will get her contract, ladies. She seemed impressed with, uh, Beloved Cupcake. She *will* be back." She offered a shaky smile that she hoped passed for confident and shook off the lingering thought that she might very well die if Ms. Donahue did *not* come back.

"Now let's get this place put back together and finish frosting the cakes. The bride's mother will be here at noon."

One last trembling glance at the door through which Ms. Donahue had made her exit, and she collected herself.

Estelle heard a round of giggling. She glanced at her employees and caught Adele snickering behind her hand. They were still standing in a cluster in the corner, regarding her with uncon-cealed amusement. This would simply not do. She must recover their respect and admiration, if only to remind them *all*, herself included, of her place and position.

"Girls." She was relieved her voice was firm and strong again. In control.

"I asked you to assist in cleaning up. When I give an instruction, I expect it to be followed immediately. Now come here."

The three young women rushed to her side, fussing and twittering, but obedient nonetheless. Better. She knew they would not dare defy her.

"Hands on the counter. That's it. Bend over. Yes, like that."

Estelle surveyed her staff, now lined up against the counter, bent at the waist, hands planted firmly in front of them. Maria, by far the most timid of the three, was trembling slightly. Estelle paused; she had never disciplined her staff, and certainly not like this. Then she heard it: all three women breathlessly begging, "Please, please. Yes. Ma'am, touch us. Yes."

Estelle walked the length of them, pausing to pull Stephanie's legs apart and back a bit more, forcing her ass up higher in the air. All three of them had plump, tasty, sweet buttocks and thighs. She felt herself flush again, remembering Ms. Donahue's hands working her over.

She picked up a spatula from the counter and went to work on the girls' asses and thighs. They squealed and squirmed, but as Estelle had suspected, none defied her or moved from their positions before her. In fact, eager cries for more filled the room, and it was obvious the girls were enjoying this impromptu spanking. Estelle found herself relishing the punishment she doled out far more than she had intended to, allowing herself to unleash her pent-up longing and frustration on her staff's willing flesh. As their skin reddened like delicious cherries and welts began to appear, Estelle found herself relaxing at last, a smile teasing the corners of her mouth. Yes. Estelle basked in newfound feelings of strength, self-awareness, and deep affection for her staff. She had never allowed herself to play out such a fantasy, but now she embraced the arousal and headiness of it. This day had become a lesson in surrender, and Estelle welcomed the peace that came once she released all inhibition. She claimed and owned her desire—and had never felt more powerful.

The ring of the phone jarred her out of the scene and back into her shop and obligations. Shaking her head at the interruption, she set the spatula down and moved to answer it. The girls remained in place, red, swollen asses held high in the air. Mmm, she might not be done with them just yet, she decided.

"Beloved Cupcake Wedding Boutique." Her voice sounded smug and self-satisfied, even to her own ear.

A pause.

"Is this Estelle? It's Olivia Donahue calling. I will be requiring a second presentation. Does tomorrow midday work for you?"

Estelle's hand fluttered helplessly in the air before coming to land on her throat.

# DIRTY GIRLS ALWAYS
# GO TO HEAVEN

Lee Minxton

"Do you think the heroine ravishes the guy in this one?"

Her husband was flipping through a vintage bodice-ripper romance in their favorite used bookstore. Laney playfully snatched it out of his hand, arching an eyebrow at him. "Are you asking me to ravish you, Erik?"

She'd seen that half-chastened, half-challenging look in his eyes more and more over the past few days. She waited for him to laugh the comment off, but he just smiled enigmatically. Finally, he turned up in their bed two weeks later wearing nothing but a white lace thong. Laney knew then that she had to give them what they both needed.

Laney had always been a good Catholic girl, but as she got older, the words rang increasingly hollow. Only God would know how perverse she really was, she vowed, trying not to let her dreams of luscious young men run wild. Temptation lurked every-where—at the hockey rink, in the library. Alone in the house, she quietly worked out a private compromise, becoming eager and

experimental over time. One day over winter break during grad-
uate school, the vibrator's rumble and the intimate curve of Laney's
fingers overpowered her discretion. She heard herself moaning,
and then a concerned voice outside the locked door.

"Are you okay?"

Let us now observe a moment of silence for what was about
to be the best orgasm of Laney's life, murdered halfway through.
"I'm fine." Laney tried to hide the embarrassed annoyance in her
voice, mind racing for an excuse. "I just . . . hit my knee on something."

It was a weak cover, she knew, and her mom threw it in her face
a few days later during a fight about holiday chores. "You don't
need to moan and groan to experience sexual pleasure." Laney
flinched visibly as the lecture began. "I'm sorry you have no other
outlet for your urges, but we have neighbors." Turning on her
heel, her mother added, "And if you're buying *erotic accoutre-
ments,* you'd better not be using our credit card."

Her mom had been so cool about everything else up to then,
so Laney was doubly stunned at being slut-shamed and virgin-
shamed in one breath. (Apparently, like Walt Whitman, she
contained multitudes.) So many responses swirled in Laney's head,
but she decided that her mother was not entitled to any of them.
No one would ever be.

She ran into a childhood friend at a New Year's Eve party.
When Kristi complained that she was in desperate need of a new
housemate, Laney took the hint.

Rooming with Kristi had seemed like it would be a relief, but
Laney soon tired of getting razzed for never bringing a man home.
Something about Kristi's smarmy boyfriends made celibacy look
good by comparison. Kristi needled her to join dating sites and
go on blind dates, but Laney blanched at equating love and the
same algorithms she dealt with each day in the lab. She didn't

budge until Kristi put her foot down one April afternoon. "I want Kevin, and he won't go out with me unless I bring someone for his friend." Kristi poked her in the chest, indignant. "So take off your big-girl panties, because you're going with me tomorrow night!"

Laney didn't expect much of the double date, especially when Kevin dragged them all to a karaoke bar. What year was this, 1986? Even so, when she saw Erik, she had to stop herself from running a hand through his immaculate long hair, dark and inviting as her desires. When they were introduced, Erik's shy smile blossomed into a grin bright as the sun.

Every time Erik opened his mouth to talk, some rinky-dink synth intro heralded another greatest hit to be butchered. To make matters worse, Kristi and Kevin's flirtation unfolded like a slow-motion train wreck alongside them. No one could blame Laney for being unable to concentrate. She nodded distractedly when Erik told her he'd be right back.

A familiar backbeat jolted her awake. Laney had never told a soul about her lifelong Iggy Pop fixation, so it was a shock to find her date onstage, tearing through "Lust for Life." Most guys would thrash and swagger to the pounding drums, but Erik's lanky hips swayed to the bass line instead. He quickly returned to his seat once the song ended (missing Laney's cheers) and turned his choirboy eyes to the waitress. "One ginger ale, please."

Kevin shook his head. "Dude, that whole display was hilarious."

"Ginger ale?" Kristi started giggling. "Gotta stop living on the edge."

"Erik, are you free next Saturday?" Laney cringed at how breathless she sounded.

"Absolutely," he replied before she could complete her sentence.

So began a deliciously frustrating courtship.

Erik passed for the black sheep of his loving but strict family.

One brother worked as a public defender, while his other brother had joined the priesthood. When Erik got admitted to a prestigious graphic design school, his father ranted about the debauchery to be found in such bohemian places. Erik was scandalized (and secretly tantalized) by such notions but discovered that his reality would be far different. Erik daydreamed of paint and clay in belle époque salons while working with pixels and programs in sterile cubicles. "I thought I'd finally get to see a naked woman in person in a life drawing class," he confided to Laney during their third date. "But . . ."

Laney didn't believe him at first. When she ran her thumb soothingly over the inside of his wrist, his soft gasp convinced her. "Never say never," she whispered.

A soft brushing of lips lingered, threatened to turn incendiary. Just as she could feel them both starting to surrender to it, a moment of mutual hesitation broke the spell. "Good night, Laney," Erik sighed into her open mouth.

The unspoken mutual promise was to go slowly, made difficult by the fact that neither Laney nor Erik really knew how to navigate the situation. No one was sure when a seemingly accidental brushing of limbs was intentional, or how to respond to a casual innuendo hanging heavy with promise in the air. Making matters worse were fleeting but insistent teases of fierce pleasure, brought about by a wayward mouth or hand before they were suppressed once more.

They'd never admitted it, but Laney and Erik's eventual engagement had felt more like a parole hearing.

The white lace thong first surfaced at Laney's bridal shower, and she hated it instantly.

Laney watched her mother grit her teeth at the sight of it, saw Erik's mother roll her eyes. When she grudgingly held it up, Kristi hollered, "It's too small!" (In the privacy of her room, she was infuriated to discover that Kristi was right. Laney had trouble pulling the cheap one-size-fits-all novelty over her curvy hips.) The room echoed with high-pitched laughter, reminding Laney of a gaggle of geese. She'd always wanted to throw the thong away, rip it to shreds, but for some reason she never had.

Now, it enveloped her husband's delectable cock. She was jealous and yet amazed at how a scrap of cloth could make Erik even more beautiful. The contrast of white nylon against his darker complexion, coarse hairs brushing against fine lace, quickened her pulse. She insinuated a fingertip under the scalloped border, savoring the feel of Erik's warm skin beneath. He shifted in response, exposing his hip to her, turning his head coquettishly to hide his passive-aggressive grin.

There was no trace of levity in Laney's voice. "You know what happens to boys who tease, Erik."

"Do I?"

She didn't take her eyes off him as she reached into the drawer, fumbling for the straps. She'd practiced this alone for what felt like a thousand times over the past two weeks, but she hadn't realized how the intensity of her husband's gaze would throw her off her game. Taking a deep breath, she found a box farther back. The semisoft silicone dildo purchased during her years of abstinence remained her favorite, but she had never told Erik about it. She blushed when she realized how much it looked like him.

"That's for me?" Erik's voice dropped. "The head looks . . . thick."

"If you need to think about it, I'll make it worth your while." Laney heard Erik gasp as she took the dildo to the hilt in one swift thrust. Grinding eagerly against it to the rhythm of his uneven breathing, she started to lose herself. Laney remembered her mission. Reluctantly, she pulled the toy out, flinching at the lewd smacking sound it made. It wasn't easy to snap the slick cock into its capture. Soon enough Laney was on her knees above Erik on the bed, offering it to his pillowy lips. He seemed quizzical as he butterfly-kissed the tip, relieved once he made a mental note of its softness. His long eyelashes fluttered as he closed his eyes, flattening his tongue against the head reverently.

*He looks like he's taking his first Holy Communion.*

The sacrilegious thought rocked Laney onto her heels. Erik grasped her waist, pushing her forward, swallowing her whole. She willed herself to keep her hips still, afraid to fuck his face, not sure if his soft mewling came from ecstasy or protest. "You're just like me, Erik," she began. "Do you know what I used to do after our dates, after those sweet kisses good night? I'd go home, lock the bedroom door, and rail myself with a dildo until I'd had enough . . . the very same dildo you have in your mouth right now." She could actually feel him tugging harder; how could that be? "Then I'd pull it out and suck it dry, imagining that I was tasting you instead."

Erik's mouth fell open as Laney wavered, pulling back so the weight of her cock wouldn't hit him in the teeth. "*Fuck*, Laney." His own cock twitched in envy. Laney looked down. The white lace was translucent around the straining flesh, drenched. She moved her hand over the taut fabric, stunned at the heat against her palm, but wouldn't release Erik from its grasp. Laney slid down his body, stopping along the way to nip at his broad shoulder, his collarbone. She rested her cheek on the hard plane of his abdomen, grateful to not have to look him in the eye for what she said next.

"Remember that night on the honeymoon, what you said? 'Let's see how far we can take it.'" Laney's voice softened at the memory and the feel of Erik's fingers nestling into her chestnut hair. "You made it sound innocent, the high school heavy-petting session neither of us got to have. I figured, why not? You'd edged me for two years straight, so a couple of hours more wouldn't make any difference."

"You won." Erik's tone grew steely. "Telling me I looked so pretty that way, flushed and panting with sap dripping down to my kneecap, that you'd never let me come again. You'd keep me naked and hard as your fuck toy forever—"

"And then what?"

"I came, Laney." His defiant voice became desperate as she caressed him through the lace. "I finally came."

Laney sat up. "That's right, you did." A lifetime of warring impulses roiled within her, and she wasn't sure which would prevail. "Now you're wearing white, like none of that ever happened." She grasped the thong with both hands and pulled. Erik heard the ripping and shuddered as the cool air hit his over-heated skin, his newly freed cock dripping onto his swollen balls. She allowed herself one long, sensual swipe of her tongue on his cockhead, lapping down his balls, lower and lower. She whispered something, breath hot against Erik's most sensitive skin: "Good thing there's one part of you that's still pure."

He moaned as she found his sweet little hole and swirled it with her tongue, feeling it get hotter and hotter beneath as she started to stroke him in earnest. He loosened under her ministrations, opening his legs. Tentatively, she brushed a fingertip against his opening, holding it still as her tongue continued to work him. His cock flowed precome like a faucet, making it impossible for Laney to keep her grip. Feeling inspired, she used his own slickness to breach him, waiting until he started to buck against one finger, then two.

"Come on." Erik winced at the ragged whine of his voice. "Just—" He had to look away to say it. "Fuck me." He raised his knees, spreading himself wider.

Laney had new respect for Erik as she struggled to find the angle. Missionary must be hell on his knees; she was starting to feel an ache in her thighs. Erik lay beneath her, expectant. She had to see his face, she knew, so she crushed the tempting impulse to flip him over and take him from behind. There was just one thing to do. She bent down to growl right in his ear.

"Then roll over on top and ride me like the cock slut you are."

She reached for a bottle, drizzling liquid over her cock, jacking herself the way she'd seen him do so many times before. Then she lay back against the pillows, overflowing and tumescent for him at once. Laney reassured Erik as she saw him bite his lip. "Feel free to take your time."

Erik did, stretching himself out luxuriantly. He tried every trick she used to drive him crazy, teasing her cockhead against his opening, circling lazily like he had all day. He braced himself on his hands, reared up so as not to bruise her tender mound, but the dildo's base taunted her clit every time he bore down. "Grind on me," she told him, "as hard as you want."

Slowly, Erik took it all, arching his back deeply. "Right there." He started to move up and down. "Rub my spot . . ."

The vision was too much for her. "Rub mine!"

As she felt his long fingers beckoning inside her, Laney could feel it building. When she saw him throw his head back, she knew her climax would go beyond any form of control. She cried out once, twice, again and again. There would be no shame for Laney tonight, just Erik's lusty screams and his spunk baptizing her chest, absolving her at last.

Erik collapsed against Laney for a moment, then pulled off slowly, his eyes never leaving hers. He licked her clean, gently kissing her nipples until he had to stop to catch his breath. "I need a minute," he confessed. "I'm totally dead."

Laney placed her hand on his heart. "It's still beating." The sudden rush of affection for him made her dizzy. "Unless we're both gone."

Erik clasped his hand over hers. "Then I made it after all." He had the sweetest smile on his lips. "Because dirty girls always go to heaven."

She enfolded him, sharing deep kisses, the taste of her pleasure fully present in its commingling with his. For the first time, and from then on, she knew it was true.

# IF THE OCEAN

**Loretta Black**

That Friday dawned bleak, and Martha eyed the gray sky as she pulled on her boots. She was bound for the fish market while her brothers began the day's work on the farm. It was a long walk down to the village but one she'd made thousands of times, and she liked it because it took her down to the water.

Reaching the sandy beach, Martha unlaced her boots and strode across, rejoicing in the slap of her soles on the wet sand, the feel of her toes sinking into it. She walked all the way down to the waterline and set her hands on her hips as she stared out at the iron-gray waves and sky. The horizon was indistinguishable behind the haze of rainfall, and the British blockade was nowhere to be seen, their ships having been carried out on strong winds. No doubt a Yankee ship or two would try to slip out unseen if the weather worsened into the evening.

Martha stood staring a moment or two longer and sighed at the dull, gray view. Just as she began to turn back, something caught her eye. She figured it for the white peak of a wave or maybe the light glinting off the wet back of a seal. But as she watched, the thing drew nearer and nearer, and she saw unmistakably a human head held above the waves for just a moment. Crying out in alarm, Martha started forward, splashing up to her calves in the water. She had never learned to swim, and there was nothing she could do for the poor soul but maybe drag them ashore if they came close enough.

She watched, her heart beating a furious rhythm in her throat, as the thing floated closer, and she was gripped by a sudden, terrible certainty that it was her Isaac. Heedless of her own safety, Martha splashed farther into the shallows, hitching up her skirts around her hips to keep them from slowing her down. The body drifted right to her, and Martha's heart sank. What she'd taken for a tangle of seaweed was a mass of dark hair, nothing like Isaac's lovely copper curls. The waves were beating against her now, threatening to topple her over and drag her down, so Martha wrapped her arms around the broad chest and dragged the body back with her to the shore. It was bitter work and exhausted her by the time she reached the surf. She crashed down into the sand, unconcerned by her wet clothing, and lay on her back, panting heavily.

As she lay there, the waves stirred the body gently, giving it the appearance of life. She steeled herself to turn it over and look, praying as she did that it was nobody she knew. But before she could move, the body stirred again, and then pushed itself up on its hands, and Martha found herself looking into a strange female face. The nostrils were mere slits, the eyes dark—the whole eye, in fact, not white at all. She startled away from it with a cry, scrambling backward through the wet sand, grit collecting under her fingernails and scraping her skin.

"What are you?" she whispered, eyes wide.

The creature blinked at her, then opened its wide mouth and made a series of guttural sounds and clicks.

"Are you a devil?" Martha asked, raking her eyes over the creature. She brought a hand up and crossed herself quickly. It was then that she finally noticed the creature's lower half. It was woman to the hip, where it transformed into the great, powerful tail of a fish. Martha's eyes almost startled out of her head, and she clapped a gritty hand over her mouth. "You're a mermaid," she breathed, running her gaze over it again.

The differences between them were more apparent now that she knew to look: the nose was wide and flat, and there were long slits like gills on either side of its throat and beneath the bare collarbone. Below, the breasts were heavy and full, each one easily the size of Martha's head, and no part of it was slender. The skin was a dull, mottled gray most places, like a porpoise, with a lightning strike of pale flesh from her face down to her navel. Between her fingers and in her underarms was a delicate webbing of skin like a duck's feet.

"What a creature," Martha marveled. She raised one hand, as though to touch, but caught herself and snatched it back. What was she thinking? She'd heard tell of mermaids before, and everyone knew they sought to ensnare foolish sailors, to take them below the waves and drain the life from them. But Martha wasn't a sailor, and she'd pulled the creature from the water, not the other way around. "Do you mean to harm me?" she asked, half to herself. "You don't seem like you do."

The mermaid tipped its head to one side, considering her. Although it couldn't speak, Martha could read intelligence in its dark gaze. It pushed itself up higher, and she was struck by how ungainly it seemed; the long tail was beautiful and gleamed in the weak sunlight, but it was useless to help the creature maneuver on the sand. It crawled closer, and a tremor of fear and excitement curdled in Martha's throat, letting loose in a soft whimper. A nearly human hand wrapped around her ankle and then slid up her bare calf. Martha wanted to kick it away, but she found she couldn't move. Her chest rose and fell sharply as she watched the creature slowly crawl up to cover her, rough hands moving up her thighs, lifting her wet skirts out of the way.

Finally it bared her to the hip, cool breath gusting over her thighs and the soft flesh of her cunny. Martha's delicate flesh began to tingle, her heart hammering in a mix of fear and arousal. Her cunny began to ache, shudders rolling through her in anticipation, surprising her with the intensity of it. As she watched, the creature lowered its head and inhaled deeply at the mouth of her cunny, turning her bright red with shame. Before she could scream or scramble away from it, the mermaid pressed its face between her legs and started to nuzzle the hot, wet flesh.

Martha cried out, her heel scraping against the sand, but she didn't try to pull away. The mermaid pressed deeper, wrapping its hands around her legs to draw her closer, spreading her wider. A long, cool tongue ran up and down her lips and then plunged into her, filling her with a dark, shuddering pleasure. Martha couldn't resist or didn't want to. She arched her back against the sand, felt her hair coming undone as the back of her head ground down. Out of her throat came a guttural cry such as she never allowed herself when she explored her sex at home.

Apparently satisfied with this performance, the mermaid raised its head again and took a firmer grasp of Martha's hips. She dizzily wondered what would come next, and then she felt water lapping at her bottom and realized that the tide was rushing up the beach. She tried to sit up, but the mermaid began to tug her back down toward the water. Martha's eyes widened. So she was going to be stolen away after all. She dug her fingers into the sand, but there was nothing to hold on to, no way to save herself. Another wave splashed up around them, soaking her to her shoulders.

"Wait, I can't swim—" Martha protested, but the thing continued to pull her forward into the water.

The mermaid chirped and made another low, hoarse sound in its throat that sounded somehow like a question. As Martha met its intent gaze, a sudden sense of peace washed over her. She knew, somehow, that the creature wouldn't harm her. She relaxed finally, letting the water take her, and wrapped her arms around the mermaid's neck.

The creature looked pleased, treating her to a series of low chirps and clicks that she couldn't begin to understand, then wrapped strong arms around her waist. The feeling made Martha shudder; it had been too long since she was held by anyone, and the sensation of those powerful arms around her sent heat shivering down her spine. The mermaid's skin wasn't soft, but thick and blubbery, almost like sealskin. The tail was smooth and strong between Martha's thighs, and Martha let herself move against it, grinding her sex against the slippery flesh.

Martha had always enjoyed women's bodies as much as men's, maybe more. Her hands shook in anticipation as she leaned back far enough to caress the mermaid's generous breasts. She needed both hands to hold just one. She marveled at the firm flesh, thumbing over the engorged nipple with an eager breath. The mermaid watched her exploration with its dark, serious eyes. When her hand slipped lower, it leaned back to accommodate her. Thick, dark hair spilled down its shoulders and drifted through the water like seaweed. Martha ran her fingers over the pale stomach then drifted across to touch the thicker, darker skin that covered the mermaid's hips. The skin darkened as the human-like torso bled into fish tail, the difference seamless as far as she could see. There was a spot where the skin was ridged and supple and exuded the same heat as Martha's cunny. She reached down, feeling for that ridge of flesh.

The flesh was much softer than elsewhere on the mermaid's body, and Martha soon discovered that it was much like her own cunny, with thick outer lips hiding a hot, slick channel. She drew her fingers up the slit, seeking out the little nub that made her writhe and kick like a horse when she stimulated herself there. The slick, fleshy lips parted for her fingers, making Martha gasp when she happened upon a large, smooth nub, easily the size of a plum. Touching it made the mermaid keen and shiver beneath her. Martha groaned, dipping her fingers into the honey-like liquid of that hot channel then stroking over the little plum. She longed to apply her mouth to it, but the mermaid was submerged from the chest down; Martha knew she would drown if she attempted it.

Instead she lifted her hands to the creature's shoulders again and positioned herself so that she could grind her cunny down against the creature's own sex, rubbing her slick folds against the little plum and watching as unmistakable pleasure bloomed over the creature's face. Color bled into its cheeks and lips and flushed the pale stripe down its chest. It was then that Martha knew for sure that they weren't so different. She lowered her head and drew the creature into a slow, lustful kiss. The soft mouth tasted salty. Its tongue was pointed, its teeth sharp, yet the creature kissed her carefully, as if aware of how easily it could hurt her.

As they kissed, the creature's webbed hands roamed down Martha's flanks then caught hold of her bottom and pressed her more insistently against its sex. She could feel the plum slipping and grinding against her own nub of pleasure, that warm honey sensation spreading out, coating her between her legs and down her thighs. It felt as though the plum was getting bigger as her pleasure mounted, and she moved her hips more feverishly, rolling them in a circle. She began to feel as though the creature's sex was breaching her. A part of her longed for that sensation of being filled, of being taken.

She drew back for a moment and, lifting one of the creature's heavy breasts to her mouth, began to kiss and nurse on it, tending the nipple gently with her lips and tongue. She glanced down as the water shifted them apart, her eyes widening at what she saw through the water. The creature's sex truly had grown, curving out from its body like a man's cock, although its shape was different, slender and tapered to the end. The creature took hold of her hips, dragging Martha back down until their bodies met again.

It was gentle when it thrust inside her, nothing like a man stuffing his cock in there the minute he got the chance. Of course Martha and Isaac had had a few goes before he got called away; there was no telling how long he'd be gone, or if he'd come back at all, and they'd both been too desperate for each other to wait and hope for the wedding that might not come. This felt better than any of the times with Isaac, even though she loved him.

The mermaid groaned and made another low, questioning sound.

"Shh," Martha soothed, cupping her hands around its face. "All is well."

Clutching her more tightly, the mermaid drove inside her, and then she felt an intense pressure and heat deep within. As the creature's shaft pulsed and swelled within her, the pressure grew, heat flushing through her. She came then, the intensity and suddenness of it taking her by surprise. Martha cried out loudly at the spasms of pleasure that took hold of her, twisting her fingers into the mermaid's thick hair, her cunny clenching around the slender shaft.

When she came to herself, they lay together in the surf, waves buffeting them gently. The mermaid still held her firm, arms wrapped around her middle, Martha's face nestled between those heavy breasts. As they stirred, Martha started to push herself up on her knees, but the mermaid held her down, keeping them joined together.

"Hey now," Martha protested softly. "I've got to hurry, I'm late already."

The creature keened and tilted its face up to her, as though asking for a kiss. Smiling reluctantly, Martha lowered her head and obliged. But this time, just before she pulled away, the creature bit her, sharp teeth puncturing her bottom lip. Martha yelped, pulling back with the taste of copper in her mouth.

"What was that for?" she hissed, lifting a hand to feel the trickle of blood on her chin. She wiped it off, frowning, then pushed herself away from the creature, separating their bodies at last. The mermaid's sex slipped out of her in a rush of liquid, more than she was accustomed to, and Martha unconsciously reached between her thighs, afraid that she might be bleeding there too. Her hand came back coated in a sticky, oily liquid, quite different to the spendings she was used to. She wiped her hand off on her damp bodice, then used her skirts to wipe down the inside of her sticky thighs. As she straightened up, she was aware of an ache deep in her cunny, of a strange sense of pressure and fullness.

There was a loud splash behind her. Martha turned to find that the mermaid had vanished into the water once more. She caught a brief glimpse of its tail flicking out of the water, and then it was gone. Still, Martha had gotten used to losing things to the sea, and she could hardly begrudge this one heading back where it belonged. She took a few steps on shaking legs, then when she found that she could stand well enough, she retrieved her boots from where she'd dropped them and headed home.

The ache didn't go away, but what else had she expected from cavorting with some strange creature like that? Besides, she appreciated the reminder that it had been real, that she hadn't dreamed the whole thing. But as weeks passed, the ache began to worsen, and then to change. She always smelled of seawater down there now, and more than once, one of her brothers accused her of bringing home the smell from the fish market on her clothes, even on days she hadn't been down to the village.

She knew something was wrong when her blood didn't come the following month. It was always so regular. And then one of her brothers told her she was looking heavier, joked about giving her more of their chores, as though she didn't already do all the cooking, cleaning, washing, and brewing. She slapped the smile off his face, but only two weeks later she had to let out her dresses to fit her growing belly.

The rumor ripped through the village like wildfire; Martha was with child. Good, hardworking Martha had let some wastrel sow his seed in her, instead of waiting for her Isaac to come home. Her brothers were furious. They demanded to know who it was, and when she stayed silent, they threw her out of the house to spend the night with the cows. She guessed they must have heard the same rumor she had, that one of them had done the deed. She would have been angry too, if she were them.

As the weeks passed, her thoughts turned more and more toward the ocean. At night she dreamt of rolling waves and dark waters and woke with the taste of brine on her lips. Her belly grew quickly, far more than a normal pregnancy, and she soon began to feel movement: strange rolling and shifting that felt like the tides stirring the ocean inside her womb. Some nights, when the wind blew in off the sea, Martha could have sworn she heard the guttural grunts and clicks of the mermaid's curious voice.

One day, passing through the village, she caught sight of a long, gray tail, hanging on a hook in the fish market. She hurried through the crowd, her heart clamoring, fear tightening a fist around her throat. A knot of onlookers had gathered and it took Martha a moment to break through, but finally the crowd spat her out and she stumbled on the slick cobblestones, looking up and shading the sun from her eyes.

"Oh," she breathed, sagging with relief. It was only a shark.

"Hey!" a voice shouted nearby. "What're you doing here, you filthy harlot? Have you no shame?"

Martha turned to the source of the voice. It was a local fisherman, the man she'd bought fish from at market for years. Isaac's father. Martha turned to him, raising her chin, and set her hands on her hips. "I've every right to be here, and you know it."

"That should've been my grandson," the man snarled, pointing an accusing finger at her round belly. "Instead you'll raise a bastard."

Martha cupped one hand around her belly. "Then I'll raise him well."

Summer drew on relentlessly. Martha's brothers no longer spoke to her, nor even caught her eye. She wasn't like them anymore, and they all knew it.

One night she woke in the darkness, with the echo of waves crashing in her ears. She dressed quietly and stole out of the house, making her way down to the shore, her gait hindered now by her huge size. As she neared the beach, a terrible flash of pain in her stomach almost took her to her knees; she grasped a nearby fence post to keep herself upright, gasping aloud. When it had passed, she straightened up again and continued her pilgrimage to the water.

More contractions followed, though none as intense as the first had been. She reached the sand and sat down to remove her boots, struggling with the bulk of her stomach in the way. The night was balmy, the gentle surf seeming to glow under the full moon. Martha's toes sank into the wet sand. She wanted to lift her head to the sky and sing.

Martha didn't know why she had come or what precisely she anticipated, only that it would come, so she sat down to wait, letting the water lap her toes.

She didn't wait long. First she glimpsed something far out amongst the waves, like moonlight on a wet seal's back, and then a slender arm raised in greeting as the creature approached. Martha didn't move; she lay on her back, propped up on her elbows with her knees spread wide. Her skirts she'd already hitched up around her waist, baring her large, pale stomach.

The mermaid came out of the water slowly, crawling toward her on its elbows the way it had the first time. Its dark, liquid eyes were just the same as she recalled them, and it chirped and clicked in greeting as it moved closer.

"This is a fine mess you left me in," Martha told it, half smiling. "I'd guess you didn't have anyone else you could trust them with."

The mermaid tilted its head to one side, then it reached out and grasped one of her swollen ankles. Martha gasped and watched as the mermaid slid its wet hands up her calves, then her thighs. It took hold of her and dragged her down into the water, until only her head and shoulders were clear of the lapping waves. Then, just as a lick of fear stole up her spine, it kissed her.

Martha sighed into the briny kiss, wrapping her arms around the creature's broad shoulders. It was the first time anyone had touched her in months, and heat poured over her and trickled down to her cunny. The mermaid drew back, nostrils flaring, and began to move down her body. It caressed her stomach gently, and Martha watched the flesh move as something within responded to its touch.

Another contraction racked her, a mix of pain and pleasure that shuddered through her body. With a soothing keen, the mermaid lowered its head between her thighs and began to stimulate her, its thick, pointed tongue tracing the stretched, swollen flesh. It focused its attention on the pleasurable nub at the height of her sex, until a soft, roaring pleasure overtook her. As the thing brought her over the edge, Martha felt something inside her give, a dam breaking. Fluid issued forth from her with the spasms of her womb and hips, and something solid wriggled out, carried on the tide. Martha exhaled heavily—half shocked, half relieved—but the creature wasn't finished. While Martha cried out, the mermaid resumed its task with determination, making her shudder and kick with an excess of pleasure. It caressed her stomach and her swollen breasts, pinching her nipples and squeezing.

Martha came again, surrendering herself to it with a loud cry, her cunny clenching and fluttering as what felt like an ocean poured out of her. Again and again it brought her to the peak of her pleasure, until she could only shake and cry out weakly, tossing her head against the wet sand and begging for mercy. At last, she was allowed to rest. Her hips and cunny ached, but her swollen stomach had shrunk to half its size, and she no longer felt the rush of birthing between her legs. On shaking arms, she pushed herself up and met the dark, intelligent gaze of the mermaid again.

"Look at that," Martha breathed, looking down at where the mermaid lay low in the water. Around it circled five or six little creatures with long, iron-gray tails, each no longer than Martha's forearm. Their human halves were not yet fully formed; they had no arms, and their heads were not yet distinct from their torsos. They reminded her of tadpoles, and she felt a tug of grief at the realization that they were gone from her now, that she could care for them no longer.

She looked up, blinking away salt water, and found the mermaid watching her closely. Martha gave it a watery smile, and the mermaid surprised her by reaching out, catching hold of her wrist. It opened her palm in its own then with one finger drew a circle, then a half circle, then the shape of a crescent moon. It repeated the motions again in reverse, and after drawing a second circle, pointed up, drawing Martha's gaze to the full moon overhead.

Martha stared, and then her mouth dropped open. She started to laugh, throwing her head back as her belly shook. It felt good to laugh, the first time she had in months. The sense of release was almost as potent as the birth had been.

"All right then," she said, clasping the creature's hand in her own. "I'll see you next month, friend."

The mermaid nodded, and with that, it was gone, taking the young spawn with it. Alone, spent, and satisfied, Martha picked herself up, wrung out her skirts, and made her way back up the beach toward home.

# SOMETHING NEW

## Emerald

"Whose car is that?" I asked as we pulled into Stan's parents' driveway and parked near a silver sedan.

He glanced at it. "It's probably Isaac and Samantha's rental car."

"Oh, of course. Oh dear, Isaac beat us here—does that mean we're late?"

"A bit." Stan smiled as he opened the car door. I followed suit, stepping into the soggy leaves lining the gravel. The rain that had greeted Thanksgiving overnight had left the sky overcast, but even the grayness didn't dampen the spectacular shades of yellow, red, orange, and green covering the hillside behind Bert and Gloria's house. There were similar hues around our home in Burlington a couple of hours away, but the color, as well as the atmosphere, was somehow more magical here in rural Vermont. Not for the first time, I gazed around and marveled at what an amazing place this must have been for Stan to grow up in.

Gloria greeted us at the door with her usual welcoming smile, ushering us in to the powerfully competing scents of pumpkin pie spices and roasting turkey. Her graying hair was wound into a neat bun, and as she stepped back from our hug, she fretted at the imaginary flour that had transferred to my blouse from her autumn leaf–patterned apron.

Isaac emerged from the hallway. "What's all the commotion?" he asked with a wink, stepping forward to give Stan a hearty hug. "And what's up with our beating you here? I'm not sure that's ever happened before. It seems good form for you to actually arrive first, given that this is your family and all."

Stan characteristically ignored his childhood friend, unceremoniously nudging him out of the way as he carried the side dishes we'd brought to the kitchen.

"Hello, Nina," Isaac said, turning his impudent blue eyes to me. "Nice to see you. Too bad you had to bring Stan with you, but I guess it's a package deal."

I couldn't help giggling. Stan and Isaac had been friends since grade school, and when Isaac's parents had moved back to their native Ireland the boys' senior year, it had been arranged for Isaac to live with Stan's family until they graduated. The two had continued on to college together on the West Coast, remaining roommates throughout. After graduation, Isaac had settled in Seattle, while Stan had returned to Vermont. Isaac was still an automatic inclusion in the family's gatherings, a virtual adoptive son of Gloria and Bert.

"Is Samantha here?" I asked. I'd met Isaac's fiancée just once, during the previous Thanksgiving before they'd gotten engaged, and I had enjoyed her company. Given that he lived on the other side of the country, I'd actually only met Isaac himself a dozen or so times in the seven years Stan and I had been married.

"She is. I think she's in talking to Bert." Isaac led the way to the kitchen, where Bert, also wearing an apron, stood near the stove conversing with the petite, dark-haired Samantha. She turned when she heard us come in.

"Nina!" She approached me with a warm smile, and I caught a whiff of a sweet, spring-like scent—lilac, maybe?—as she hugged me. "You look wonderful," she said graciously as she backed away, managing to sound as if she really meant it. Silently I returned the compliment, unsure how to frame it out loud without gushing. She really was a beautiful woman, her magnetic green eyes set in smooth features offset by the dark chocolate shade of her hair.

My father-in-law leaned forward to kiss my cheek before announcing that dinner was almost ready. Low-level pandemonium ensued as the six of us converged on the dining room and found our chairs.

"Is Diana coming this year?" I asked Gloria, referring to Stan's younger sister, who lived with her husband and their two kids in Florida.

Gloria shook her head. "They're with Kellon's family for the day, and they and the kids will fly in on Saturday to spend the next few days with us. So it's just the six of us today."

"I'm sorry to miss them." I saw Stan enter the dining room and pause to pull out Samantha's chair for her as he made his way to our side of the table. I smiled at him as he approached and did the same for me.

"So, have you been to Ireland to meet your future in-laws yet?" I asked Samantha as sweet potatoes, stuffing, cranberry sauce, and green bean casserole started making their way around the table.

She smiled and shook her head as she handed me a wicker basket of rolls. "No, but I met them when they visited Seattle over the summer. We're planning a trip out there after the new year for a couple of weeks. Then they're coming in about a week before the wedding in April." Her cheeks flushed as she discussed the forthcoming nuptials, and I found myself smiling at her enthusiasm. Her engagement to Isaac really seemed to agree with her. The radiance that emanated seemed utterly unpretentious and unforced.

"Will you have a traditional Irish handfasting ceremony at your wedding?" Gloria asked from the end of the table.

Isaac snorted. "No, and we're not having shamrocks on our cake or carrying a horseshoe, either," he said as Samantha giggled. "Seriously, my mom would rather we get married in Ireland among a small army of Riverdancers."

"We did agree to get married in April instead of May," Samantha commented with a grin at her fiancé. "In Irish tradition, May is apparently a bad month to get married."

"Well, you are marrying Isaac, and the month you do it in won't change that, but it's nice of you to concede something to Jean's wishes," Stan said mildly. "I'm sure she's simultaneously thrilled and astonished that someone as lovely as you agreed to marry him. I know I am," he added as Isaac pretended to throw a roll at him.

Stan's understated ribbing next to Isaac's unabashed mockery was a metaphor for their respective characters. Physically, Isaac was both taller and considerably stockier than Stan, but his youthful features and unkempt blond hair contributed to his seeming the younger of the pair, even though they were the same age. Stan's more refined appearance matched his more reserved demeanor. Indeed, it wasn't just the closeness of the two that made them seem like brothers—Isaac's irreverence and occasional impetuousness contrasted with Stan's inclination toward seriousness gave them a stereotypical younger brother/older brother dynamic.

When the meal drew to a close, Stan stood and started to clear the dishes with Gloria close behind him. Bert and I were each carrying a leftover side dish to the kitchen when I heard the garbage disposal give an earsplitting grind before halting abruptly.

I entered the room to see mother and son standing at the sink peering into it. Gloria squeezed her hand through the black rubber around the drain and winced.

"Oh, the garbage disposal's clogged. All those potato peels . . . oops."

"Let me take a look," Stan said, already rolling up his sleeves as he crouched down and opened the cupboard. "Hey, Isaac, make yourself useful and grab the tools from the basement, would you?" he called to the next room. Then he glanced at me. "We may need the drain snake. It's probably in the shed. Could you go get it, honey?"

Agreeably I headed outside and across the lawn, glad I was wearing flats as I avoided the worst of the mud the earlier rain had left under the fallen leaves. The sun had found its way out while we'd been eating, and the surrounding light was now golden instead of gray.

The shed door creaked mostly closed behind me, and I blinked as my eyes adjusted to the dimness. Looking around for the drain snake, I frowned when I saw it up on a shelf the generator had been parked in front of. I would have to move the generator if I was going to reach the drain snake.

I had little experience with generators, but it certainly looked heavy. I approached it and swiped a finger across the dust covering the orange handle. Even in the dim light from the tiny window, a stripe several shades brighter appeared on the metal where I'd touched it.

Bracing myself, I grasped the generator's handle and hoisted. A gasp of part exertion, part laugher escaped me as it was instantly obvious I would be moving the machine exactly nowhere.

Glancing around, I saw a stack of empty five-gallon buckets and grabbed one. I could turn it over and stand on it to reach over the generator to the drain snake. Flipping the bucket over, I set it beside the generator and pressed my foot against the top to check the stability before hoisting myself up and balancing on what suddenly felt like a rather flimsy plastic cylinder beneath me. As I reached forward, the door creaked behind me. I turned, a shaft of sunlight thwarting my vision, and felt the sole of my shoe slip on the bucket. I shrieked as I grabbed futilely at the shelf, milliseconds from tumbling off my precarious perch.

Whoever had opened the door was at my side in a flash, and strong arms gripped me around the waist just in time. I cringed as my full weight bore into the shoulder of the individual who quickly steadied me and braced me against them. As they allowed me to slide safely to the floor, I found my breath catching for reasons beyond the fear of falling. The panic from having slipped transferred seamlessly to arousal as I felt the hard muscles pressed against my body and the strength holding me in place. I swallowed, concerned that I knew who my rescuer might be and uncomfortable with this visceral reaction to his closeness.

I was right. Isaac's expression was a combination of amusement and concern as he released me.

"What the hell are you doing?" he asked with characteristic bluntness, and I smiled ruefully.

"The generator's in the way."

He glanced at it, his face registering understanding of my predicament. Reaching down, he grabbed the handle and, with a quick grunt, shoved it a few feet to the left and out of the way.

My cheeks heated. My breathing changed, too, though, and I knew it was more than embarrassment that was making me blush. Isaac's biceps flexed beneath the T-shirt he wore (he had apparently shed his button-down shirt during the kitchen repair proceedings inside), and I bit my lip as I remembered how his arms had felt around me seconds before.

Internally shaking myself, I looked away and moved forward to grab the drain snake.

"Let me take that," he said gruffly, sending a sidelong look at my blouse as his large hand closed around the handle. "You're not dressed to get dirty."

For some reason the words made my breath catch. What the hell was the matter with me? I'd been experiencing all manner of hormonal shifts as I neared forty, but crushing on my husband's best friend had not thus far come up. Granted, I'd always recognized Isaac's attractiveness in a purely physical way, but that was it. It wasn't something that had made me feel active interest before.

The door creaked again, and both of us turned—a little too fast, it seemed to me. Had I jumped slightly? The heat filled my face again as I saw my husband standing in the doorway.

"What on earth is taking you two so long?" he asked after a slight pause in which I was sure he looked at me with some sort of suspicion, recognition, or something that indicated he had looked right into my consciousness and seen what was there. Guilt momentarily hindered my speech, and I was grateful when Isaac spoke up.

"The generator was in front of the shelf with the drain snake, and Nina was trying to stand on a bucket to get it out from behind it. She was just about to take a tumble when I walked in."

"Are you okay?" Stan asked me.

"Yes, she's okay," Isaac spoke again before I could open my mouth. "I caught her."

"Ah," Stan replied. His eyes sparkled. "I come out here and you've been manhandling my wife, is that what you're saying?"

I managed to keep the strangled sound that formed in my throat from escaping into the air and somehow concocted a smile at the last minute. I hoped it looked more innocent than I felt.

Stan approached me and slipped his own arms around my waist as he kissed my cheek. I took solace in knowing Stan at least wasn't the jealous type in general; at times throughout our relationship, we had kept company with swingers and both observed and considered casual polyamorous play that had always taken place in the same room.

Still, that was different from my lusting after the man who was practically his brother. I finally deigned to look at Isaac, who didn't appear embarrassed by Stan's expression of affection and instead was smirking at his childhood friend.

"As tempting as it would be to do so, Stanley, no. I was simply trying to help her."

I blinked. Isaac had never given any indication he found me attractive, and the compliment had me blushing yet again. Really, my cheeks seemed to have procured their own tiny space heaters within the last half hour, and I was growing impatient with their open announcement of both the arousal and the embarrassment I was experiencing.

"I'm sure she appreciated it," Stan said smoothly, his light sarcasm contrasting with the intensity that had me squirming. "She's a tempting lady indeed," he added, intertwining his fingers in mine and snaking our joined hands behind my back. After a beat, he continued, "Such handling could be arranged under agreed upon circumstances."

Oh god. Had he really just said that?

Isaac's reaction was similar, though he recovered almost instantly. It was a mere split second before he guffawed and said, "Well, look who picked up a sense of humor for the holidays."

I was sure, though, that the spark of hope I had seen in his eyes for that split second wasn't my imagination. The energy in me that had been divided between guilt and arousal now gathered all on the "arousal" side and made me wet as I stood there.

Behind my back, Stan squeezed my hand. I knew that was my signal to squeeze back if I needed him to slow down or stop. There was still time to play his comment off as a joke if I wanted him to.

I also knew then that he would pursue it if I wanted to as well. I took a deep breath and allowed my hand to remain slack.

Stan raised his eyebrows. "Are you saying you wouldn't be interested in fucking my wife?"

I almost smiled at that. Isaac's quick wit was both well-known and often on display, but my husband possessed a cleverness that, while not always obvious, was at his disposal when he wanted it to be.

Isaac's eyes shifted from Stan's to mine and back. I could see him looking carefully for signs that Stan was joking.

"Is that a trick question?" he finally answered with a wry smile.

At that moment I regained both my voice and my composure enough to join the substance of the conversation. "It's a sincere one," I said evenly, meeting Isaac's gaze.

One didn't have to have interacted much with Isaac to recognize that it was rare for him to be left speechless. I almost smiled again at having inadvertently accomplished such a feat.

"Samantha would never go for it," he said finally, his gaze moving back to Stan's.

I studied Isaac from under my lashes. Even his stance somehow conveyed his brashness, his impulsiveness, the audaciousness that seemed to exemplify the stereotype of the younger brother. Stan had a more classic handsomeness, a more understated temperament, about him. One I clearly found appealing, as I had married him.

But Isaac's appearance, as well as his demeanor, pulled at me a different way right then. It wasn't something I felt I'd ever find appealing enough to want to marry, or even be in a serious relationship with. Just something I wouldn't mind spreading my legs for now and then.

Unabashedly. Wantonly.

Now.

I took a deep breath and nodded. "Understood. The offer's open if you happen to be wrong." I let go of Stan's hand and walked ahead to the shed door, letting my breath out as my swollen clit throbbed with each step.

Back in the house, the garbage disposal, which I'd nearly forgotten about, had apparently been fixed with one of the tools Isaac had produced from the basement. Bert was putting them back in the toolbox as we entered the kitchen, where Gloria and Samantha sat together at the table. Samantha smiled at me, and I found myself hoping she wouldn't be too upset that Stan—and I—would offer such a proposition. Given the response he had anticipated from her, perhaps Isaac wouldn't even mention it to her.

"Want to help me serve pie?" Gloria asked as she got up. I followed her to the counter and added ice cream to the generous slices she handed me, then carried the small plates to the dining room in pairs.

"Where did Isaac and Samantha go?" I asked when I'd finished.

"They took the drain snake back to the shed," Stan said, meeting my eyes.

At that moment the subjects of our conversation walked back in the door. Isaac's presence was noticeable as usual as he led his fiancée into the room, and I stilled as his intent gaze, completed by the subtlest of smiles, landed on mine.

When I looked at Samantha, there was an unmistakably different energy in her countenance. Her eyes had changed, from lively and friendly to darker and intense. Abruptly I found myself captivated by her even more than by Isaac, transfixed by the intangible allure she now radiated. I watched her look at my husband with obvious hunger, and I smiled.

I, fortunately, was not the jealous type either. And I had a feeling Isaac had just learned something new about his soon-to-be wife.

* * *

Stan and I had planned to go home after dinner, coming back out on Saturday to spend the day with the family before the non-locals flew back home.

But plans had changed.

Samantha and Isaac's hotel room in the nearby town had two queen beds. It was obvious which one they planned to sleep in, making it just as obvious to me which one Isaac was about to fuck me in. Elsewhere in the building, my husband was in the room he had just checked in to with Isaac's fiancée.

Isaac stepped forward and grasped me around the waist, his hand sliding solidly up the back of my neck as he kissed me. By the time he backed up to pull off his shirt, I was breathless, lowering my eyes and trying to feign indifference as he reached for the top button of my blouse.

I looked up at him and saw the hard lust in his eyes. I didn't need to feign anything. He wanted me. And he wasn't about to hide that.

I knew then that he would be holding nothing back, and I ran my tongue over my lips, suddenly wanting the tip of his cock pressing between them. Before I could move, Isaac pushed my now-open blouse from my shoulders and dropped his hands to the button of my slacks. He made short work of undoing them, and I slid my panties down after them as they dropped to the floor.

Isaac took a breath as he stared at my nakedness in the dark. Ripping his own fly open, he grabbed a condom from the box on the table and kissed me hard as I heard him tear it open.

Seconds later he lifted me by my waist, spearing me with his hard cock as he pushed me against the wall. I gasped at the suddenness of the penetration, recognizing the wetness that invited him in and made the moan I emitted involuntary. His impetuous, demanding nature was already showing, and it wasn't something I was used to.

But it was certainly affecting my body. Breathlessly I squeezed my legs around his hips and clung to his shoulders as he flexed in and out of me slowly, his muscles tight as he held me against the wall.

Gripping my ass, Isaac turned and lowered me to the bed. I spread my legs wider, waiting to feel him on top of me. Instead he slid down my body, and I caught my breath as his tongue touched my clit. He flicked it rapidly, steadily, almost insistently, and the physical sensation built in me faster than I could mentally process it. His motions were straightforward, in no way narcissistic but not wrapped in sweetness, gentleness, the give-and-take of a couple attuned to each other's nuances and vicissitudes. They were about sex. Wanting. Now.

About what we were, indeed, both there for.

As it had in the shed, my body responded with no input from me. My hands clutched the blanket on either side of me as I felt myself writhing, heard the moans from my throat and the word "Yes" escaping my lips over and over. Just as I was about to come, Isaac pulled away and mounted the bed, turning me over by my hips before I had even reoriented.

It didn't matter. I felt myself scramble shamelessly to my hands and knees as my sex pulsed desperately, as though reaching to try to pull him deep inside. As he pushed into me, I cried out and pressed my chest and shoulders into the bed, straining to push back against him, get him ever closer to my pussy, though he was just about as close as he could get at the moment.

Isaac was more demanding than his best friend, banging into me from behind with complete abandon, his strong hands clenching my hips. It wasn't something I'd usually wanted, but right now my body simply couldn't get enough. The sounds of my wetness were discernable even among the slapping of his body against mine and the involuntary moans pulsing from my throat.

As intense as it was, though, I recognized the strangely impersonal nature of the sensations electrifying my body. I realized I wasn't thinking about Isaac, the man, but just about the body that was fucking me, the cock that slammed into me in a way somehow different from how Stan's ever had. Stan was more of a "take his time" kind of lover, and I felt like I had suddenly boarded a sexual roller coaster after years of a very satisfying lazy river. It was a purely physical ecstasy my brain didn't have the framework to process faster than my body—which, for the time being, seemed to have taken on a life of its own.

Isaac's hand slid from my hip to caress my buttock, the touch gentle but not in a substantive way—as though it was just teasing, just sneaking, not an actual caress of affection but one of preamble, intended as a distinct contrast to what was about to come. I somehow knew what he was going to do and also knew he wouldn't without knowing I wanted it. My face heated as I wondered how to express to him how much I did.

Beating me to it, Isaac leaned down to whisper in my ear.

"I think you need a spanking, Ms. Nina. What do you think?"

Words were rather beyond my capacity by that time, but even I recognized the desperate enthusiasm in the shriek I let out. Spanking was not in my usual sexual repertoire, and I didn't even know how I would respond to it. Isaac let out a low chuckle as he rose back up, and before I could even prepare myself—

*Smack.*

Isaac landed a solid spank on my right buttcheek that left me breathless, barely able to do anything but scream and try to spread my legs wider as his hand came down on the left side of my rear. I held on to the sheets for dear life as he alternated gentle but solid blows, until suddenly I realized I was going to come. The revelation almost startled me out of my ecstasy—I almost never came solely through intercourse with Stan. A tingle of guilt ran along my senses. What would my husband think?

But as the surprising but unmistakable sensation built, something in me knew Stan wouldn't have initiated this if he didn't want me to enjoy it, to experience something unique that he knew might not happen with him but that he also knew wouldn't threaten anything I felt about him or our relationship.

Indeed it didn't. The intensity centered in my core grew like a cresting wave, and as it peaked, I screamed long and hard into the pillow I clutched, shaking as the swell crashed over me.

Isaac's breathing was frenzied above me and knowing how hot he obviously found fucking me almost overwhelmed me. I worked to catch my breath as he pounded into me, his speed increasing with the pace of his breath as I could tell he was right at the edge, fucking my cunt with a desperation to come, to fill the condom inside me with an orgasm I suspected would rival the power of the one that had just ravished me.

When he did, he let out a guttural moan that I was sure made me wetter, made me ready to come again as I reveled in the simplicity of being wanted, of being purely, carnally taken. With nothing but a connection founded on casual respect and physical desire that wasn't concerned with other aspects of our lives, with the intimacy of a shared life together. Isaac didn't need to consider how his life fit with mine beyond the sexual way our bodies just had. None of us did.

The freedom of that took my breath away anew as I felt him gently pull out behind me.

"It's hot to fuck someone and not feel concern about long-term aspects of how you relate," I said to Stan on our way home. "You know, how it all interacts together." I stalled, not sure I was articulating it well and suddenly even less sure Stan wouldn't find what I was saying offensive. I wasn't saying I wanted that. Or only that.

On the contrary. It had been such a long time since I'd fucked someone like that, I had almost forgotten what it was like. Or maybe more accurately, before Stan, I hadn't really experienced what it was like to love someone on all levels and for sex to be a part of that rather than somehow separate, unrelated to a whole.

When I looked over at him, a smile played on my husband's lips. "Yeah, it is," he said, his eyes on the dark road in front of us.

I studied his features, the familiar goatee that so complemented them, the blue eyes I adored looking into when we made love. I had no idea yet what had transpired between Stan and Samantha.

Was I jealous? I didn't think so. It didn't feel like it, though I supposed that would be something I would eventually be faced with.

I hadn't had the impression jealousy was on either of our minds during the brief exchange I'd had with Samantha in the lobby restroom before we'd left. She had excused herself to visit it as we'd said good-bye, and I had followed her, almost sensing her beckoning me.

There had been no talk of specifics. I got the impression she just wanted to speak with me alone, to relate in a way unique to the two of us. It was as though we both knew we were checking in with each other, though neither of us spelled that out.

I smiled as I recalled one of the few direct statements she had made about her experience. "He's . . . sensitive," she had said of my husband, wrinkling her forehead in a way I was sure indicated uncertainty of how to articulate what she wanted to say.

I'd nodded. "He is that." Stan did embody a sensitivity that seemed less prominent in Isaac. I suspected Samantha found it fascinating and appealing in the same way I found Isaac's brashness. She and I clearly had different tastes as far as what we were looking for in a life partner, but we could appreciate such traits under less committed circumstances. Sensitivity was appealing in a sexual encounter. So was brashness.

"Have the two of you ever fucked the same woman before?" I asked Stan now, suddenly curious.

He shook his head. "No. Not that I know of, anyway," he added.

I smiled. Samantha and I had each had a taste of what the other experienced regularly. So had Isaac and Stan. The memory still had me abuzz with headiness, and I suspected it would for some time to come. But as I reached for Stan's hand and he squeezed my fingers in his, I was unquestionably aware that the real shared experience had been between the two of us.

Wishing them the best as they embarked on their life together, I hoped Samantha and Isaac felt the same.

# THE SUMMER OF 1669

Jayne Renault

*Ville-Marie, Nouvelle-France, November 1682*

It was a bright Sunday morning when Marguerite Bourgeois walked up Rue Saint-Francois-Xavier with her four little ones in tow and a babe swaddled tightly in her arms. Though the chill of a killing frost had passed through not days before, the sun was unusually warm as she guided her flock to church.

Her husband had journeyed there often to trade his pelts over the years but the Bourgeois family was new to Ville-Marie. Between the fire that had engulfed Québec City that summer and the increasing demands of Luc's profession, it seemed as good a time as any to relocate farther down the river.

Luc's company had set out for their winter hunt the same day as the frost, and Marguerite was already anxious for their return. Luc Bourgeois was a fine husband and worked very hard to give her the life he'd promised when he first presented himself all those years ago. But with that came many days of praying for his safe return from the wilderness and many cold nights without her handsome *coureur de bois* warming their bed.

Despite the pang of longing this stirred in her, she smiled. With the sun on her back and baby Angélique at her front, she had much thanks to offer God. Life wasn't always easy in the New World, but having grown up an orphan in Paris, she never anticipated such fortune to come her way.

When she rounded the corner at Rue Notre-Dame, the sunlight caressed her cheek. She spied the fresh stone facade with its proud new steeple towering up before, and she smiled a little wider.

It was a perfect day for their first Mass at the new church.

When Marguerite looked over her shoulder, she was struck by a moment of panic. There were only three little boys looking back at her.

Jeanne had disappeared.

"Roland!" she barked at her eldest, a boy of twelve who was the spitting image of his father. "Where is your sister?"

"Just there, *Maman.*" Roland pointed up the road to where Jeanne seemed to have struck up a conversation with another girl her age.

Jeanne had always been brave and gregarious in ways that filled Marguerite with pride and apprehension in equal measure.

Marguerite gathered up her skirts with her free hand and hurried to her wayward daughter. Just as she reached the pair, the other girl turned around, stopping Marguerite cold with her fiercely dark gaze.

### La Rochelle, France, May 1669

Three weeks had passed since Sister Bourdon arrived at the Pitié-Salpêtrière hospital, offering a handful of girls the opportunity to change the trajectory of their lives forever—to become *Filles du Roi.* As symbolic Daughters of their King, these otherwise unmarriageable girls would have their dowries paid by the crown to help bolster the budding colonies overseas.

Amongst the girls to receive an invitation was Marguerite Têtu.

Marguerite was an unlikely hospital resident for there was a time when her family was held in high regard. That is, until her grandfather found himself on the wrong side of a Huguenot rebellion. The accusations against him were, in fact, false, but it made no difference. Their name was damaged beyond repair and they would find no sympathy from the staunchly Catholic crown.

As the youngest of four girls, there would hardly have been a chance of Marguerite marrying under the best of circumstances. But without enough wealth to pay her entrance to a convent, never mind a dowry, her father was left with very few options. Her parents were likely still breathing somewhere, but she was just as much an orphan as any of the girls found destitute and alone on the streets of Paris.

Marguerite was certain that this opportunity was a show of God's mercy. When Sister Bourdon gave her the invitation, she accepted it before she could think herself out of it.

When the *Saint-Jean-Baptiste* arrived, many girls just like Marguerite, all *Filles du Roi*, were already aboard the handsome galleon. On that fifteenth day of May, the long string of girls followed the gray-robed Sister Bourdon onto the ship to embark on the adventure of their lifetime.

Looking out to the faces waving at them from the docks, Marguerite became suddenly and painfully aware of the weight of her journey into the unknown. She hiccupped on her realization and rubbed a tear away with her thumb. In doing so, she caught the dark eye of a fierce-looking girl not much older than herself. With wild, dark curls poking beyond the fringes of her bonnet, the young woman offered her a slight smile. Marguerite quickly looked away, too shy to respond.

As the first days passed, any glamour Marguerite imagined about adventures on the high seas washed away with the waves.

The food was awful, the cramped sleeping quarters even worse, and Marguerite, like many others, did not handle the sway of the ocean well.

Curled up into the hull next to her bunk, she hung despondently over the bucket between her knees. This was an unnecessary precaution; she only occasionally retched up air because she hadn't kept food down since they left dry land.

"You'd feel better if you came up for air."

Marguerite looked up to see the fierce-eyed girl standing there, but said nothing.

"If you don't do something, you'll die down here," the girl insisted.

"So be it," Marguerite barked at the girl, who left without another word.

On the fourth day, Marguerite awoke with the most ghastly headache and the girl's words still ringing heavy in her ears.

With every ounce of resolve she could muster, Marguerite gathered up her skirts and ambled up the ladder through the hatch. She could barely hold herself upright, and the shock of the sun was blinding. However, after a few kisses from the breeze on her cheeks, she began to feel better than she had in the dank, dark underworld below deck.

Marguerite noticed several girls gathered around her would-be savior at the base of the main mast. It was clear that she, like Marguerite, was amongst the eldest on the ship, and these little ones took to her like a surrogate mother goose. The girl waved her arms about, and her face displayed a whole range of expressions. She seemed to be telling great stories. Her audience was riveted.

Not one to wedge herself into a moment, Marguerite moved away from the vibrant show. Leaned over the taffrail, she watched for a long while as the ship cut through the waves as smoothly as a knife through a decadent Brie.

"You look terrible." The fierce-eyed girl gave Marguerite a start when she sidled up next to her and flashed a smug smirk. "Here."

Marguerite turned to find an offering of a hardened biscuit and a cup of water. She noted the girl's proud aquiline nose and the darkest pair of eyes she'd ever seen on someone so fair. Short and slight in frame, this girl held herself like a woman well beyond her years, although she couldn't be much older than Marguerite, who had passed her twentieth birthday only days before she'd been invited aboard this very ship.

"They say it could take three months to get there," the girl said, nudging the twice-cooked bread closer to Marguerite. "Would you rather have an upset stomach or starve to death?"

Marguerite let out a sigh of defeat but was still too stubborn to respond.

"Oh, la-la." The girl blew air through her lips and shoved the biscuit into her front pocket, revealing in its stead a rough silver coin. "Fine. We will leave it to our Papa then—*pile ou face*. If his face is revealed, you must be a good girl and do as he says. *D'accord?*"

Marguerite was taken aback by the girl's forthright demeanor but couldn't help but nod.

With a smirk, the girl flipped the silver coin into the air and let it land on the planks between them. As it fell flat, Louis XIV glared proudly back up at them.

"*Et voilà!* Our Papa has settled it. And he insists." She thrust the cup into Marguerite's hand. "Be a good girl and take small sips. If you gobble too quickly, you'll make yourself sick again."

Marguerite nodded and did as she was told.

"Little bites," she forced the biscuit into Marguerite's other hand, "and when you're done with that, take deep breaths and look at the horizon."

"Thank you," Marguerite said nibbling on the hard, lackluster biscuit.

"It's nothing," the girl said in a tone almost as dry as the biscuit, yet infinitely more lustrous. "What is your name?"

"Marguerite Têtu."

"Ha! A perfect name for such a stubborn girl. Jacqueline Perrault. *Enchantée.*"

Whether it was the sustenance, the deep breaths, or the presence of this intense yet comforting force next to her, Marguerite found herself settling for the first time since they set out.

"Will it really take three months to get there?" she asked between bites.

"I'm not sure," Jacqueline said with a little shrug of her shoulder. "How long should it take to get to the other side of the world?"

The next day, Marguerite woke to find her stomach less angry.

"You are no longer green, at least," Jacqueline said with her hands on her hips, her countenance smug as ever.

"I even managed to swallow some salted meats at supper last night," Marguerite quipped back. "What were you doing with the little ones yesterday?"

"I tell them stories to pass the time," said Jacqueline.

"What kind of stories?"

"Stories of great adventure in far-off lands, of brave knights and beautiful princesses. Fairy tales. Love stories."

"Where do you find these stories?"

"My uncle told me some," she said. "The rest I make up myself."

"That is very impressive."

"It's nothing," she said with another shrug.

Having found a friend, Marguerite's time passed more enjoyably. The girls compared fantasies of their new lives, and at Jacqueline's invitation, Marguerite even joined the audience during the storytelling performances.

Watching the ease and fervor with which Jacqueline delivered her tales, Marguerite was in awe. One day in particular when Jacqueline locked those dark eyes on her in the middle of an epic love story, Marguerite found her throat tightening in a peculiar way. She coughed through the sensations just as quickly as they came on and sloughed them away. Unnerved though, she silently excused herself from her seat. Jacqueline told her rapt listeners of how the prince's blade sliced through the gnarly thorns surrounding an old castle, but it was the narrator's glare that pierced Marguerite as she walked away.

In bed that night, Marguerite's thoughts didn't drift too far before landing back on Jacqueline—her courageous spirit, her infinite well of stories, her musings on the rugged men their husbands would be, of grand homes made from giant trees; of what it would be like to be the mothers of the *Nouveau Monde*.

Marguerite couldn't fathom how this girl could be so bold in the face of such a great unknown.

Her thoughts sank deeper to how soft Jacqueline's delicate hands seemed and how piercing her dark eyes certainly were. The long black curls of her hair, how they tumbled when she freed them from her bonnet.

The longer Marguerite thought about her, the more intensely she felt . . . everywhere.

She couldn't distinguish where her thoughts ended and her dreams began, but she woke with a start when images of unholy lewdness appeared to her. Sweat had swelled to her surfaces, her heart beat too quickly, and an uncomfortable tension tugged between her legs. She was keenly aware of how tight every corner of her was. Heat flashed in her ears and shot chills down the back of her neck. Her forearms clenched, as did the pit of her stomach. While her thighs squeezed involuntarily, the indistinct pain looming in her loins was reluctant to subside.

While Marguerite battled with tension and sleep, a fever began to creep its way through the ship. Over the next several days, at least half of the crew and a good many more of the girls saw their fair share of night sweats and gut-wrenching agony. Though most managed to weather the storms waging inside them, one of the younger girls took too ill and never recovered.

The mood was somber the morning after they wrapped the girl in a sailcloth and slipped her overboard. Marguerite found the stark silence unnerving. For the first time since they left La Rochelle, neither Jacqueline's face nor her voice was anywhere to be found.

That night, Marguerite was unable to sleep under the weight of a boatful of grief. Somewhere in the darkness, she heard an unsettling sound rise above the slosh of the waves.

Before she realized what she was doing, she rose and wound through the cramped sleeping cabin. She was surprised to find that it was her fearless Jacqueline who was sniffling so softly. The space next to her was empty; the girl who once lay there now slept on the seabed. Marguerite approached quietly, not wanting to wake anyone else or to startle her friend.

She wondered if she should proceed, but her overwhelming need to return Jacqueline's generosity and care, maybe even to hold her through her upset, outweighed any fear of rejection. Without further hesitation, Marguerite stretched herself out along the edge of the bunk, allowing Jacqueline to register the extra weight next to her.

"*Pile ou face?*" she whispered into Jacqueline's back.

Immediately, Jacqueline turned and pressed her forehead to Marguerite's.

The mere touch paralyzed Marguerite, but after many, many close breaths in the dark, the tension racking her body dissipated, replaced by some softer comfort.

Marguerite watched as peace washed over her friend's face before finally drifting to sleep herself.

When Marguerite awoke, she found Jacqueline's face, smiling anew in the soft light of day.

"*Mon amie,*" Jacqueline said, warmly pressing a cheek to Marguerite's shoulder. "Thank you for your kindness."

Marguerite tried to respond but her throat was too dry to say anything.

"Might you sleep near me again tonight? Your company was most agreeable."

Marguerite simply smiled and nodded, trying to contain her elation and stifle whatever it might mean.

All day, Marguerite imagined confessing to Jacqueline what she felt when they were so close. But what might Jacqueline think of her if she did? What if she shunned her or, worse, betrayed her to Sister Bourdon, who would surely send her right back to the hospital to live among orphans and witches and prostitutes for the rest of her days?

Lying next to each other again that night, Marguerite avoided Jacqueline's face, staring awkwardly at the low overhead, petrified by nerves. She shifted restlessly on the bunk like she was trying to shimmy her frantic thoughts out through her feet. When Jacqueline's hand moved in the shadows and rested on her arm, Marguerite nearly fell out of bed.

"Is something wrong?" Jacqueline whispered.

Marguerite held her tongue for fear of saying . . . anything.

"What is it?" Jacqueline pleaded gently.

Reluctantly, Marguerite turned to her side and faced Jacqueline.

"I was just thinking about . . ." Marguerite paused, holding the weight of her silence as long as she could before it crushed the words from her chest. "How I will miss you."

Though it was dark, Marguerite made out the shadow of Jacqueline's smile as it curled slowly upward.

"Ah, yes," Jacqueline said, warm and knowing. "I . . . often think about . . . missing you, too."

Tears immediately swelled in Marguerite's eyes. She was overwhelmed with as much fear as joy. She knew that such feelings couldn't be proper of a good Catholic woman, a future wife, a Daughter of the King himself.

And yet . . .

Before she could stop herself, Marguerite swallowed hard and inched her hand over her until she found the tiniest edge of Jacqueline's finger and waited.

When Jacqueline's finger twitched, welcoming her closer, Marguerite's breath caught in a gasp. Their foreheads touched, and slowly their faces tilted, welcoming one another until their lips met with as much certainty and as little sound as they could muster.

When they parted, their pinky fingers entwined and breaths heaving, a smile tore through Marguerite's face. Her eyes glossed behind her lids, and she fought off sleep for as long as she could to marvel at the moment.

### Québec City, Nouvelle-France, June 1669

One week later, the *Saint-Jean-Baptiste* was greeted at port by a throng of excitable young men trying to get a look at their future wives. Sister Bourdon guided her flock of girls through the chaos, straight to the Ursuline convent. Marguerite would stay there for the three months it would take her to meet and marry Luc. For Jacqueline, who was already promised to an officer in Ville-Marie, it was merely a place to rest for a few days until she began the next leg of her journey.

Before leaving them for the night, Sister Bourdon warned the girls not to leave the convent grounds, with allusions to dangers lurking in the shadows.

Jacqueline flashed Marguerite the most diabolical smirk.

"I would like to explore these shadows, I think," she said.

"But Sister Bourdon said—"

"I know what she said," Jacqueline cut her off, drawing the coin from her apron pocket. "But what does Papa say?"

Marguerite couldn't help but smile at her audacious friend. Jacqueline grinned and flipped the coin. Both girls followed it until the Sun King's face beamed up at them.

"See? Papa says be a good girl and follow me."

Marguerite's cheeks burned at the words, but she took Jacqueline's hand without hesitation.

After slinking down the hall and out the door unseen, the pair found themselves on the deserted courtyard. Though they were surrounded by high stone walls, the aroma of pine trees and nocturnal wood fires drifted freely around them. Marguerite watched as Jacqueline twirled, her skirts lifting to reveal the whites of her fresh stockings.

"Marguerite, we made it!"

But Marguerite found that she couldn't return her friend's smile.

"What's wrong?" Jacqueline said, closing the distance between them. "You look like you did your first day on the ship."

Jacqueline took her hand. Despite its pleasant warmth, Marguerite looked away.

"Come now, *mon amie* . . . There is still some time."

Marguerite scoffed and squinted away the tear swelling at the corner of her eye. "There will never be enough time," she blurted back.

When Marguerite found her gaze, it wavered for the first time. For once, Jacqueline was speechless.

After an eternity of bloated silence, Marguerite couldn't stand it any longer. She tugged on Jacqueline's hand, inviting her closer. "Look, you leave for Ville-Marie very soon. And me? I will be staying here until I find a husband of my own. We are likely never to see each other again." Jacqueline sniffled softly and wiped away a tear. "And I would like to thank God for you—I don't think I'd have made it here without you—but I can't."

Jaqueline looked hurt and pulled her hand away.

"Why not?"

"Because I don't think He appreciates how much I want to kiss you."

They waited just long enough to be sure that God hadn't hurled any thunderbolts at them for the blasphemous confession. Then, emboldened by this defiance of everything she had ever known, Marguerite moved toward Jacqueline, who mirrored her movements until they met in the middle. With their bodies flush and nervous fingers interlocked, their foreheads found familiarity in each other. Tears swollen with love and disbelief streamed down their cheeks until finally their mouths came softly together. Bound at the lips in the middle of the quiet courtyard, they rocked and swayed with each other like they were still on board the ship until dizziness overtook them.

Pulling apart, they giggled incredulously, and Marguerite took Jacqueline by the hand, pulling her into the shadows where two walls met.

Fueled by the darkness, Jacqueline took Marguerite's face between her hands and, pressing Marguerite into the bricks, kissed with the same fervor as her storytelling, weaving fresh tales with her tongue. Marguerite wrapped her arms around Jacqueline and pulled her in so close that she was certain the only reason she could still breathe was because Jacqueline was doing it for her.

The tension between Marguerite's legs was ten times what it had been in her bunk. But here, in the open air of this wild new world, she felt free to explore. Cautiously, she ran a hand down Jacqueline's side, into the crook of her waist.

"Ah, yes," Jaqueline swooned with encouragement. She ran her fingers around the exposed back of Marguerite's neck in response, drawing shivers with her touch.

Despite the layers of skirts between them, Marguerite felt a distinct clench as Jacqueline straddled her thigh.

"It's . . ." Marguerite stammered, finding words impossible. The pulse between her legs was deafening.

"Very intense, yes." Jacqueline's whispers were tight in her throat. "And I think"—she giggled, losing her own words now—"I may be so excited that I wet myself."

Marguerite was oddly relieved to hear her say so, for she too was wet between her thighs.

"But you feel all right?"

"Yes." Jacqueline's throaty whisper softened. "More than all right."

"Might I . . ."

"Yes?"

"Touch you . . . under your skirts."

"Yes."

Jacqueline hastily gathered the bunch of her skirt and lifted it so Marguerite's hand could snake under. The skin on her inner thigh was soft on Marguerite's fingers as she slid with careful curiosity toward the bare juncture of her groin. They both breathed deeply through their noses all along the way.

"Your touch is so gentle," Jacqueline cooed. "Yet I feel like I might burst."

*"Moi aussi."*

Their next kiss was slower, more patient than before, giving room for their bodies to take over. Marguerite cupped Jacqueline's fleshy mound and absorbed the warmth through her palm.

"You are so . . . hot?"

Despite the shadows, Jacqueline's face flushed an even deeper shade of red, and she ground herself down into Marguerite's hand, rubbing the generous wetness into her palm.

"May I touch you like this too?" Jacqueline said between soft moans.

Marguerite barely had time to nod before Jacqueline was tugging at the skirts to bury a hand under in the same fashion. Her fingertips were cool as they followed the same ginger path Marguerite had traced on her.

Like the vines climbing up the stone wall, their upright bodies wove tightly together—a chin hooked on a shoulder, lips pressed to a neck, hidden hands roving uncharted areas while the others held them steady. Grinding and rubbing and learning the lay of their own land and each other's body . . . until the excitement of it all made the pressure between Marguerite's apparently very wet folds too much to bear. Just as she was about to ask Jacqueline to stop, light flashed behind her scrunched eyelids and she choked on the breath she had been holding. Her right leg began to shake of its own accord. Meanwhile, Jacqueline was rubbing herself harder and harder into the heel of Marguerite's palm, and her body seemed to be gripped by the same sensation that had overcome Marguerite.

Holding all the potential of the *Nouveau Monde* in the palms of their hands, they collapsed into each other, laughing intermittently.

When Jacqueline pulled back to look Marguerite in the eye, her face was so soft and round, glowing with perfection and hope and more magic than all of her stories combined. When she smiled, Marguerite couldn't help but bury her face in Jacqueline's shoulder and cry.

"*Merci,*" Marguerite said between sobs. "For everything."

Jacqueline wrapped both arms around Marguerite's neck and whispered for the last time, "It's nothing."

Marguerite barely noticed the little girl run off to meet a dark-haired man in uniform, standing near his horse-drawn wagon. It wasn't until she had entered the church that Marguerite finally broke from her reverie.

"What is it, *Maman?*" her youngest boy, Henri, asked with genuine concern.

"Ah, it's nothing, *mon petit.*"

Henri furrowed his brow, fully unconvinced by his mother's response.

Marguerite guided her brood to a pew in the middle of the church. Filing in first, she knew Roland would play his father's protective role and match her at the outside edge. As she arranged the little ones in their seats, she felt the comforting weight of a fellow congregant on her other side doing the same. While she took count of their little heads, Jeanne, who was snuggled up next to her, leaned over Angélique and waved to someone beyond them.

"What is it, Jeanne?"

"*Mon amie,*" Jeanne said, beaming.

When Marguerite turned, she found the face of the fierce-eyed girl from the road sat snugly between two more girls and two boys. Their smart-looking officer of a father held them in place from the other end, while right next to Marguerite was a tiny infant in the arms of the woman whose leg was pressed flush to hers.

Marguerite's pulse caught in her throat. Though the years had drawn new lines through it, the face Marguerite looked into undoubtedly belonged to Jacqueline Perrault.

The sermon began, but Marguerite, so dizzied by the impossibility, could barely make out the words ringing out from the altar. Marguerite caught Jacqueline's smile from the corner of her eye when the zealous new parish priest warned them to beware the blasphemous sinfulness of inebriation and sorcery. She pressed her leg lightly into Jacqueline, who responded with the whisper of a knowing shoulder nudge. Marguerite then clenched her thighs together, fearing the entire congregation could hear the pound of her pulse striking the pew beneath her.

Following the service, Marguerite watched Jacqueline's family file out of the church before hers. She was desperate to talk to her, to hold her, to kiss her timeless lips. But how could she?

As she walked down the front steps into the road, she looked down at Angélique, still sleeping soundly in her arms.

No, Marguerite told herself. They weren't lost girls caught up in a fairytale anymore. They were wives, mothers. They had a responsibility to their families, to God, to their King.

And yet . . .

When Marguerite looked up again, she caught Jacqueline glancing over her shoulder, and a spark of silver flashed in the sunlight, landing on the ground behind her.

Marguerite hurried over to the glint on the road, happy to find Louis XIV's face looking back up at her.

*Well,* she thought to herself as she dropped the coin into her apron pocket, *a good girl always does as Papa says.*

# BROKEN THING FIXED

Anna Mia Hansen

"You're not going to Bjorn's tonight?" my mother asked me, as she entered our small kitchen. She smiled inquisitively at the messenger boy, who was standing on our back doorstep, light from the last rays of the setting sun making his tattered tunic look like spun gold. He smiled back at her shyly as he waited for me to hand him the things I wanted him to deliver.

It was a fair question. I went to Bjorn's every night. Under cover of darkness, I'd cross the cobblestone road in front of our house, risking the Guardians' detection to follow a rocky path down to the roaring seaside where Bjorn's cottage sat, nestled among the boulders. He kept a candle in the window to guide me up the steps, but I never needed it. He always opened the door before I'd reached his front doorstep, to usher me in out of the cold, as though he'd been standing by the window, watching for me.

"After dinner," I said to my mother. I gave the boy stew in a travel bowl and then handed him my jewelry box, which I'd already emptied of the few pieces I owned. To the boy, I said, "Be careful with this. It's not worth much, but it's precious to me."

Bjorn had made it, engraving it with my name—Sigrid—and had given it to me when I'd turned eighteen. I'd accepted it when I'd turned down his proposal. Bjorn would understand why I now sent it to him.

"Why after dinner?" my mother asked, ever curious. "You've never done that before."

"I don't want to talk about it," I said. My mother knew everything about Bjorn and me, from my crush on him in my youth, to my turning down his proposal, to the most recent development—my working for him in his woodwork shop during the day, plus keeping house for him in the evening. But there were some things I wasn't prepared to discuss with her.

"You're not going to break his heart again, are you?"

I refused to answer. Instead, I started serving our own dinner, dishing up two bowls of stew and placing them on the table. But my mother was unrelenting. "You should never have turned him down in the first place."

I was setting the cutlery and I slammed the spoon on the table at her place harder than I'd planned, but I was on edge. "You think I don't know that?" I asked. "I said I didn't want to talk about it and I don't. Now, eat." And then, when my mother glared at me, I softened, repenting. "Please."

I regretted my flare of temper. My mother was worried, too. But I was nervous. And my mother's questions only agitated those nerves. I had a history of messing things up with Bjorn. I was about to do something extreme, and I feared that instead of fixing things between him and me, I was only going to make them worse.

As I sat at the table, I considered the reason I was on edge.

I regretted rejecting Bjorn's proposal. That was true. Even at the time, it'd felt like a mistake. I'd loved him even then, and I had wanted to marry him. But just as he'd proposed, I'd heard he'd informed on my brother who was then forced into hiding.

I'd doubted Bjorn, had questioned my trust in him, had decided I couldn't possibly marry him.

But Bjorn had never informed on my brother. He'd proved that in the most extreme of ways three months ago, when the Guardians had arrested him, dragging him from his cottage in the middle of the night. They'd kept him confined for a week inside a tiny cell, alone but for the rats, interrogating him. He hadn't betrayed my brother. Not when they'd threatened him with pain. Not even when they'd shattered his kneecap. I realized now, without a doubt, that Bjorn was trustworthy.

But the realization had come too late. Bjorn's shattered kneecap wasn't healing properly. He'd be left with a limp. And now it didn't matter how profusely I proclaimed my love for him, Bjorn thought I only pitied him. It didn't matter that I helped in his workshop or in his home; he thought I did that only out of sympathy. And he'd made no move toward me, even though I'd hinted I wouldn't turn him down this time. Half the people in the village thought we were a couple. Even my mother had been surprised to learn we weren't lovers. But Bjorn kept me at arm's length, because he didn't believe I really wanted him.

Tonight, I was going to show him how wrong he was.

After dinner, I cleaned up. Then I went to the washroom to remove the grime of the workshop from my body. I needed the extra time that evening to prepare and I took it. I dressed carefully.

By then, the moon had risen. I went downstairs, grabbed my coat, and closed the door on my way out.

I crossed the cobblestone road and followed the rocky path to the seaside. Luckily, the moon was bright, because the tiny flame in Bjorn's window, by the time I reached it, had dwindled to such a hopeless flicker it was barely visible from the path. I should have taken that as the first sign something was wrong.

The door didn't open on my approach. I had to knock.

Knock and wait.

That was the second sign.

When the door did finally open, Bjorn appeared. He looked a mess. His hair was disheveled, his face gaunt. For a moment, he just stood there and stared at me. Then he pulled me inside so quickly, he made my head spin. He hauled me against him. The door closed behind me with a bang. "Oh god, Sigrid," he said. "Oh god." I felt him tremble, recognized it as a sign of fear, and wondered if the Guardians had returned while I was gone. Then he said, "I thought you weren't coming." And I realized what had happened.

I'd messed up again. I'd sent him his dinner, giving him the wrong idea.

"No, no," I said. I rubbed my hands up and down his arms. "I told you I was never going to leave you. Don't you believe me? I was just delayed, that's all."

He pushed me away as soon as I said this. There hadn't been pity in my voice. But pity he'd heard.

I sighed, trying not to feel defeated, and removed my coat. He took it, saying, "Why did you send me the jewelry box, then?"

I'd already stepped away from him. "You don't know?" I asked. I was contemplating my explanation when I turned. It was my first glance at the room, and I froze. "What the hell happened here?" I didn't often swear. But the scene before me warranted it. The stew I'd sent to Bjorn sat on the table, untouched. And the jewelry box—my jewelry box—lay in pieces on the floor.

Of course, I didn't need to ask the question. I could tell what had happened.

Bjorn had built a set of wooden shelves on the wall next to the fireplace, where he kept his ornaments—the flawed ones he couldn't sell. He called them his misfits. Bjorn had hurled the jewelry box at the shelves, knocking off some misfits and splintering the box itself.

Bjorn came up behind me. "I thought you weren't coming back," he said, as though this explained everything.

I glanced at him, unable to hide my astonishment.

I didn't know what to do. I'd come to Bjorn's cottage planning to convince him of my desire to stay with him, but it seemed I'd done the opposite.

In my confusion, I decided the only thing to do was start cleaning up. I picked up a few of the misfits and placed them on a low shelf. I didn't touch the jewelry box. I couldn't even bear to look at it.

At first, Bjorn helped. But it was soon obvious the strain hurt his knee. I sent him to his armchair, which only made matters worse. He hated being treated like an invalid.

He sat and watched me in silence.

It was while he was watching me that I decided I might as well go ahead with my plan. I had a history of messing things up. But surely I couldn't mess up more than I already had.

I stood before the ramshackle shelves, gathering my courage.

Then, I left the room, returning a moment later with a short stepladder that Bjorn had constructed himself. It was thigh high and ended with a top cap that could double as a seat. I cleared a space on the floor and positioned it so I could return some misfits to the highest of the shelves. Then, I picked up one of the misfits, climbed up the ladder, and placed it. I was aware of Bjorn watching me, and as I climbed down, I feigned a stumble.

"Careful," Bjorn said, rising out of his armchair, as though readying himself to come to my aid. Then he groaned, grimaced, and fell back, rubbing his knee.

I did feel a spark of sympathy for him then. I couldn't imagine how he felt now. Three months ago, his body had been strong, able, in the prime of life. He'd flexed and angled his muscles according to his desires. Then, overnight, by cruel hands, his body had been changed. I could see it frustrated him. But I could also see he took it too much to heart, rejecting his entire body when he just needed to learn to adjust to its new limitations.

I realized I could help him learn, and that gave me confidence. "Silly me," I said. "I must be tired. I'm getting clumsy."

Bjorn continued to rub his knee. "The bottom rung's the problem," he said. "I used to stumble over it myself. It's so close to the ground, it's tempting to skip it altogether. But then you trip. Just make sure you use all the rungs and you'll be fine."

I smiled, but I didn't promise to take his advice. He must have been in too much pain to notice.

And in too much pain to notice the tremor in my voice when, a couple of minutes later, I finally gathered the courage to move on to the next step in my plan. "The problem is my tunic," I said nonchalantly, feigning a stumble on the bottom rung again.

Bjorn looked at me in surprise. "No," he said. "I really think it's the bottom rung."

I shook my head. "No. It's my tunic. I wear a more practical one to your workshop. This one's looser. Longer. The skirt tangles around my knees whenever I climb up or down."

Bjorn raised his eyebrows. "I hadn't noticed."

"You might not be able to see it, but I can feel it," I said.

I could tell he disagreed but wasn't willing to argue. "Well," he said, speaking in his most reasonable voice, "there's nothing you can do about it now. I've nothing to offer you but my own tunics, which are even bigger. I'd suggest you move carefully. Or leave the misfits. I'll put them back myself when I'm rested. Unless, of course," his voice caught, as though the thought had just occurred to him, "unless you want to return to your own house to change?" His Adam's apple bobbed as he swallowed. "Is that what you want?" he asked. "Do you want to go home?" And then, the thought that really bothered him. "You'll come back, won't you?"

This wasn't the turn I'd wanted the scene to take.

"No," I said quickly, trying to save the moment. "I mean . . . Yes, I'll come back if I go. But no, I don't want to go." I saw relief cross his face. "But I think I'll just . . ." My voice quavered. My confidence faltered.

I closed my eyes, trying to imagine myself as a seductress. Instead, I saw myself the way I was: young, a virgin, and inexperienced with men in all the ways that, in this moment, counted. It wasn't what I wanted to be and I tried to think of who I would have been, if I hadn't lost trust in Bjorn, if I'd accepted his proposal. I would have been his wife. By now, I'd already know what it felt like to have him inside me. I tried to pretend I was that person. A confident woman, not an unsure girl. "I think I'll just take the tunic off instead," I said.

The expression on Bjorn's face changed to astonishment. "Don't do that," he said.

But I'd already started undoing the buttons.

I looked at him with wide eyes. "Why not?" I asked. My fingers fumbled.

His bottom lip quivered. It was the only thing that gave him away. "You know why not," he whispered. "Sigrid . . . It'll drive me crazy."

I undid the last button. "That's what I'm hoping," I said. I lifted my chin, gazed directly into his eyes, and shrugged the sleeves over my shoulders.

The garment dropped to the ground in a single, liquid movement.

The material pooled at my feet.

And I just stood there, breathing rapidly, my chest rising and falling, the warmth from the fire licking my newly exposed skin.

He said, "My god. Sigrid."

Beneath the tunic, I was wearing nothing at all.

He'd never seen me like this. For the first few moments, all he could do was stare.

And I waited. An unexpected thrill ran down my spine. I thought I'd be self-conscious. But the way he was looking at me, I only felt excitement.

After a moment, he stood up. I could see desire in his eyes. He moved toward me. Slowly. Limping. In pain. His eyes didn't leave me.

I remained where I was. Shoulders back. Chin high. Offering myself to his gaze.

He didn't try to hide the fact that he was looking at me. His glance skimmed across my neck, my shoulders, my arms. It paused at my breasts, lingering for so long I wanted to squirm.

But I refused to budge, to collect my tunic from the floor, or to cover my most private parts with my hands.

He was close, now. So close, I felt his heat. So close, the coarse grain of his tunic brushed my bare nipples. He placed his hands on my shoulders delicately. I didn't know what he planned to do. Then, he lowered his mouth to mine. And kissed me. A faint kiss. Fluttery. Ticklish. Such a sweet thing. But it sent a ribbon of desire coursing from my heart to my groin. Unbearable. I wanted to throw my arms around his neck and beg him to push me to the floor and take me. But I knew I hadn't won him over yet. Knew he was still afraid.

"I love you, Sigrid," he said, quietly, his lips next to my mouth.

I'd closed my eyes when he'd kissed me. I opened them now to look at him. And saw sadness swimming in the depths of his blue irises. I was going to tell him I loved him, too. But he stopped me with a finger against my lips. "Do you have any idea what I want to do to you?" he murmured.

"Yes," I said. "And I *want* you to do it, Bjorn."

"Oh, Sigrid," he said. "Oh god, Sigrid." He closed his eyes.

I thought he'd take me in his arms. But suddenly, he opened his eyes. He looked angry. "I can't," he continued. "I won't let you hand yourself over to me out of pity."

I couldn't believe it. He thought I'd go this far—stand naked before him—out of pity?

I wanted to pull him into my arms myself, force him to see the truth. But I knew, instinctively, that now I'd made the first move toward him, he had to make the next move toward me.

"This is what I want," I said.

"What you want?" he said. "What you *want?* You want me to fuck you out of some ill-conceived sense of honor, that's what you want. I didn't squeal on your brother, and now you think you owe me. But if I do that, Sigrid—if I take what you're so beautifully offering—no decent man in the village will want to marry you. You'll be ruined. And god help me, I don't want to do that to you."

I was supposed to be offended by his coarse words. I knew that. I was supposed to run. But I didn't run so easily. "Well," I said, "I guess you'll just have to fuck me and marry me yourself, then, won't you?"

"Don't turn this into a joke."

I touched his chin. His stubble scraped my fingertips. I wanted to feel that scrape against my thighs. "It's not a joke," I said.

"You don't want to marry me." A flat statement.

"Who says?" I asked.

"You do. You turned me down."

"That was years ago," I said. "Before—"

I broke off. I was about to say the wrong thing. Again.

Before I could reclaim my sentence, Bjorn finished it for me. "That was before the Guardians arrested me, broke my knee, and gave me my limp. Before you decided you wanted to warm my bed with pity." He faltered. "I don't want your pity." He sounded broken. "But, god help me, Sigrid, I do want *you*. Please put your clothes back on. Please? Before I do something we'll both regret."

"I don't pity you," I argued, not bending to collect my tunic. "I'm trying to make you see that, Bjorn. I don't."

Bjorn groaned. I was tempting him. I knew it. He bent his head to nuzzle my neck. "I want to believe you," he said. He ran his lips along my throat. Then, lifting his head, he reached for my hips. His touch jolted me. I could see his face. He looked torn. He lifted me, sat me on the top cap, spread my knees. Stood, fully clothed, between them. "Oh god, I want to believe you so much."

He stood there like that for a long moment, stroking my hips, struggling with his thoughts.

I didn't want there to be any question in his mind. "Touch me," I said. "Touch me and then you'll see I'm telling the truth."

He smiled wanly. "I *am* touching you." He slapped my hip. Gently. Teasing. A bit like the old Bjorn. "Can't you tell?"

"Not there, you fool," I curled my arms around his neck, looked up into his face. "Between my legs. Feel me."

He stiffened in my arms.

I'd always considered him the experienced one when it came to sex, for no other reason than he was a man and a couple of years older than me. Now, I realized he was on new ground, too.

I resisted the urge to guide his hand with my own, but I spoke gently. "Go on. Touch me."

He didn't need me to ask again. His hand left my hip. Shaking, it fumbled toward my thigh, hesitated for a moment at my pubic mound. And then moved downward.

All of a sudden, he pressed his whole palm against me, flattening it against my opening.

I gasped and arched into him. He felt so warm and wonderful.

He cried out, "Good god, Sigrid, you're so wet."

I wanted to giggle at his surprise, but I was too aroused. "See?" I said. I wriggled my hips so that my crotch slipped against his hand. "What do you suppose pity feels like? Do you think it feels like a woman's sopping wet pussy sliding against your palm?"

It wasn't a slow dawning. Rather, it was like he'd been asleep and someone had shaken him awake. His eyes suddenly sparked. Hope sprung there. And he smiled at me. I was delighted. It'd been a long time since I'd seen him happy.

"Sigrid," he said. He moved his hand against me, back and forth, reveling in the sensation, making me giddy. "No," he said. "This isn't pity I feel."

"Then will you go ahead and fuck me already?" I said, pressing against him, urging him on, tortured by the sensation yet wanting more.

His mouth stretched into a big, wide smile.

"What?" I asked.

"You have a dirty mouth, you know that?"

"What are you going to do about it?" I teased.

He pulled me in for a kiss. "I think some reprimands might be in order," he said, as his lips met mine.

I liked his sudden confidence. "You'll have to catch me first," I replied, breathless as I pulled my mouth away.

Too late, I realized what I'd said. But he delighted me further when he pressed his forehead against mine and said, "You think I'm actually going to let you go?"

I smiled into his face. He smiled back.

Quickly, he became serious again. "Sigrid," he said, "we don't have to make love if you're not ready. You've proved your point. But if you are ready . . . I'd really like to . . ." Words failed him. He dropped his hands from my crotch to his belt buckle, showing me what he wanted. "But this is the point of no return. After this, even if there is someone else who wants to marry you, I won't let him." He pressed his cheek against mine. "I won't let you go. You'll be mine. Do you understand? Mine."

I'd been gripping his arms. Now, I lowered my hands until they rested on his, on his belt buckle. I caressed his knuckles gently, encouraging him. "I understand," I said. "It's what I want. I promise you."

I felt him undo his belt buckle then. He pulled his trousers down while I leaned my forehead against his chest and watched. His penis sprang out. Long and hard and marvelous. "You're beautiful," I said, without thinking.

He chuckled. Nervous and embarrassed and unmistakably aroused.

He shifted. When the wet tip of his penis accidentally brushed my hand, I took the opportunity to stroke it with my thumb. Bjorn groaned. Not a small groan, but a big, agonized, carnal one. Suddenly, he was in a hurry. "Last chance, darling," he said. His hips rocked against my hand. "Tell me now if you've changed your mind. In a moment, I don't think I'll be able to stop."

I continued to stroke him, bold after his cry of pleasure. "Does it feel like I've changed my mind?" I asked.

He groaned again. "No. It doesn't. I hope . . . Darling, I hope you never regret this." He paused. "I never will."

Then he lifted my hands from his penis to settle them onto his shoulders, straightening me in the process, so I sat high on the stepladder. He spread my legs so wide they almost ran in line with the rungs. He stepped closer to me, looked right into my eyes. I knew what he was about to do. I had a moment—a single moment—of trepidation. I wanted to remind him that I was a virgin, that he needed to go easily or he'd hurt me.

Then I realized I didn't need to remind him. "It'll be all right," he said, to reassure me, as though by looking into my eyes he'd read my mind.

I believed him. I returned his look. He drew his hips back. Slowly. And then thrust forward. Fast. A single, rapid movement. Hard.

I screamed.

And closed my eyes.

I'd torn immediately. And certainly it hurt. I cried out in agony. But Bjorn captured my cry with his mouth, kissing me gently, so I knew he was there with me. And I felt him. Inside me. Deep. Nestled. The pain quickly gave way to a euphoric pleasure. He kept kissing me, his hands on my hips. I whimpered against his mouth. The grind of his cock inside me felt so good. I soared, held on to him for dear life, bucked against him. Grunted. And groaned. Trying to get something from him. But what? More pleasure? More ecstasy? Release? No, not release. I never wanted this to stop. "Dear god," I said, pulling my mouth from his.

"I know," he replied, voice strained.

He bucked into my body just as hard as I bucked into his.

"So, so good," I said.

He didn't reply. I didn't know if he was capable of speech. Then, suddenly, "So. Much. Better. Than. That."

His thrusting intensified. He grabbed my ass, hard, fingers digging right in. The pressure felt incredible. I gasped over his shoulder, spouting nonsense words. He pounded into me, again and again. I would have fallen off the stool if it weren't for his grip. He cried out my name, over and over, as though he had no other word in his vocabulary. His teeth nipped the skin at my neck. His stubble scratched my shoulder. His huge, thumping body felt bestial in my arms.

Then he cried out—and me with him. We shouted. Our voices mingled. We clung to each other. So tightly I thought we'd merge.

Finally, his knee gave way. He fell backward. I toppled with him, falling onto his chest. Breathless.

We lay like that for minutes. I, with my head on his chest, listening to the thud of his heart. He, with his hand in my hair.

"Mine," he said.

"Yours," I agreed.

It was a long, long while later that he said, "Why did you return the jewelry box?" He was kissing me softly, and I was dizzy with elation so I wasn't expecting the question. But I could tell it mattered to him.

"I accepted it when I turned down your proposal," I said. "So I returned it to you as a way of letting you know I wanted to undo the past, that I wanted you to propose again."

"Uh-huh," Bjorn said. He chuckled. "In future, do you think you could just tell me what you're thinking, rather than offering coded messages? I don't think I got the meaning of this one right."

I glanced sideways, to where the box still lay on the floor in pieces. "I see what you mean," I said dryly. "Okay."

He laughed but there was no bitterness in it. What had happened between us was so joyous, he could begin to move on from his pain. "I'll make you another one," he promised.

"I don't want another one. Can't you repair this one?"

He looked down his chest at me. "I can," he said slowly. "But don't you want one that's new?"

I shook my head. "Broken things fixed are better than new."

# ONE INTERPRETATION

Stella Harris

Cassandra hates wasting time. She's barely able to finish her lecture and allow questions on the best of days, so losing ten minutes is especially frustrating. Feeling on the spot, she apologizes to her class for the second time and continues to pace between the podium and her desk, her heels clacking on the linoleum floor with each step.

Finally, right when she is about to call the university office and complain, a man bursts through the loud metal doors of the classroom and strides up to her. With a shock, she recognizes him as the man she'd been eying in the staff lounge just days before. She'd thought he was a new professor, and she wasn't sure what he was doing here now.

"Sorry I'm late, Professor Basset," he says, and there's a glint in his eye, though she isn't in on the joke.

"You're the interpreter?" Cassandra asks, collecting herself.

"That's right, Philip Reed. I'm the new adjunct English professor. But I don't have any classes this session and I got a call that you needed someone," he says hurriedly, holding out his hand for Cassandra to shake.

She's still fixed on the "needing someone" comment when she realizes she's leaving his hand hanging between them. She grabs it on instinct but almost immediately looks down; his hand seems impossibly smooth and supple in hers.

There is a fine art to a good handshake. You must be firm but not too firm. Hold long enough but not too long. Sweaty hands are a no-no, but too chapped and dry is no good either. It's a skill she's been careful to cultivate as she's climbed the academic ladder. She's never wanted to give any administrator a bad first impression. After all, you can tell a lot about a person from a handshake. And Cassandra's body is reaching quite a few conclusions about Philip from this one.

Too late, Cassandra realizes she's broken at least one of her own rules for a good handshake by holding on too long, not to mention the lack of eye contact. But when she does look up, she's not at all prepared for the deep blue eyes and mischievous twinkle fixed on her. She'd gotten the impression he was handsome from her brief glimpse before, but his eyes are something else.

"Are you ready to begin?" Philip asks, and Cassandra realizes that his voice is far deeper than it had seemed when he first spoke, still out of breath.

And she's doing it again, or rather, still doing it. The rules of the handshake are out the window at this point. They are more or less just holding hands—in front of the full lecture hall. This man's smooth hands, blue eyes, and deep voice have destroyed her focus in just minutes, and she hasn't even begun to lecture yet.

Slowly it sinks in that she was asked a question. "Excuse me?" she asks, helplessly.

"The lecture. Are you ready to begin?" he says again, clearly trying to keep any sign of amusement out of his voice.

"Oh yes. Of course." Cassandra tries to gather her composure, even if it's too little too late. She can hear the students shifting in their seats and even a few pointed coughs.

Philip frees his hand from Cassandra's grip, dragging his fingertips across Cassandra's palm far more than seems absolutely necessary. Cassandra shudders in response to the touch, but having a roomful of eyes on her is excellent motivation to get her act in gear.

Gathering the notes from her desk, Cassandra steps up to the podium in front of the class as Philip takes his place several feet to the left, giving Cassandra a perfect view.

Cassandra gathers the pages together and taps them on the podium several times, ostensibly to tidy the pile, while making one last desperate attempt to get ahold of herself. Finally, when she thinks she can speak without her voice cracking, Cassandra launches into today's lecture on the nuances of Ancient Greek architecture.

But as soon as she begins speaking, movement to her left catches Cassandra's eye and she can't stop herself from watching as Philip's hands move along to her words, interpreting the lecture. There's a fluidity and grace to his movements she's never noticed from other interpreters she's had in class.

Cassandra also notices that during the brief moments when she wasn't watching, Philip had removed his coat and rolled up his shirtsleeves, drawing attention not only to his hands but to his delicate, slender wrists and forearms. She had never realized how erotic hands and wrists could be.

With effort, Cassandra pulls her eyes back down to her notes, determined to make it through at least the next page before looking at him again.

She makes it about three paragraphs before her eyes move of their own accord to the man standing to her left. Apparently Philip isn't just translating her words but is gesturing to illustrate her points. As she talks about the way the architecture takes into account the bright sunshine and deep blue of the ocean, his hands move to indicate the expanse of sea and sky. When she explains the precision with which marble surfaces were polished and smoothed, making curves that allow the eye to track through the space, his hands move as though they are indicating the curves on a body, making the class giggle.

When he looks at her again with that same twinkle in his eye, she can't help but feel she's being teased. Cassandra manages to continue speaking while casting surreptitious glances to the side. She's never been happier that she knows this material so well.

The way Philip's hands move is proving ever more difficult to ignore. She can't help but imagine what those hands would feel like on her body or how his smooth skin would feel sliding against her. Cassandra clears her throat repeatedly and adjusts her glasses in an attempt to disguise the fact that she has become distracted and lost her train of thought, again.

But every time she pauses, it makes matters worse. Because every time she stops speaking for even a moment, Philip turns to look at her with his piercing blue eyes and Cassandra's mouth goes completely dry. She's beginning to think she's not going to make it through this lecture.

When she begins to doubt her ability to focus any longer, she spares a glance down at her watch and breathes a sigh of relief that the class period is nearly over. Never has an hour felt so long. Deciding to cut her losses, she sets her papers aside and announces that because of the late start they are going to spread that day's topic across two classes and will finish the lecture next time they meet.

She asks if there are any questions. Luckily there are very few; most of the students look as eager to leave as she is to have them gone. After a few more tortuous moments, she announces that they're done, and the students stand as one and hurry to the doors.

Cassandra straightens her papers for the umpteenth time as she watches the last of the students file from the room, the doors slamming shut behind them. The finality of that sound grants her some relief.

When at last she turns away from the podium, she finds Philip waiting behind her, standing well within her personal space. "I just wanted to apologize again for being late. I only got the call at the last minute that they needed someone to fill in."

"Oh, don't worry about it. I appreciate you coming on such short notice," Cassandra hurries to say, kicking herself for being so accommodating.

"It was my pleasure," comes his smooth reply. Philip is just inches from her now, blue eyes drilling into her, showing no concern for the silence building between them.

Then, without warning, Philip turns and walks away, going to collect his coat. Cassandra's heart is pounding so hard she thinks Philip might hear it from across the room. But not knowing what to do, or what to say, Cassandra simply walks back to her desk and drops her notes haphazardly, the pages scattering to the floor.

Hearing what sounds like a suppressed chuckle behind her, Cassandra spins around to find Philip within inches of her once again. As if choreographed, they both kneel to gather the fallen papers, their hands bumping when reaching for the same sheets. They gather the pages in silence, neither commenting on the way their hands linger every time they come into contact.

Finally standing, Philip hands over the pages he'd collected and offers his hand to shake once more. Cassandra pauses, considering the implication of touching him again. This time when they grip hands, it doesn't feel like either of them intends to let go.

Reaching forward with her free hand, Cassandra clasps Philip's wrist, marveling at how slender it is, her fingers spanning the whole circumference, delicate bones easily felt beneath the skin.

"Professor?" Philip prompts, and his voice sounds more intrigued than alarmed. Using her title rather than her name feels like he's giving her the upper hand, even though apparently they're colleagues now.

Cassandra takes her time, deciding what to do next or how to respond. While she thinks, she absently massages Philip's hand, her thumb making circles against his palm.

"May I?" Cassandra asks, though she's already raising Philip's hand to her mouth, holding eye contact and kissing the back of it in an old-fashioned gesture, though with the roles reversed.

She waits for Philip's eyes to widen in alarm, or for him to pull away, but he does neither of those things. Instead he just smiles serenely, waiting to see what Cassandra is going to do.

Emboldened, Cassandra next kisses Philip's fingertips, each one in turn. She can't remember ever being so forward, but something about him brings out a part of herself she's unfamiliar with. She keeps watching his eyes, and she sees them go soft and then flutter closed as she parts her lips and takes two fingertips into her mouth up to the first knuckle.

Cassandra slides her tongue between Philip's fingers while watching his reactions. She takes in the sight of Philip's mouth falling open and his head tilting back as encouragement, and continues to suck, lick, and explore, taking his fingers deeper and deeper.

When Cassandra has taken his fingers all the way down into her throat, Philip's eyes shoot open and he groans and steps forward, pressing his body up against Cassandra's from knees to hips. The very clear reaction his body is having provides further encouragement. Cassandra smiles around the fingers in her mouth and applies a bit of pressure with her teeth, causing Philip to press harder against her, knocking the back of Cassandra's legs up against her desk.

She slides her ass up onto the desk, and since she's still holding Philip's wrist, he steps forward with her, now standing half between her parted knees.

He reaches out for Cassandra's shoulder as if to steady himself, and his eyes slide closed. Cassandra thoroughly enjoys the sight of Philip coming apart, after having been driven crazy by him for the last hour. Turnabout is fair play.

Cassandra finally lets his fingers slide out of her mouth with a pop and nibbles her way down to Philip's wrist before biting the tender flesh she finds there. He makes a small sound and her eyes meet his, seeing the same arousal and desperation she feels.

Still holding his hand, she glides his fingers slowly down her neck, down her cleavage and lower still, to the hem of her skirt.

As she moves she keeps a close eye on Philip's face, looking for any signs of hesitation or discomfort. She doesn't find any. So she keeps moving until she's led his fingers all the way up her skirt and between her legs. The look on his face when instead of encountering panties his fingers are pressed directly against her wetness is priceless.

Cassandra struggles to maintain control when what she really wants to do is throw her head back and let his hand work at her. But she's leading the way, and if she stops, he might stop, too. And that's the last thing she wants.

She pulls on his wrist and he simultaneously steps forward and plunges his fingers inside her. They share a look of surprise at the escalation, but neither stops. Instead he leans forward, in a motion that's almost a swoon, and their lips brush against each other in a brief kiss.

Philip is taking initiative now, his fingers curling inside her and finding the spot that makes her squirm. His thumb focuses on her clit and makes small circles at the same time. Cassandra is delighted to find that he's as good with his hands as it looked like he'd be, and she barely holds his wrist now, letting him drive the action.

He makes short work of her, the whole lecture having operated as foreplay. And before she knows it, she's letting out a shaky gasp and leaning forward to rest her head on his shoulder.

As she comes to her senses, she feels his breathing against the side of her neck, coming in short gasps. She's had her release, but he's still on edge.

She drops her hand to the front of his pants and finds the bulge there, stretching the fabric to capacity. She gives him a gentle squeeze and he moans, pressing forward into her hand. She traces the outline of his cock with her fingers, enjoying the slow tease now that her own sense of urgency has passed.

Cassandra leans forward to whisper in Philip's ear, "I'm pretty good with my hands, too. Come home with me?"

Philip nods his assent, and she grabs his still slippery hand to pull him out of the classroom.

# PERIPHERAL VOYEURISM

A. Zimmerman

Music pounded through the room, the bass strong enough to start syncopating heartbeats but not loud enough to drown out club attendees. Divided into a series of wide hallways, smaller rooms, and little nooks, it was impossible to tell where any one noise was originating in the club. It was not, however, impossible to tell what the noises were.

Beneath the music there was the soft grunt of someone putting effort into a swing followed by the gasping reaction of someone being hit. The snap of skin hitting skin. The sharper sound of leather. The softer whistle of rattan canes. The hard rattle of metal chains. Together they composed the erotic sound of sexual sadism, and it was enveloping Claire.

She hadn't known what to expect; Ryan had simply said they were going out. There wasn't a name on the building, just an address. The front door opened into a neutral hallway with a closed door at the end. The second door opened to a flight of stairs going down. Once on the stairs, Claire heard club music playing.

At the bottom, Ryan checked in at a ticket window before

being allowed through yet another door. Only then had it become clear it wasn't a dance club. Leading her past the bar to a sitting area of chairs and love seats, Ryan directed Claire to sit on the floor as he dropped into an overstuffed chair.

As his submissive-in-training, she didn't question but she did hesitate, fussing with the black skirt he had dressed her in, tucking the unfamiliar sweep of fabric under her curled legs as she sat. Ryan threaded his fingers through her shoulder-length hair, encouraging her to lean in. With the reassurance of his touch, Claire relaxed, resting her head on his denim-clad thigh, her arms looping around his shin.

Over the curve of Ryan's knee, Claire studied the platform-style stage across the way. A blindfolded woman stood with her arms over her head, wrists in manacles hanging from the ceiling, every lingerie-clad pudgy curve lovingly lit by stage lighting. Clearly Claire wasn't the only well-rounded woman in the club. Claire watched those watching the stage. Obviously, here one didn't need to be model-thin to be beautifully on display.

From the shadows, a single-tail whip snaked out, the woman writhing as it struck her hip. The next time it found its mark, she cried out with abandon. Claire understood one person's pain was another's pleasure, but even so . . . Vaguely appalled by the show, she dropped her eyes to the floor only to discover it had become a different kind of stage.

Within arm's reach a man lay on his back, trussed in a tight leather harness, his chest serving as a footrest for the six-inch spike heels of the woman he was accompanying. The end of the leash in the woman's hand was fastened to the man's bound genitals, the slightest flick of her gloved fingers causing him to squirm. Stunned, she stared until he caught her eye and winked.

Embarrassed, Claire buried her face against Ryan's leg. He stroked her hair, bringing her to heel with the absentminded authority of his touch as he began conversing with the woman holding the leash. Eventually Claire propped her chin on his knee, studying the interaction between the man on the floor and the woman controlling him.

Ryan tugged her hair, bringing her focus back to him.

"Stand," he ordered, his voice pitched under the music.

Claire obeyed. Being careful to not step on the man on the floor, she stood in front of Ryan, automatically folding her arms behind her back. He studied her, trying to make her fidget and failing.

"Your shirt is pretty—"

"Thank you, Sir."

Ryan ignored the interruption.

"Take it off."

"What?"

"Take it off."

Claire squirmed, breaking the traditional waiting stance. Nervously, she crossed her arms over her stomach. Ryan waited, eyes unwaveringly on her, making the two-inch steel ring of the leather collar she was wearing weigh heavy against the hollow of her throat.

Ryan had fastened it around her neck one night about a month after they had begun dating. It was a physical acknowledgment that they had reached an agreement about their relationship, that she agreed to defer, trust, and submit to him. He had then gone home, after instructing her to think about it and telling her that he would be back with breakfast.

The following morning Ryan had removed the leather collar and, with Claire's agreement, replaced it with a silver necklace. Claire vividly remembered the soft kiss that followed the change and could still hear Ryan's whispered words: "You're going to be mine, all day, every day." He had traced the necklace where it lay on her collarbone while explaining it was his job to decide what would go around her collar, and it was her job to wear the collar.

Claire absently fingered the ring of steel as she listened to the cadence of issued instructions and the particular silence that followed as they were obeyed. She knew she should be part of the gaps of silence. The atmosphere of the room began pressing in on her, physically collapsing her. She leaned in, the ring on the collar swaying, her head coming to rest on Ryan's shoulder.

"I can't."

"What?"

"I can't."

"You can."

"Can't."

The quaver in her voice pulled Ryan's protective instincts. He wanted to gather her close, holding her until her uncertainty vanished. He also wanted her to obey. He cupped the side of her neck, tipping his own head to lean against hers as he spoke, using logic to guide her through the resistance.

"Why?"

Claire shook her head.

"If you don't have a reason to not do it, you do it."

"I can't."

"Why?"

"People."

He responded to what she wasn't saying.

"You're mine. You do what I want. Everyone here understands."

"Body."

Ryan's heart melted, hearing what she wasn't saying. He kissed her temple.

"You think I'd let anything be said about my girl?"

Claire shook her head.

"Who owns you?"

"You."

"What's your concern?"

"You."

"Which means?"

"Nothing else is my concern."

"Exactly—"

Ryan changed his mind, biting back the rest of his words. He waited for Claire to make the next move, giving her time to come into submission on her own. Finally Claire put a shaking hand on his thigh and pushed herself upright, locking eyes with him. The club became a blur in her peripheral vision, her potential owner filling her world.

Claire lifted her hands to the top of her shirt, fingers brushing the collar around her neck as she caught the fabric. Trembling, she pulled the shirt over her head, offering it to him. After he took it, Claire folded her arms behind her back, slipping back into a waiting stance. Ryan tucked her shirt into the small duffel bag half under his chair.

"Take off the skirt."

She obeyed instantly, not giving herself time to think. Standing in bra, panties, and sandals, Claire handed him the skirt. He took it and turned back to the duffel bag. Claire knew she was on the fringe of Ryan's awareness; any unwarranted move would snap his attention fully to her. She stood still, her mind sinking into the nothingness of waiting.

Ryan messed with the contents of the bag, buying time to debate how to manage what was happening. He needed to harness the energy surging between them, which was going to be tricky as he was distracted by the rush of power. Claire trusting him enough to strip in the middle of the club, making herself vulnerable in so many different ways, resonated in a way he hadn't expected. He wanted to stop and wrap his arms around her.

Ryan knew he had a huge romantic streak. Other submissive women had left him because of it, claiming he wasn't dominant enough. He would never understand how giving flowers or politely holding a door open for the woman you were with could make her decide to leave.

Although he wasn't concerned about Claire leaving, he was concerned with building on the current momentum. The intimate energy humming between them was the opportunity to push her in the direction they both wanted, guiding her into accepting his encompassing personal ownership.

He snagged a polar fleece headband and stood, completely filling Claire's personal space. Sliding the headband over her head, he combined dominance with romance, taking extra time to smooth and straighten her hair as he tugged the fabric into place.

"How's that?" he inquired, tracing the edges of the headband-turned-blindfold with his fingertips.

She nodded in slow response, her ability to think muffled by the power of Ryan's control.

"Don't move."

Without waiting for a reaction, Ryan walked over to the bar. She continuously amazed him. He had no idea where she found the strength to trust him so completely, to have such utter faith she would stand alone and exposed in a room of strangers.

Behind the blindfold, Claire closed her eyes, letting the noise of the crowded club wash over her, concentrating on staying centered in the moment. She refused to think beyond her next breath and steadfastly ignored the fact that there had to be voyeurs around. Technically she had been one herself; of course there were more.

Claire's shoulders twitched, the possibility of putting on a show for strangers making her skin crawl. Abruptly she couldn't get the idea of perverts watching her out of her mind. As the saying went: what I do over here is wonderfully erotic, what you do over there is outrageously perverted. She didn't want to be some stranger's pervert. She wanted to be Ryan's pervert.

She forced herself to remain still, staying under Ryan's control. It was a small but vital step forward, staying where Ryan put her even when he was gone. Claire wasn't the only one experiencing halting progress. Ryan knew he led their relationship only for as long as Claire followed. Having been involved for six months, they had less of a relationship and more a game of trials and errors. Coming to the club was basically a trial Ryan was hoping wouldn't turn into an error.

Watching Claire stay in place loosened the knot of tension between Ryan's shoulders. Even from a distance he could see Claire's growing discomfort was cracking the surface of her composure, creating a fissure in her defenses. It was the opening he needed to start pulling her in, to have her become completely absorbed in a power relationship with him.

He returned to her, fishing an ice cube out of his glass of carbonated water as he walked. He traced her lips with the edge of the ice, the heat of her skin making it melt faster. Initially Claire jerked back, startled by the cold, slick touch. A second later she relaxed, flicking her tongue over the cube. Ryan's eyes locked on to her mouth, his cock stirring as he imagined her mouth doing to his balls what she was currently doing to the piece of ice.

"All right." He had to clear his throat. "Enough."

Recognizing the catch in his voice, Claire laughed delightedly, licking her lips provocatively as she responded with an overly obedient, "Yes, Sir."

Ryan hooked his fingers through the collar's ring, giving it a teasing jerk.

"Stop," he warned mildly, his voice gone hoarse with passion.

He used the collar to pull her head forward, pressing a lingering kiss to her cooled mouth. He kept the tension around her neck, twisting to set his cup down before reaching down into the duffel bag to pull out a length of chain. Straightening, he clipped the chain to the ring in the collar and wrapped some of the extra links around his hand as he leaned forward to whisper in her ear.

"Collared and leashed." He tugged on the chain. "Follow."

Still blindfolded, Claire aligned herself with the direction of the leash, moving with the tension of the chain. Ryan shortened it, putting himself within the boundaries of the area he thought Claire could peripherally sense. Proving his estimate correct, the change in distance between them changed Claire's body language, her steps coming without hesitation as she confidently followed his lead.

Ultimately disoriented, Claire stumbled to a stop as Ryan turned toward her, clasping her by the shoulders. He turned her, pushing her until she was stopped by something about waist high.

"It's a long padded bench," Ryan told her, his soft tone cocooning them together. "Lean over it facedown, flat on your torso."

Claire slid her hands along the length, feeling her way as she followed Ryan's directions. She squirmed into a comfortable position, the shifting of her hips distracting Ryan from his preparations. He stopped what he was doing and leaned over Claire, one hand resting on the small of her back, his lips brushing the shell of her ear teasingly.

"What a wiggle."

"What?"

Claire moved unexpectedly with her question, bumping him in the nose. Ryan ducked away as she propped herself up on her forearms with a vaguely worded apology. He slid the heel of his hand up her spine until it rested on the back of her neck, his fingers spread across her head. He pushed her down with a low, sharp warning.

"Did you request to move?"

Aware of the scattering of people moving around the edges of the room taking in the vignette he was constructing, the same way he and Claire had watched others, Ryan leaned over her, his hard-edged words for her ears only.

"Don't embarrass me."

"Nosir," Claire slurred, her voice muffled by the padding on the bench as she buried her face in her arms.

"You haven't," Ryan amended, his tone softening. "But you need to be the well-trained slave I know you can be."

Claire nodded into her crossed arms, the hand Ryan could see shaking uncontrollably. Leaving one hand on her head, he folded her fingers into his other hand, squeezing tightly. He held on until he felt her squeeze back. Disentangling himself, Ryan turned and reached into the duffel bag, catching the handle of his favorite crop.

He traced the soft leather flapper across her shoulders and down the center of her back. His slow, teasing start gave Claire a chance to recognize what toy he had selected as well as giving him the opportunity to make her shiver in anticipation. He chased the shivers with the crop, one response feeding the next, creating a circle of sensation.

Ryan began flipping the crop against her, generating a light, smacking rhythm that brought heat to her skin's surface. The heat echoed through Ryan's groin, pulling him to an erotic edge. With careful concentration, he systematically increased the intensity of the cropping until he was making a design of red slashes over the blurs of pink from earlier marks.

For no discernible reason, Claire occasionally flinched as the crop landed but she never changed position. Ryan knew the ability to have his words bind Claire into place was the foundation of their relationship. Her willingness to stay put provided him with such a deep rush of power it momentarily took his breath away. This was what he had been hoping would happen. This was the actualization of control he had been wanting so badly for so long.

His cock surged hot and hard, pressing against the fly of his jeans, the fast spike of sexual excitement making his hands tremble. Knowing the slight shake in his hand would compromise his ability to correctly guide the crop, he dropped it in favor of a flogger, its three-dozen braided leather cords providing a larger margin for error.

Ryan rolled his wrist, swinging the flogger gently so it landed on Claire's head with a soft thump, the cords twisting with her hair to hang like dreadlocks. Continuing the rolling motion he rotated his forearm, pulling the flogger down the length of her body.

Ryan's attention narrowed to Claire. Even with the music covering the sound of her moan, he saw the change in her breathing, correctly interpreting the deeper exhale as a pleasure response. Letting the heavy weight of the flogger drag naturally down from her hips, Ryan again continued the pattern of rotation. He rolled his entire arm back and around, circling the flogger up and over to gain a full swing as he landed it across her shoulders with an audible thud.

This time Claire's harsh exhale could be heard over the music as her skin, left a delicate pink from the attention of the crop, flashed into red lines, one for each cord of the flogger that bit into her shoulder. Her involuntary noise, so clearly saturated with arousal, made Ryan's achingly hard cock surge in reaction.

As she was still inhaling, he windmilled the flogger, landing it with precision across her other shoulder blade. Working into a rhythm, Ryan began moving around the lower half of the bench in a slow half circle, the flogger arching into a continual blur as he lashed Claire. Within a few strikes he developed a pattern, landing diagonal blows from left to right as he moved from her shoulders to her thighs and back again, the leather cords crisscrossing nonstop.

Before Claire could fully register the heavy blow and the stinging snap of the knotted end of the cords that followed, the flogger was whirling around, landing an overlapping blow. The seconds of pain smudged together, the totality equaling an erotic endorphin rush that sent her senses spinning into overload, her clit pulsing in time with the stinging lash, her pussy wantonly melting in response to the heat of the flogger over her skin. Losing all sense of time, Claire sank into silence, pushed into the support of the bench by the inescapable weight of the flogger thumping across her body in countless repetition.

Ryan also lost track of time, his concern shifting from minutes to minutiae. It wasn't about the amount of time or the number of strikes. It was about the authority to manage Claire's reactions and his split-second ability to decide whether she was going to flinch or sigh next. He was even regulating the color of her skin, choosing the shade of red warmth across her back while creating a pattern of deeper red lash marks. Along with his physical management, Ryan knew he had mental command of Claire; she wasn't moving until he gave permission. Eclipsed by the eroticism of absolute domination, his erection faded.

The small part of his mind not riding the rush the power created by his control made specific note of Claire's left arm sliding out from under her head to hang off the edge of the bench. She was so deep into her own version of the rush created by the flow of power between them she was going completely limp.

Not wanting her to slip off the bench and land in a heap on the floor, Ryan began easing back, gradually decreasing the intensity of the flogging, slowly bringing them both back from the intimate depths of their power exchange.

On his next backswing, Ryan was suddenly brought up short, the flogger tangling behind him. He jerked around, startled to find a man being pulled out of range by others standing along the edge of the space. Several people silently waved him back toward Claire, the potentially awkward situation clearly under control. Without a second thought, Ryan turned his back on the crowd, refocusing on Claire to the exclusion of the rest of the room.

The interruption provided Ryan with the perfect way to segue from what he was doing, using the break in rhythm to alter how he was using the flogger. His next stroke landed as a caress around her shoulders, shimmying the cords down her back. He repeated this move a dozen times, each one coming a little slower and lasting a little longer until there wasn't enough momentum to lift the flogger. He let it drop, freeing both hands to cup her hips.

Kneading lightly, he worked his way up her torso, the warmth from the flogging and latticed design of welts he could feel on her skin arousing him. Claire moaned, her right arm slipping to dangle off the other side of the bench.

"Careful there, slave," Ryan whispered, his mouth brushing her ear.

Claire gave a muffled groan, then sighed, stretching her back luxuriously. Ryan stroked one hand down her spine, ending with a pat on her ass. With the other hand, he dragged the blindfold off her head while continuing to speak quietly to her.

"I want you to get up, get dressed, and put all the toys back in the bag. Check this area very carefully. When you're finished, come to me."

He waited for her faint "Yes, Sir," before moving to a seat against one of the walls of the room. He stretched his legs out comfortably and folded his arms behind his head, monitoring the dazed way Claire followed his instructions.

"Nice scene," a stranger commented as he stepped around Ryan while staying well away from Claire.

Ryan smiled and nodded, his eyes never leaving Claire. The thundering music began to change, dropping in volume until it cut off, allowing the announcement that the club was closing in fifteen minutes to be heard. Caught off guard, Ryan checked his watch, surprised to find it was after two in the morning. At the same time, Claire glanced at the ceiling, acknowledging the announcement as she zipped the duffel bag.

She then hesitated, clearly at a loss for what to do next, the bag hanging from one hand. Just when Ryan was getting ready to catch her attention, she remembered and scanned the room, smiling as she found him. Ryan stood to greet her as she approached, taking the bag from her unresisting fingers.

"It's later than I thought," he admitted. "You good?"

Pushing a hand through her rumpled hair, Claire nodded, her body leaning toward his. Ryan held his hand out to her, and she looked at it blankly. Ryan smiled, pleased to see her so indolent. Obviously she was still flooded with endorphins, the erotic high making it difficult for her to quickly process new information. He wiggled his fingers, and Claire laced her fingers with his.

Ryan tugged her hand, leading her through the club, catching her elbow to help her keep her balance as she tripped on the stairs on their way out onto the street. Still mostly disoriented and more than a little disinterested in the basic mechanics of navigating home, Claire stood, completely passive to everything on the block but Ryan.

He waved down a cab, assessing Claire as it came to a stop in front of them. He was going to tell her to get in and slide over to the other side but thought better of it, doubting her ability to follow directions without the guidance of his touch. Instead, he handed Claire through the nearest door and walked around to the far side to climb into the cab. Leaning forward, he gave directions to the driver. A second after he sat back, Claire fell sideways into a boneless heap, causing Ryan to jerk the duffel bag up and out of the way a second before her head came to rest on his lap.

Ryan chuckled, one hand once again on her head as he used the other hand to balance the duffel bag on his knees, wedging it against the back of the front seat. Sighing, Claire slipped a hand under his thigh, the intimacy of the gesture making his cock rise. He shifted, pushing the bag another few inches against the seat-back as he spoke quietly, his words pitched under the radio the cab driver was playing.

"Lift your head."

Claire moved to rest her head on the bag. Ryan slipped his hand down, the soft rasp of his jeans unzipping causing her to turn so she could watch him fish his cock out. Leaving his hand wrapped partially around the shaft, he made a "come here" gesture with two fingers, the motion just visible in the flickering streetlight.

Claire obeyed, dropping her head between the bag and his stomach, her mouth smoothly sliding down his hard length until the head of his cock nestled into the back of her throat. Ryan tipped his head all the way back, fighting to swallow a guttural groan as her sizzling mouth encased him fully. He cupped the back of her head in one hand, holding her still as she stroked him with her tongue.

Although he was certain that between the darkness of the backseat and the position of the bag there wasn't anything to see, Ryan felt a nagging doubt. He opened his eyes a slit, angling his head just enough so he could see the cab driver and verify he was driving rather than watching. His doubt put to rest, Ryan dropped his head back and let the hot arousal pooling in his groin flood the rest of his body, his heart thundering in time with the deep pull of Claire's mouth.

Claire crushed her tongue along the underside of his shaft, forcing the length of his cock to follow the curve of the roof of her mouth as she sucked harder, creating an unbelievable tension. A low groan escaped through Ryan's gritted teeth, the nerves in his cock singing. His balls tightened, growing heavy with sexual excitement, his body surging to the edge of climax.

Not wanting to come in the back of a cab, Ryan regretfully lifted his head, searching out the window for something to focus on other than his impending orgasm. Catching sight of a familiar storefront, he tugged on Claire's hair and spoke, his voice gone gruff with lust.

"We're almost home."

He kept gently yet steadily pulling on her hair until she sat up, his cock slipping from her mouth with excruciating slowness. Claire curled herself up on the seat, pressing a kiss to his jaw before pillowing her head on his shoulder, one arm draping across his chest. Ryan cautiously pushed his throbbing cock back into his jeans and untucked his shirt to cover the open zipper as the cab came to a stop.

Ryan fished his wallet out with one hand and paid the fare while giving Claire a friendly shove with the other one, ushering her out of the cab in record time. Keeping the bag awkwardly in front of his hips, he joined her on the sidewalk. He wrapped one arm around her tightly as he spoke, his voice vibrating with passion.

"As soon as we get upstairs, I'm going to fuck my slave until she begs to come."

Claire slung her arms around his neck, pulling his head down so she could whisper in his ear, the cadence of her quiet words shooting straight to his cock, making him glad he hadn't zipped his jeans. Ryan laughed breathlessly, hip checking her toward the door of their building.

"I want to hear it again when I'm buried in you to the balls."

"That and more," she agreed saucily, slipping a hand into his pants to caress his cock as he unlocked the security door—and with it untold sexual possibilities for the rest of the night.

# DANCING WITH MYSELF

Quinn LeStrange

I can't believe I'm here again.

If someone had told me a year ago that I would be exposing myself in front of a live audience of strangers, I'd ask what kind of drugs they were on so that I could acquire a small stash for bad days. A year ago, I was insecure, fragile, and afraid to be myself in this world because I was scared that it would make others uncomfortable. All of that changed, however, when Jackson found me and made me his. Sometimes it seems like it was just yesterday that he walked into my life and turned it upside down, introduced me to so many things. Taught me things about myself that I'm not sure I would have ever stumbled across on my own. He pushed me to do things I never would have had the guts to do.

And I loved it all.

Our first meeting was complete serendipity, two missed exchanges landing us in the same art gallery at the same time. I had intended to meet a blind date, he to meet an artist about a commission for the social club he owned. I had been so transfixed by the erotic scenes on the walls that I stayed and got lost a while, not wanting to waste a perfectly stimulating experience. It had felt naughty, suggesting this place as a first encounter with a complete stranger. If anything, my date's absence without notification gave a better indication of his comfort with all this than any conversation would have. In my mind, I had dodged a bullet. There was nothing to be gained from those who were uncomfortable in the presence of the naked form, so I satisfied my own curiosity.

After some time spent wandering, I found myself standing transfixed by the image of a woman delivering one hell of an O face. Her back was to the camera, as she lay spread invitingly across the chaise. Her head dangled over the arching back, hair nearly brushing the floor. Thickly muscled arms banded like vises on her thighs, holding them wide. Only a whisper of dark curly hair in blurred motion hinted at what was going on through the picturesque valley between her breasts.

Overall, the black-and-white was tastefully done, but what cranked this photo up from sensual to breathlessly erotic was the look on the woman's face. The wild-eyed look of shock warred with the lustfully glazed expression hovering around the edges of her eyes, mouth artfully shaped into the telltale expression of screaming orgasm. She looked as though she had been startled into her climax, wholly unprepared for the audience that had come to capture the moment. I was having one hell of a time speculating whether the orgasm amplified the shock or the shock amplified the strength of the orgasm, and it was making me incredibly hot just thinking through those scenarios.

It was then that I began to feel as though I were under just as much focus as the image on the wall. I had half thought for a moment that it was my intended date for the evening until curiosity got the better of me, and I snuck a peek in my peripheral vision. I was utterly lost then, bowled over by the sex and intensity radiating from the man so obviously not the one I had intended to meet. Instead, I found my curiosity had taken another turn, and I was suddenly compelled to get inside the mind of this man. I needed to know what that look in his eyes meant, the depth of what he thought he knew about me reflected in those dark eyes.

An hour had gone by before Jackson actually approached me, but I constantly felt the charge of his presence around me. We were like magnets in the space. I was the point to his counterpoint; the charge between us persisted no matter our proximity as I moved throughout the gallery. I felt hunted, constantly under his gaze, anticipating his approach, needing it in a way. When he finally obliged my silent request, I felt the physical relief of the break in anticipation. I had returned to the woman in shock, and had mentally begun running numbers in my head as I contemplated purchasing the piece. I took my inability to leave the image for very long as a sign that I should take it home. I was so transfixed that I didn't sense him approaching until it was too late. He was suddenly so close that I felt the warmth of his body at my back, and I found myself holding my breath waiting for him to speak. He didn't disappoint. And he didn't pretend as though he didn't already know that we had been at this dance for a while. He skipped the pleasantries, joined my study, and got right to the point.

"Tell me what's so compelling about this one." His tone suggested that he fully expected an answer, as though we had been speaking for hours. It mildly chafed, even though I found my interest wouldn't allow me to deny him.

"I can't figure out which triggered which, the shock or the orgasm," I admitted, still refusing to look away for other reasons, the heat at my cheeks and throat a dead giveaway.

"Talk me through your reasoning," he said.

"Well," I hesitated. "She's clearly enjoying herself before this moment. But the look of shock in her eyes seems completely unprepared, as if the startling is what took her over the edge. Alternately, she could have been unprepared for how strong the orgasm was, hence the shocked expression. It could go either way."

"And if it were you." It was a question without being a question, no inflection but leading me nonetheless.

I didn't have to consider that long.

"I imagine the former scenario would be more accurate than the latter."

"Because you're turned on by the idea of being caught mid-coitus." Again, not an actual question.

"Because I have enough awareness of my body to know an orgasm like that is going to roll me over before it hits me."

"I see," he said, the hint of challenge evident in his tone. "That's . . . curious."

I could not say precisely when he moved. But in one instant he was standing a distance away, the next the warmth of his breath coated the back of my neck, sending hot chills down my spine. The warmth of his hand enveloped mine, depositing a crisp note I soon identified as a business card. The action placed much of his body in close proximity with mine and left me wanting so much more.

"I'd like to find out for myself," he said and sent a fresh round of chills through my body. "Call me when you're ready."

I didn't make him wait long. And he totally blew my mind.

My transformation with Jackson started slowly, beginning with subtle comments he'd make about how sexy I was, how much he wanted me—whenever and wherever. It wasn't until later that I realized how literal that declaration was. The transition was so seamless I barely registered that the dynamic had shifted. The little sexy bits of nothing he would buy for me subtly nudged me to find comfort in the exotic world in which he thrived.

Things slowly escalated from there, my insatiable hunger for him propelling me onward as his adventurous nature captured my curiosity. I remember the day he took me to the ballet and tasked me to keep quiet as he fingered me to orgasm in the crowded theater. Before it was all said and done, I had been convinced that the man playing the role of the doting husband at my other side knew exactly what Jackson had been doing to me underneath the cover of his jacket. Even though his expression hadn't given him away, the thick bulge in his pants definitely had.

Soon after, he asked me to meet him at this little dim sum place near his home. He told me it was his favorite because of the soup dumplings they served. I suspected that it was due to the fact that this exclusive place was partitioned in the old traditional style, for private party reservations only. I had been tasked with showcasing my oral skills in between course deliveries. It seemed as though he timed it perfectly, fucking my throat with abandon one moment and then righting me the next.

This session was almost therapeutic as I began to anticipate the rhythm he had set. It was precisely this sense of security that left me caught off guard when I heard the flustered gasp of our waiter returning as Jackson's thick shaft glided down my throat, making no move to slow its pace. Surfacing from the haze, I peeked through my thick lashes up at the young man as Jackson fucked my face. I had been completely unprepared to see the fierce look of lust on his face, the pent-up energy, his implicit eagerness had we asked him to join in. That look alone was enough to undo me, and in that moment I came harder than I ever had before.

I admit that I had quite a hard time reconciling the way I felt about these tasks. Even though I enjoyed the outcome of the things that Jackson asked of me, I often felt out of place doing them. That is, until one fateful encounter. A few months after our meeting he took me out on a romantic date. An hour into our meal, I was relaxed and comfortable and much too horny, to be perfectly honest. He had teased me mercilessly with his fingers at home and had not allowed me to come. Then, out of nowhere, his hands were lifting my ass and pulling off my panties under the table right in the middle of the restaurant. His fingers teased and worked me over so well. I, of course, was meant to play coy, not to betray myself to those nearby. For the first time, I was eager to play his game from the start.

That night, Jackson made me come between courses. By the end of the meal, I was melting, begging him to fuck me. He paid for our meal, then dragged me through the rear entry doors. Rather than directing us to the parking lot and driving back to his place, he took us on a detour. He guided me in the other direction to the alcove where the lush courtyard terminated at the brick alleyway. Had it been warmer, this area would likely have been bustling with traffic and the lanterns lit. But in the cool fall air it was perfect for what he had in mind. He pressed my back against the chilly stone. In one smooth motion he had my legs around his waist and was pressing his thick, hard shaft inside me. The heat of his cock wrung a groan from deep inside me, and I felt his hand suddenly over my mouth, stifling the sound.

"Shh," he whispered into my hair, barely enough for me to comprehend over his deep but unhurried thrusts inside my freshly orgasmed pussy. The sensitivity there made me want to climb the walls; it was almost soul shattering. I maintained a delicate balance, hovering between enjoying Jackson's pleasure and the terror of possibly giving myself away by getting too caught up in my own. When his thrusts gained tempo without losing an inch of depth, I clung to him fiercely, drowning my sound in his shirt. My adrenaline was pumping, scorching an inferno through my blood. I had no idea how much time had gone by.

Out of the corner of my eye, I noticed a younger man hugging the wall close to the adjacent corner, trying to be invisible. Though it should have been almost impossible in the darkness of the alcove, there was no mistaking the telltale motion of his hand near his crotch and the way his chest quietly heaved as he pushed himself toward orgasm.

The knowledge that he was getting off to our show was the nudge I needed to bowl me over the edge again. Sensing how powerful my orgasm would potentially be, I warned Jackson the only way I could, with a gasp of his name as he stuffed my dripping wet cunt. He seemed to sense my impending explosion and crushed his lips to mine, muffling the scream as the first wash of intense pleasure blew through me. Jackson didn't hold back then, the strokes he delivered forcing my orgasm on and on, robbing me of breath. I could feel myself beginning to float and belatedly felt the warmth of Jackson's seed pumping deep inside me, eliciting a smaller wave of ecstasy as he stayed buried in me until the twitching stopped.

I might have been mildly delirious and absolutely come-drunk after that encounter, but it was such a revelation for me. I needed to be watched, craved knowing that I inspired lust in others. I needed to feel that again. And again. Being watched while experiencing the kind of intense sexual pleasure it evoked was the headiest of drugs. However, after that night, something clicked for me. Soon the tasks Jackson set before me became less and less daunting. I found that rather than overwhelming me with my fears, he was pushing me to my limits. I was eagerly participating, wanting the same.

So yeah. I lied. I can definitely see why I am here again. I stare at my own body swaying softly to the music, my dark fall coat cinched tightly around my waist. I know that as I revolve in this faceted octagonal space, my Jackson is on the other side of one of these mirrors, only I don't know which one. Eight panels of myself wink back at me as I allow my body to feel the music, deepening its gyration. I want to dance for him, to put on a show for him.

Therefore, I must put on a show for them all. I know that on the other side of these panels of two-way glass are strangers—men, women, couples, who knows. And they are all watching me. They want to see the show as much as I want to perform.

I can't help but let my hands travel up my body, caress my exposed skin. It is getting warm in this space, and I need to be free. I tug on the tie at my waist, drawing out the moment before I reveal myself. I take a gamble, slowly spin two panels clockwise, and allow the coat to slip from my shoulders. Sliding two more, I allow gravity to take the coat to my hips as I arch my back prettily and undulate my thick hips to the beat. I begin to feel a thin sheen of sweat coating and cooling my skin, the chill twisting my hard nipples even tighter. Through the gauze of the sheer black teddy, it's impossible not to notice. I shift slowly once more, allowing my jacket to slide down my body and drop to the floor, lifting my hand to cup my ample breasts, rolling my nipples between my fingers to calm them a little. I brush the dense curls from my face, turning, allowing my hands to explore my increasingly sensitive flesh. My fingers tentatively hover near but never actually touch my pussy.

I continue my slow rotation, maintaining eye contact with myself, hoping he is staring back at me on the other side. I hope that he is enjoying this as much as I am. I slowly make my way up to the chair seated on the platform that I have strategically danced around all this time in my six-inch heels. Once I step onto the base, it begins its revolution at the speed of thick molasses. I lean over the chair, poking my ass out in the air to tease. I stifle a moan when my pelvis bumps against the back of the chair on the way up. The music dims noticeably, the patrons clearly interested in hearing me more than the driving drum solo accompanying me on my dance. I begin to realize then that I can hear them as clearly as I am sure they can hear me.

I swing myself over and then down onto the cool leather,

grateful for the support of my suddenly weak knees, wondering slyly if anyone happened to notice them shaking through my controlled attempt at grace. I'm completely unprepared for the lusty sounds of decadence beating out their own cadence alongside mine. They make me hotter than I ever would have expected. They swirl around me all at once, their sources impossible to distinguish as the sounds echo around my head. Breathing takes effort, the thickness of lust clouding my airways. I smell the sex in the air, oblivious to the fact that it's only my own, not so oblivious to the fact that the only thing saving this expensive leather from a puddle of my wetness is my soaked teddy. It, like my sanity, barely hangs by a thread. I don't know what possesses me, but I picture Jackson's head between my soft thighs, sucking me through the thin, glazed fabric. My breath catches. I feel my heartbeat in my ears and stare a moment at myself in the polished ceiling.

It's impossible not to touch myself.

It's impossible not to *watch* myself touch myself.

My hands are ahead of my thoughts, dragging themselves up my sweat-dampened arms and grasping my shoulders, the warm embrace I need to calm myself a little. I notice then that my hands no longer shake from my nerves, but in anticipation. I no longer question whether what I'm doing is what I want. I need this connection like I need my next breath.

It's a heady thing, knowing that I'm the sole focus of so many people's desires, even if only as background entertainment. It feels as though Jackson and I are again of one accord. Through glazed eyes, I picture him looming over me, the heat in his gaze enough for me to combust on the spot. I don't need to see his true face to know what he would tell me to do next. I smile up at us both. His phantom lips move but nothing can be heard over the raucous sounds of play around me. I feel his command radiate through my trembling frame.

*Show me those beautiful breasts, love,* he would say.

*I'd love to,* I'd purr back.

I drag my hands down my body, exposing myself, enjoying the feel of the tingling warmth dragging a lazy trail down my skin. Only when I feel the anticipation peak do I reach for the straps of my bra and complete the same circuit with them in tow, allowing my breasts to spill free, the cool air almost too much on my sensitive skin. A rush of sensation washes up my body, and I find it's become difficult to control my breathing again. I cup the tender flesh of my breasts, squeeze the skin in a futile effort to soothe. It's much too late for that. My therapeutic touch grows hungry quickly, my want overwhelming my senses, and for a moment everything goes blank. All that I can feel is my desire. I am nothing but my desire. I am burning from the inside out, every touch and caress all at once too much and not nearly enough. I open my eyes and look out at myself, unsure of how to feel about the agonized expression on my face.

I am unrecognizable even to my own eyes, the fire inside me peeking through, showing her true self for the first time. We know even in this state what our Jackson wants from us. We do not mind. We want it as much, if not more, than he does.

I lift my hips slowly off of the seat. I do not move slowly because I want to put on a show. I move slowly because I cannot bear the friction that speed would bring with it. With my ass off the soft leather of the chair, my shoulders brace against the chair back so I don't fall. Gingerly, I pull the fabric from my soaked body, let the scrap of ruined material slide over my knees and down my legs. I stay that way a moment, my elbows now braced on the arms, bare pussy glistening, thighs parting ever farther as I slowly spin around on the dais.

Jackson loves my pussy. He calls it beautiful all the time. I wonder briefly if he is behind one of the panels getting an eyeful right now. I picture him, eyes aflame, with his cock gripped tightly in hand. Like me, he's waiting, allowing his need to build. He, like me, knows how much better it will be for the waiting. However, there comes a time in everyone's life where the waiting becomes too much. I can't take it anymore.

I need.

Something.

I finally draw my attention over my shoulder, to the short table accompanying me along my spin. I can no longer ignore its presence while I feel this way. On the table sits exactly what I need. Exactly what I asked for. My favorite toy. Glistening in the twinkling lights, it is like a beacon guaranteed to guide me out of the stormy haze of lust that I've created for myself. I cup my hands to my sex, squeeze her to incite calm, but the sudden pressure only jolts a flurry of sensation through my body. I find my hips are ignoring me, pressing my sensitive bits into my hand, gently circling. It's clear that my body could give less than a shit about control. And frankly, I can no longer argue. I reach for the silver wand, thick and knobby on either end of its gentle curve. I put it to my lips and let the heat of desire rush through me, enticing my tongue out of its warm depths, lightly tracing the ridge of the larger end.

I wish I could see my husband's face watching me. I wonder if he's jerking off to me at this very moment, losing himself in my dance. He'd love to be here with me, moving my hands out of the way and thrusting deep into me. The thought makes me smile as the slippery metal pops from my mouth and I draw a wet path back down to my pussy. I can no longer stand the wait. More forcefully than I intended, I fill myself with the slickened toy. It's thick, slightly warm from my mouth, and fits exactly right. My head falls back against the chair as I gyrate my hips up farther onto the toy, the delicious tingles racing up my spine. I rock into it and let it work for me, massaging my G-spot and taking me home. Before long I am lost in the sensation, feeling the phantom caress of Jackson's curved shaft plundering my depths, awakening a monster of an orgasm from slumber.

On my periphery, I can hear the raucous symphony of sounds, my keening cries blanketing them all. My hips move faster, and I can feel my orgasm just out of reach, antagonizing me with its nearness. Out of instinct rather than want, I circle my clit and deliver a firm slap over the sensitive skin. That proves to be the perfect catalyst. My orgasm rips me apart from the inside, my body splintering into a million little pieces. I can't stop rocking into the toy as each stroke prolongs the bliss. Copious fluids are wrung from my body and shower the poor leather beneath me. Tears spring from my eyes involuntarily at the magnitude of the release issuing from me. Coming down, body twitching, I finally let go of the toy. The weight alone causes it to slip from my pussy and clatter to the floor. I lie here for quite a while, continue my slow rotation as I float outside of myself in the tingles of electricity.

The lights come down in my room then, and the sight of the myriad scenes of fornication around me nearly undoes me again. Groups of ones, twos, threes, and even one group of four are losing themselves in each other all around me. My dais slows to a halt as I face my love, his eyes blazing and a satisfied smirk on his lips. His self-control is astonishing. He stands there showing no signs of attempting to relieve the huge erection straining behind his dark blue jeans. He saved it just for me, and I will savor every second of it once I get out of this room. He doesn't need to say anything. I rise and gather my things, the call of that man too intense to ignore. He's just outside the door of the Mirror Palace when I exit, pulling me in for a smoldering kiss. His fingers are like heat-seeking missiles underneath my coat, going straight to play in the fresh juices at my hungry opening.

"Damn, woman," he groans into my sweat-dampened hair, plunging two fingers into my pussy. "I should make you a regular headliner here."

I don't say anything, just pull his head back down to mine and ravage his mouth. He doesn't need any confirmation. We both know I will be back.

# VINTAGE TREASURES

Angora Shade

Corrine sighed as she flipped the switch for the cellar, flooding the rickety stairway with muted fluorescent light. She wasn't looking forward to today. They'd been warned. The trouble with buying a house at auction was sorting through the junk the former owner had left behind and attempting not to feel ashamed in unloading someone else's memories into the trash.

"Move your ass, Corrine."

David whisked by in his excitement, the fresh scent of his after-shave mixing with the musty smell of old cardboard boxes, stale air, and packed earth flooring. Corrine heard him sputter as he descended the final, creaky step, watching him wrestle an invisible cobweb when she reached the bottom.

Laughter eased her tension. "That's what you get for being in a rush."

David's bright teeth contrasted starkly against the dark tones of his handsome face, his honest enthusiasm filling the room with an energy even Corrine couldn't deny.

"I know what you're thinking, Mr. Carson . . ." She shook her finger at him with her most serious your-wife-knows-best, hand-on-hip attitude. "But there's no guarantee you'll find any ancient baseball cards down in this mess."

David scanned over recessed shelves of spoiled preserves standing behind a waist-high wall of boxes, faded newspapers, and a solo bicycle wheel. "I dunno, honey. There's sure to be buried treasure in here." He reached into a box and coughed as a layer of dust ballooned into the air like heavy smoke. But he smiled again as he held up a thin, square object. "Aha!" He cleared his throat. "Barry Mann! *Who Put the Bomp*, 1961!"

Corrine set down her empty plastic storage tubs on the floor and tackled the area near the cellar's single, tiny window. A sturdy wooden workbench stood underneath, cluttered with rusty tools, bolts, and heaps of random objects in various stages of decay. She shook her head, lifting a worn-out boot by a rotting leather shoe-string, wondering what type of people used to live here. She tossed it behind her into a bin.

"One for garbage, David, and one for donations; just like the attic. I'll take this corner. I just hope we have something to show Father William and Suzanne when they get here at five o'clock. They were so excited to hear we had contributions for the parish."

David was busy sifting through more records, mumbling lyrics and studying his finds. "Damn, I love this song."

Several hours of labor saw many trips up and down the stairs, to the curbside and back, and black-bagged hauls to their pickup, but the cellar was still a clutter-filled shop of chaos. Corrine managed to clear the old workbench and David his wall of boxes—even finding a functional record player—but the space behind the stairs and the far corners of the room had yet to be explored.

David popped the top off a cold beer and leaned against the stairwell, watching Corrine sweep her hair from her brow and scoot a stained cardboard box closer to the light. He absentmindedly tossed a record onto the machine while he stared at his wife, bent at the waist, the material of her worn summer shorts buckling at the back and unknowingly sending the string of her thong into view. "That is one mighty fine rear, Mrs. Carson."

Corrine arched an eyebrow as she glanced over her shoulder, grinning while she deliberately swayed her ample buttocks side to side. "What is that? Folk music?" She screwed up her face a bit and spoke in a mock-sexy voice. "That's *so* hot."

"Don't tempt me, woman. . . ."

Corrine laughed and went back to sorting while David headed toward the boxes under the stairs. When he shifted a few out toward his wife, he spotted something surprising.

His piercing whistle made Corrine look up, her curiosity piquing with the look of wonder plastered on her husband's face. "What'd you find?"

"Didn't the auctioneer say an elderly couple used to live here?"

Corrine threw a few pieces of retro sports equipment into her designated donation bin and nodded. "Yeah. They both moved to a retirement home."

David rubbed his hands together in excitement. "We've got something good here, baby! I can feel it. This is the only thing down here that looks important." He pulled off a protective plastic covering and sent a fresh plume of dust into the air. "It's an old steamer trunk." He ran his hands along the seam and threw two latches open, but his face fell when the lid remained firmly shut, a shiny keyhole staring him down. "Shit. It's locked. Look around for the key."

Corrine grabbed a rusty hammer from the workbench and tossed it on top of a box near David's feet. "Like I always tell you, Mr. Carson: 'When life closes a door . . .'"

David chuckled and whacked at the latch, hearing the satisfying ping of old metal shattering and finishing his wife's modified words of wisdom. "'Break yourself a window.'"

David stood a moment staring at the contents, the stagnant silence sending Corrine's heart racing. "What's in there?"

A boyish grin stretched wide over David's face, touching his eyes in a way that spelled mischief with a capital M. "Old folks maybe . . ." He held up a pristine purple box the size of a toaster. "But they must've had one hell of a sex life."

Corrine sputtered over debris in her way and snatched the item from his grasp. "No way." She turned it over in her hands, reading: "*The innovative Steel Rectal Plug is designed for the beginner anal enthusiast. Easy insertion and cleanup.*"

"Wait, there's more."

Corrine's shock intensified.

David could barely contain his amusement as he read the inscription of an odd object reminiscent of a hairdryer with a two-foot electrical cord, still encased in its original packaging. "*Personal Wand Massager—for all your intimate needs.*"

Corrine yanked the heavy trunk out from its hidden corner for more light. Everything inside looked store-shelf fresh, the pastel coloring and dated retro imagery the only indicator of true age. She rested her arm above her against the stairs while she gazed over the shocking contents. A set of metal handcuffs, outdated boxes of condoms, lacy mismatched lingerie, and several items Corrine had never seen before sat atop a partially crushed red feather boa.

"You have got to be kidding me," she whispered.

"Saving for a rainy day, I bet," David smirked.

"1969 . . . 1971 . . . 1973 . . . David, these are all vintage."

Corrine felt the cool snap of metal encase her wrist.

"No-o way, David. You know I don't do kinky."

David leaned in close and pulled his wife's hand toward his face by the cuff he held tight in his grip. His lips met her knuckles while his features grew deep with desire. "You got something better to do, woman?"

The energy around David's body was electric. They'd been so busy with the move: packing, unpacking, cleaning, decorating, and remodeling; it left them too exhausted for more than a five-minute quickie at the end of the day, if at all. But she'd swear to high heaven she hadn't seen David this lustful since before they were married. His facial muscles were set, his mouth a sly, devilish smile, the bulge in his shorts caught in the restrictive hold of his jeans. She imagined how that must ache. But she loved his hungry stare. Tingles broke out over her bare arms, and a needy pull in her pelvis betrayed her mission to stay on task. She had to admit she was curious. After all, nothing she saw in the trunk looked truly dangerous.

Perhaps Mr. and Mrs. Former-House-Owners had perfected marital bliss.

David leaned over the trunk between them and brushed his lips lightly against Corrine's mouth. She could smell the sweet scent of beer on his breath, taste the warmth of his pursing flesh. She heard a scrape and felt movement, giggles breaking from her mouth as feathers wrapped about her shoulders, tickling her neck and jaw.

"What're you doing, Mr. Carson?"

"Damn, woman, I love when you call me *Mr. Carson.*" He twirled her in a circle as a saxophone sang crisp tones from the record player, then he smacked her round bottom until she giggled again. Their eyes met when she spun back to face him, a long moment hanging in the air like the modern dangling bracelet from her wrist. Another smile broke over David's face, all his pristine teeth reflecting the thoughts in his head as he grabbed another item from the box. "You should try this on, honey," he said.

She looked at the barely there, lacy pink bra he dangled from a finger. It looked clean, the original tag still attached by its short, cotton thread. But she paused a moment, aware of Father William and Suzanne's visit, wondering what they'd think if they knew about the ridiculous box of depravity she and David had found. She thought back on how she'd never ventured past a tiny egg vibrator that had been a gift at her bachelorette party years earlier and how devastated she'd been when the tiny motor finally gave out. Too much of a prude, she'd skipped out on heading to an adult store to replace it for fear she'd be recognized. But sex with David had always been good. She didn't need all the silly extras. . . .

Corrine sighed. Good, maybe, but everything they did was slowly becoming as rote as multiplication tables ten years into their marriage.

She decided she spent too much time thinking and pushed past rules of propriety and her own ideas of traditional until her jaw was set and she reached the tipping point: *Why not?*

Throwing her T-shirt over her head in a burst of energy, she slipped out of her sports bra and turned her back to her husband, eying him like a skilled tease. He shimmied in place with his focus locked, appearing ready to pounce.

"Does it fit?"

Corrine spun around with her hands cupping her chest, hiding the sexy garb. "Come find out . . ."

David took a step forward, and Corrine took a step back, forcing him to follow. She darted left when he reached for her arm, and then right to sidestep obstacles, until her game had them both chasing in circles around the cellar. He finally caught her with her back against the old workbench, pinning her hips with his body, mildly out of breath.

He kissed her neck, and still she held her hands across her front. He kneaded the flesh of her naked biceps down to her elbows while he nipped at her chin and scissored his legs between hers. She finally melted when their lips met and the bulge in his pants pushed up against her thigh. Seeking to bring him closer and explore the contours of his muscular back, her arms snaked away from her front and found the hidden ripples of youthful, abdominal perfection beneath his shirt.

David spun her around and held her back to his chest while dragging his hands from her shoulders to her breasts. He nuzzled into her naturally thick hair, loving the sweet scent of her labor mixed with her everyday lotion, until he found the surprise pink treasure fitting like a snug glove, encasing her with soft lace that gave under his fingertips.

David bent his head to kiss the delicate skin of Corrine's ear. She pushed back into him, following the edges of his waist until her hands fell low upon the swell in his shorts. The saxophone stopped playing, replaced with their deep exhales and sighs.

And a click.

Corrine hadn't felt David direct her arm forward atop the workbench or seen the iron ring attached to the edge until she'd opened her eyes to the strange sound.

"David?"

The warmth of his body had already moved away. She pivoted to see him grab a length of old clothesline peeking out from a box, unwinding several feet and dragging it slowly toward her across the floor.

She laughed. "You're not serious . . ."

David eyed her like a piece of meat, licking his lips. "New house, new toys, new adventures."

She laughed and rolled her eyes.

But David was the delicious devil. "Tell me you want to play with me, Corrine."

Tension began building in her core as she pulled against her wrist at the table and watched David step closer with his make-shift rope. She wondered what he might do. She was a novice to the *more,* her thoughts flickering only to what she'd seen in a few

X-rated movies. A rush of heat enveloped her face and between her thighs as the possibilities ignited her mind. Maybe this was the opportunity to explore past a simple egg toy. Maybe this was how *rote* became the new *adventure* David suggested. Besides, the watch on her wrist read just after three. Father William wasn't due until five.

Corrine followed the edge of her plump mouth with the tip of her tongue, gauging David's lusty, rigid stance. All he needed was a go. "Only if you agree to trade places next time . . . *Mr. Carson.*"

David inhaled deeply, stretched the line taut between his hands, and dropped his voice. "With boxes full of goodies, we could be down here *for days.*"

Corrine laughed, pivoted toward the wall, and allowed her husband to bind her other wrist to the same metal ring and remove her shorts. She stepped out of them while he proceeded to gently spread her legs and wrap her ankles to the right and left legs of the workbench. Enough slack in the material allowed her to pivot at the hips and peer back over her shoulder, but not move farther than a few inches from where her waist bumped over the rough table's edge.

David slid back to the record player and tossed on another tune. "Love Me Tender" played quietly while he disappeared. She heard his footfalls thump against the old stairs and the faint creak of floorboards over her head in the kitchen. A moment later his presence filled the cool cellar again, and the unmistakable crackle of plastic crinkling and slide of cardboard moving alerted her something had been opened. She didn't know what he'd taken from the box, and her whole body broke into gooseflesh despite the comfortable temperature below ground in high summer.

She jumped when she felt David wrap his large hands around her toned waist. His bulge pressed into her thigh again, his warm torso covering her bare back. She sighed when his kisses fell onto her shoulder and his fingers slid down her sides. A moment later the fabric of her thong was stretched to the side and the warm pressure of David's steady digit traced the line her panties usually followed. Corrine felt her rectal muscles pucker when he found her sweet hole.

He whispered into her ear. "I've got this neat beginner's toy in my hand . . ."

She tensed when the cool slip of metal slid against her.

"And a jar of oil . . ."

A cap was unscrewed softly and the aroma of coconut wafted about them. The scent reminded her of baked goods, sugar in her mouth, and vivid visuals of slippery slickness when the common kitchen item was exposed to the slightest bit of heat. She took a deep breath and wondered how she'd feel, slick, plugged, and full. David's long, thick girth was always exciting when he drove deep into her wanting cunt. Fresh tingles of desire awoke the goose bumps that had fallen away, anticipation causing all the hairs on her neck to stand as erect as her husband's primal urge.

David rubbed her left buttcheek with his left hand while he dotted slow kisses down her spine. "I want my favorite hole as tight as this one."

Corrine swooned hearing his husky tone, her muscles relaxing. David probed with the same light pressure his tender mouth made as he continued to descend. There was little resistance. It was only when his tongue drew circles over the upper half of her right asscheek and her muscles flexed of their own accord that she felt the narrow space of her exit trapped with a pleasant fullness.

David stood and pressed himself against Corrine's back again, reaching around to cup her left breast and inch his way into the lacy pink garment. He pinched her perky, hungry nipple while his right arm brushed over her shoulder and toward an electric outlet. The personal massager looked nothing like the modern things

Corrine had seen, but the purpose was clear; she just hoped it worked. She hoped it would drive them both wild.

Corrine pulled at her arms only to remember they were harnessed to the table. She desperately wished to touch David, to give him the same affection she was receiving. It was so different being restrained, giving him all the power. He was a creative lover. Her blood burned wondering what would come next.

The sound of his fly unzipping and the light fall of his shorts against the floor told her what she couldn't see. His fleshy member rubbed against her backside, and warmth in her middle filled her with unbridled anticipation. But she didn't know how ready she was until she craned her head over her shoulder to meet David's lips while his cock slid against her vulva.

David tilted his hips and pushed Corrine's waist tight against the workbench while his marble cock probed between her spread legs. Her buttocks tilted up to meet him as he entered, the metal toy in her rear giving the usually comfortable fit a more compact feeling. Every inch of her greeted his dick like a desperate hug, and soon his thrusts had him balls-deep in formfitting pleasure.

Corrine moaned and met him with each beat of Elvis Presley's love song. She relished how her man kneaded the flesh of her ass and the needful way he slid his hand up her neck and into the thick of her untamed hair. Her internal skin felt more sensation than ever with the toy and David's cock working in unison. She barely noticed the hard tabletop or her restraints.

Until she heard the buzz.

The vintage toy wiggled to life with its loud vibrations. She saw David bring it down out of sight and felt the soft plastic head jiggle into the skin of her torso.

David held her tight to him while he dove in deep again. He grunted and pulled out, drawing his tool down in front of Corrine's waist and between her legs. She tensed, but his fingers massaged her abdomen while he directed his tool lower, his lips suckling the arch of her neck.

The moment she relaxed, her body responded.

"David," Corrine breathed, "that's amazing." So much better than the little egg toy.

Vibrations teased her clit while David's cock slid back into her tight folds. The internal ball of combustion she always felt close to orgasm was growing, compacting, jabbing at her with determination of its own. Elvis sang something sweet but Corrine only heard David's lustful moans mixing with the peaking, unintelligible cries sputtering from her lips.

The sweat of David's body crept into his shirt and stuck to her back while her limbs flexed against her resistance. His balls thwacked her ass; his hand encompassed her waist, his cock straining for release. Corrine began to tremble, but he held the vibrating massager to her clit until she screamed, his cue for her to unleash.

Corrine came hard, her legs wiggling, her toes clamped together fast inside the trainers still on her feet. She didn't feel the uncomfortable pull of the handcuff at her wrist or the way the clothesline stretched and squeaked. There was only the constant, agonizingly delicious pulsing of her orgasm hitting her on repeat. Her knees buckled slightly as her body went limp, but David held her aloft, his member ramming home hard and fast, finishing with his own verbal roar.

He laid Corrine gently against the table, one hand still at her belly, the other lifting his wand to the table and switching it off.

"Mr. Carson . . ."

David looked down at his wife and bent her head up to kiss her lips. Sweat beaded at her forehead and the smell of their sex was stronger than the odor of forgotten treasures and cellar.

"That happened so fast . . ."

"Don't worry, babe. There's a whole house left to christen." He untied her rope-bound wrist and legs and twirled her to the side to feel the full embrace of her body, minus her lone, handcuffed wrist.

Corrine bent her knee around David's calf and dragged her free hand down the length of his back. "I think I like toys, Mr. Carson."

David smiled. "*Vintage* toys."

"Do I just pop this out?" She put her hand behind her to touch the metal object still in her rear.

"Yeah." David grabbed the handle and gently rotated the toy out from Corrine's backside. "I hear there are ones that vibrate. . . ."

Corrine chuckled, but her middle was growing hot again, the flush of desire returning to her face. She glanced at her watch. It was only a little after four. They had almost a whole hour to play. David had agreed to go next. . . .

Corrine watched her husband smirk. A moment later he was rummaging through the contents of the trunk again, digging elbow-deep along the bottom. He spoke to the floor. "If there's not one in here, we could always add to the collection."

"Only if we drive out past the next dozen counties, David. What if we saw someone we know?"

He shrugged, his flaccid member perking up slightly as he raised a neon-purple strap-on into the air.

No sound came out of Corrine as she mouthed, *Oh my god.*

Both their heads whipped in unison as the dong of the doorbell rang somewhere overhead.

"Shit! Get dressed!"

"No-no-no." Corrine shook her head, her horror freezing her in place. "They're way too early!"

But David was already sliding his shorts back up and tucking his cock in. A moment later he'd bounded to the steps, his footfalls smacking overhead, his words muffled but his tone a genuine greeting to the pious, kindhearted preacher.

Corrine snapped to attention, realizing she should be there too, but she couldn't reach her shorts at her feet. She was held fast by the wrist to the metal ring on the workbench. She felt her face blanch as she raised her voice. "Hey, honey? Where's the key?"

# SHEER PLEASURE

A. Z. Louise

"Oh my god. Oh my *god.*"

"What is it?" asked Aidan.

"*Oh my god.*"

"Billie, what?"

"I'm *dying,*" I said. "These *looks.*"

"Show me." He stretched his leg from his chair to the couch, nudging my knee with his foot. It was cold, since it was the weird in-between time where you didn't want to turn on the heat, but the warmth of summer was beginning to fail.

"Get your hoof off me, I'm still scrolling."

"At least tell me what you're losing your shit over."

"Plus-size fashion show pics. They look like beautiful, fat, slutty witches, and I want to be them. Or smooch them. Or both? I'm unclear." There was so much sheer fabric, so many gorgeous exposed bralettes, so much skin. I let out a wistful sigh as I reached the bottom of the page and handed my phone over to Aidan.

His thick brows drew down just a little as he scrolled—they always did that when he was focused on something—and a small smile quirked the corner of his mouth, making his dark-skinned cheek dimple.

"These are great looks, Billie. It's almost your birthday, maybe you should buy something like this for when I take you out. I might want to smooch you."

"I couldn't wear something like that."

"Too feminine for my enby princex?" Aidan asked. I toyed with one of my red yarn braids, not wanting to talk about it. I'd resigned myself to wearing feminine things ages ago; you can't have J-cups and wear masculine clothes without a binder, and those made me feel like I was suffocating. "Do they not make them in your size?" Aidan persisted, in his sweet, clueless, straight-size way. He was a pretty thick guy, but he wasn't fat at all. He was Instagram thick. "These models don't look that much smaller than you."

"I mean, some of them do. But I'm just not confident enough to wear any of it."

"Billie, you love your body."

"I do. Other people don't," I said.

"You can just wear them in the apartment," Aidan suggested.

"If you think I'm wearing anything more than pajamas in this apartment, you got another thing coming." I'd just taken my flannel pajama pants out of the closet for the cool weather, and the only thing I'd rather wear to bed was nothing.

"Hmm." Aidan went silent, scrolling through the pics long enough that I picked up my tablet, knowing I wasn't getting my phone back any time soon. "Maybe we should add it to our sexy repertoire."

"What?"

"Well, if you're not confident, that means you're afraid to embarrass yourself, right?" asked Aidan.

"Yeah, I guess so."

"So you love humiliation and degradation stuff when we do it."

"That's completely different, Aidan. It's not in public," I said. "It feels safe."

"You don't think I'd keep you safe out in public?" Aidan asked.

"What are you going to do, beat someone up for looking at me funny?"

"No, but I'll roast them within an inch of their lives," said Aidan. I couldn't help laughing.

"This is your worst idea, and I love you."

"All I'm saying is that if we make it sexy, it won't be scary. It'll just make you look like the slutty piece of garbage we both know you are inside."

"You're so charming."

I joked, but just hearing Aidan casually throw out an insult made my heart skip a beat, because he usually only did it in bed. It was a Pavlovian response that made my brain conjure up what he would say if I wore any of the mesh or lace pieces I'd loved. If it was half as filthy as anything I could think up, it was possible I could die. I didn't need any more than that to shop, and found myself scrolling through my favorite stores in hopes of finding something. Soon I had so many tabs open that I couldn't even see the titles any more.

"Why are you pouting?" Aidan asked.

"I'm not pouting, I'm frowning," I said. "There are so many good things, I can't choose. Plus I'm nervous, and thinking about wearing any of it kind of gives me anxiety, but at the same time I super want to do it, and this is all way too much."

"You don't have to; I just think that it would be fun and give you the chance to do something a little outside your comfort zone. You know that's my job."

"Stretch zone daddy."

"That's me," Aidan said, laughing. "I can choose and pay for it. Then it'll be me humiliating you, not your own bad fashion choices."

I looked down at my tabs, biting my lip. That was the point of it all, really. To put things in his hands, to let him spit back everything bad I'd ever thought about myself so that it didn't hurt so much anymore. If he dressed me in something he thought worthy of ridicule, the anticipation of what he might say could be enough to get me out of my own head about it. I passed him my tablet, letting out a long, calming sigh.

Waiting for the package was almost like waiting for a report card. There was no way to be completely sure what was inside, but it could get me in trouble. I mostly worried that I'd put the clothes on, see that I looked like a horrible, hideous lump, and not even want to show them to Aidan. It wasn't derision I feared from him, it was pity; if he felt sorry for me, it would mean I really looked awful, too bad to even mock.

The clothes were waiting on the welcome mat in the hall on Friday night when I got back from the office. The apartment was dark; Aidan must have had errands to run before he came home. I tore the plastic sack open, rushing into the bedroom to try everything on before he got back. That way if I hated it too much, I could just tell him to return them without having him try to sympathize.

There were three pieces in the bag: a black pair of leggings with mesh panels, an oversized top cut from the same sheer fabric, and a black strappy bralette that I'd definitely wear if the rest of the outfit didn't work. I stripped out of my cardigan, shirt, and pencil skirt to try everything on, the tiled bathroom floor cold on the bottoms of my feet when I went to check my reflection.

My side rolls were way more out there than they ever had been before, but at least Aidan had clearly been thinking about comfort. I focused on the softness of the fabrics, because the rolls were a little too much. I could imagine people eyeing the folds of my flesh the way they glared at my fat thighs on the bus, disgusted that they had to look at me or even share space with me.

"Hey, Billie?" Aidan's voice came from the front room. The thud of his shoes coming off followed, and I felt a moment of panic.

"Hey, babe," I called back.

"I saw the tracking, get your ass out here."

I caught a glimpse of my own smile in the mirror as I turned away from my reflection. He knew me too damn well. Aidan's face lit up when he looked at me, and something fluttered inside my stomach.

"Lord," he said, making me laugh.

"It's okay?"

"Billie. William. Trilliam. You could make a garbage bag look good. Let's go get early birthday dinner."

"I don't know if I want to be out that long."

"Dinner soft serve?" Aidan asked.

"You want me, a fat fatty, to go out in half an outfit to eat ice cream for dinner?"

"You love ice cream."

Something brave and foolish came over me. I *did* love ice cream, and I'd have eaten it after dinner, in my normal clothes, without even thinking about it. The second it became irresponsible, I got scared, and that made no sense. Strangers had no idea whether I'd had dinner or not, and I was shaped the same no matter what I was wearing. Plus I was starving.

"Okay. Let's go."

The soft serve place was only a few minutes away, standing alone in the middle of a parking lot as night fell around it. There were a few people sitting on benches or leaning against the building as they ate. The air was balmier than it had been the night before, but a cool breeze snuck up on us as we waited for our sundaes. I was afraid that if I shivered, someone might notice I hadn't thought about a hoodie. Then they'd notice how I was dressed and start staring, judging, hating.

The weathered picnic table we picked was on the still side of the building, and that made me feel marginally better. Aidan wasn't paying attention to me at all, playing with his phone before he started eating. Sudden tears welled up in my eyes before my phone went off. I fumbled for it, taking a shaky breath, and almost laughed. It was a text from Aidan.

*Quit being a pussy and eat your ice cream, slut.*

He grinned at me over his sundae, his eyes promising more. My heart juddered against my ribs, making me breathless, and relief flowed through me. It was working. The shame remained, but it had shifted into something exciting rather than scary. Hunger too had begun to fade into the background of desire, but I ate. Aidan said nothing, and anticipation built as I wondered what he was holding back because we were in public. He picked up his phone again.

*Don't fill up. I'm gonna make you drink my come like the filthy bitch you are.*

I felt that one deep down inside me. I dropped my plastic spoon in my bowl, unable to choke down another bite.

"Finished?" Aidan asked. I nodded. As it melted, the last bite of vanilla soft serve left my mouth bone-dry. "Let's go."

In the car, Aidan's hand pressed against my left thigh as he drove, fingernails making a soft scraping noise as they drew across the mesh panel. Drawing my attention to the exposed skin, making sure the shame didn't drain out of me. My breath snagged in my throat, and I reached for his hand, needing comfort at the thought of how I'd gone out with so little on. Instead of holding my hand, Aidan slid his fingers between my legs.

"I bet you can't wait, can you?" he asked. He had to know that wasn't why I'd reached for him, but he turned the question into a little white lie to make me squirm, to take my mind off things. It made the last couple minutes feel like an hour, and nervous energy burst out of me when I jumped up out of the car.

Aidan was right behind me as I rushed into the safety of the apartment, his hand touching my back, moving to my stomach to pull me toward him once the door was shut. His lips brushed my ear, making me shiver.

"You love flaunting your body, don't you? Making me want you." His cock was hard against the small of my back, his voice hungry.

"Yes," I whispered, surprising myself.

Aidan's lips were cool on the side of my neck, his fingers cold as they slid under my shirt. He pulled up my bralette, making my tits spill out heavy and warm. Aidan kneaded at them hard, fingers searching out my nipples. He teased and tortured until they felt like two scalding coals, until my knees were weak. I moaned, writhing against him until he stopped and slipped a hand down into my underwear. My legs almost gave out as he stroked my pussy, before Aidan finally took his hand away, putting his wet fingers into my mouth.

"You like that?" he murmured. My answer was smothered by his hand, and he laughed, low and husky. A shudder worked its way down my spine. "Since you wanted to go out dressed like a ho, I'm gonna make you ruin these clothes."

He pulled his fingers out of my mouth, letting them trail back down between my legs. When he found my clit, I almost lost my feet, but his left arm looped under mine, keeping me upright as he teased circles around the sensitive little node. I clutched his arm, grinding against his hand as pleasure built inside me.

"Squirt for me, you filthy piece of trash."

Aidan's words put me over the edge, pure, electric sensation filling me until hot liquid spilled down my thighs, soaking my leggings. When he let go of me, I fell to my knees, panting. Aidan stepped back, walking a slow circle around me once, twice, before stopping in front of me.

"Look at the mess you've made," he said. "Disgusting. You think I want anything from you after what you've done?"

"Please," I begged. "You said you'd make me drink your come."

Aidan laughed. He unzipped his pants, pulling his dick out, and grabbed a handful of my yarn braids. I didn't need his hand to guide my mouth to his cock. I kissed its smooth, hard length, wetted it with my tongue, took it in my mouth until it pressed against the back of my throat and almost made me gag. Aidan made no sound, but his hips began to thrust forward, driving deeper. The smell of him—sweat and soap and faded cologne— filled my head, and my soaked leggings had gone cold against my thighs. The humiliation of being made to sit in my own mess made the exhaustion of my climax fall away. It was replaced with fresh desire, and a small moan was muffled against his flesh. Aidan pulled away.

"You want more?"

"Yes," I hissed.

He let go of my hair, letting me stand, and tucked his dick back into his pants. He pushed me toward the bedroom where I tried to sit down on our unmade bed.

"No," Aidan said sharply. I snapped upright, face heating. I'd completely forgotten that my leggings were drenched. "Take your clothes off."

I had to bend down to take off my boots, my eyes brushing the hand that stroked his dick through his jeans. He loved making me stand naked in front of him while he was fully clothed, touching himself while he made me wait for him to give me something, anything. I took off my shirt and bunched-up bralette, peeled away my cold, wet leggings and underwear.

"Give me your panties," Aidan said. I obeyed, and he put his hand on the back of my neck, pulling me closer. "Open your mouth."

He shoved the wad of wet fabric into my mouth, bathing my tongue in my own juices, and stood staring into my eyes. I almost couldn't take his gaze as it took in my cheeks, bulging with my own soiled underwear. Prickly tears began to well up in my eyes. Aidan pressed his lips against my forehead, offering a moment of comfort, as a few tears spilled out. I wiped my cheeks, not wanting him to see. I liked to cry when he did this—it felt cathartic—but it overwhelmed him with guilt when I did.

"Get on your knees and show me your pussy," he said.

I got up on the bed, spreading my legs for Aidan, heard the soft noise he made, and felt a tug deep inside. He slowly pushed inside me, the zipper of his jeans scraping against my skin. The pressure pushed a moan into my dirty underwear, soaked through with come and spit. I didn't want to swallow, but I didn't want to drool all over the sheets.

"God, your nasty little pussy feels so good," Aidan said. His cock began to drive deeper, and all thought fled. "You love it wet and messy, don't you, you disgusting bitch? Yeah, you do. You know this is all you're good for."

I tried to say yes, but all that came out was a desperate moan. Aidan yanked at my braids, pulling my head back and making me tighten around him. He fucked me harder, making heat rush through me until I couldn't stand any more. I screamed into my wadded-up panties as an orgasm pulsed through me, and another, and another.

Aidan let go of my hair, letting me fall forward onto the

mattress. He only let me rest for a few seconds before he told me to sit on the edge of the bed. When he pulled the soaked fabric from my mouth, spit spilled down my chin and dripped into my lap. I tried to wipe my face, but he grabbed my wrist. Aidan's other hand cupped my chin, and I opened my mouth for his dick, his other hand releasing my arm to move to the back of my head.

"Oh god, yes," he moaned, sending a jolt of excitement through me.

I loved this part, when Aidan was too lost in pleasure to come up with an insult. The wetness on my face smeared my hand as I worked his dick with my fist, sucking fast and hard. I put my other hand on his thigh, encouraging him to thrust into my throat, but he pulled away without warning, holding my head steady as he stroked with his other hand. Come burst onto my tongue, ran down my spit-slicked chin, and he gave one last groan.

For a few seconds, Aidan just stood there, catching his breath and stroking my hair. He dropped down next to me, making the bed squeal, and put his arm around me, pulling my head against his shoulder. I wiped my chin on the back of my hand, not wanting to dirty his shirt.

"You were so good, princex. You were so brave."

"I got kind of scared for a minute while we were out."

"I know. But you did it," said Aidan. The pride in his voice filled me with warmth, but I demurred.

"Only because of you," I said.

"Not really. I just kind of tricked you into letting your confidence out."

"Jerk." I nuzzled my face into the side of his neck, listening to the sound of Aidan's laugh as he squeezed me tighter. I didn't know whether I'd wear that outfit in public again, but I knew he'd have my back if I did.

# THE FIRST MOMENT I SAW YOU

Caridad Piñeiro

His presence rocked me like an 8.9 earthquake.

I had caught a glimpse of him from the corner of my eye as he approached the bar, weaving and bobbing his way through the throng of people mobbing the space. Unlike the bearded wannabe hipsters and scruffy grunge types, he was clean shaven and impeccably dressed in a bespoke navy-blue suit, white shirt, and a silk tie the color of a fine burgundy. Wavy, raven-dark hair was carelessly tousled, a shock of color against his fair skin. His looks screamed *GQ* model, and my insides clenched at the thought of breaking past that fashionable veneer, not to mention what we might do with that tie.

I gave undue attention to my glass of twelve-year-old Macallan, shifting the glass back and forth on the surface of the bar until someone jostled me. Hard muscles brushed against my back and a citrusy masculine scent teased my nostrils. Both had me salivating.

"I'm sorry. This place is a zoo," he said, his voice deep and slightly husky.

I knew who it was even before I glanced up at him, taking

my time, playing coy, not that I typically did that. I was usually more direct, but maybe it was time to change things up. Especially as amazing ice-blue eyes locked with mine and had my insides melting with heat.

Smiling, I raised my glass and said, "*No problema.*"

He grinned and somehow eased into the spot beside me, earning a muttered complaint from the man whom I'd already shut down earlier that night. With a quick look around, he said, "Do you come here often?"

I laughed and shook my head. "You know that has to be the worst pickup line ever, right?"

Even in the dim light, it was impossible to miss the flush of color that swept across his cheeks. It only made him sexier. "Worse than 'If I told you you have a nice body . . .'"

"'Would you hold it against me?'" we both said at the same time and chuckled. He had a nice laugh. Unrestrained, it melded with a devilish dimpled grin that had me imagining that mouth doing other naughty things.

The DJ came back onstage and cranked up the music, intruding on our moment. I frowned, wishing for the quiet again. As if he had read my mind, Sexy Guy leaned over and whispered, "How about we go somewhere we can talk?"

I had no doubt what he meant by "talk," and I was all for exploring what might happen.

I nodded, slugged back the watery remains of my whiskey, and slid off the stool. As I walked toward the door, he placed his hand at the small of my back, the gesture almost possessive. His hand was as hot as a brand against my bare skin, and large, since it nearly spanned my waist. Now that I was standing beside him, I felt almost delicate against his tall, nicely muscled frame.

As we stepped out of the bar and into the hotel lobby, the noise faded away. Sexy Guy applied gentle pressure and guided me toward the elevator bank. I slowed and shot him a silent question he answered by pulling a keycard out of his pocket and holding it up.

I narrowed my gaze as I peered at it. "Presumptuous much?"

As he inched closer, his lean body and oh-so-masculine scent rocked me again.

His voice was low and threaded with need as he whispered into my ear. "Babe, that dress screams, 'Fuck me,' but I won't do anything you don't want to do."

He eased away and locked that clear gaze on me. I couldn't deny I had worn the clinging sheath of red silk to say just that. I also couldn't deny that I wanted him to fuck me. I had since the moment I first laid eyes on him. And if he was going to give me control, I was going to take it.

I grabbed hold of his tie and drew him down until his mouth was barely an inch away from mine and his warm breath spilled against my lips. "So you want to play?"

He laid the rough pad of one finger on my mouth and traced the edges of my lips, the touch stoking desire in my core. "Most definitely," he said.

"I call the shots," I reminded him, defiance in my tone. With a tug on his tie, I yanked him toward the elevators.

He keyed us in and up to his room, one of the expensive suites on the top floor. The room was dark except for a small desk lamp in the foyer and the intimate light that spilled in from a floor-to-ceiling wall of windows with views of the city below. The bedroom was at the far side of the space, but I doubted we'd make it there. At least not the first time.

I strolled toward the windows and peered down. He followed and stood behind me, teasing my back with the firm wall of his chest. As I met the reflection of his gaze on the glass, it was impossible to miss the desire on his face and mine. That icy blue gaze had darkened to the color of the sea at night and his lids had grown heavy.

I reached for his hand and brought it around to lay it on my thigh. His hand trembled beneath mine. I urged him to shift upward, past the silk stockings and garter to flesh warm and damp with the beginnings of arousal.

His body shook behind me as he moved his rough palm ever higher until he laid it over my neatly trimmed bush. If my dress had said, "Fuck me," my lack of panties said, "Now!"

"Fuck," he muttered, then splayed his other hand across my midsection and drew me tight to his body. As the long, thick ridge of his cock pressed against me and between my legs, my pussy wept at the thought of having him inside. But not yet.

"Touch me," I commanded, my gaze never wavering from his. His pupils were so wide, his eyes almost appeared black.

He brought his big hands to my hips and urged me around to face him, forcing me to gaze up. He topped me by half a foot even with my four-inch heels, but then he bent and closed the distance between us. He brushed a quick kiss across my lips before moving downward, dancing his lips across the swells of my breasts, his mouth blazing hot against my skin. My nipples were tight in anticipation of his lips blessing them with his kiss, but he ignored them, earning my groan of complaint.

He arched a brow and teased, "Impatient?"

"Yes-s-s-s," I responded, sounding like a balloon losing air. The pressure of desire built as he kneeled and slipped his hands under the hem of my dress. He slowly drew it upward to reveal the barely there curls at my center; my insides clenched in expectation.

He cupped my ass with his hands as he moved forward and nuzzled the short curls with his nose a second before he licked my clit. That single stroke of his tongue nearly undid me, I was so hot and ready for him.

"Sweet," he said before he buried his head against me, licking and sucking until my knees were weak and my drenched pussy pulsed on emptiness, begging to be filled.

"Please," I pleaded, and he answered, driving first one finger and then a second into me, his strokes gentle at first until I moved against him, seeking my release. My hips urged him on as I arched against the wall of glass, one hand splayed against it for stability while I tangled my fingers in his hair with the other, holding him close. My knees and thighs trembled as the climax built inside with his mouth eating me alive and his fingers expertly fucking me.

I didn't care who could see us through that wall of glass. If anything, it excited me to think about how we looked. The big powerful man kneeling and pleasuring me, groaning against my clit as he tasted my sweetness, and his fingers, wet with my passion, drove me higher. As he stabbed his tongue into me and then retreated with a teasing love bite at my clit, I came, my body shaking. A sharp cry of pleasure escaped me as I held him to me, and he lapped up my release greedily, like a thirsty man at an oasis.

My knees gave way, but he was immediately there, lifting me up into his arms as if I weighed nothing.

I wrapped my legs around his waist, and he strode with me toward the bedroom, the insistent pressure of his cock between my legs, each step reminding me that the time for pleasure hadn't ended.

Gently, he eased me to the edge of the bed where I sat and peered up at him as he shrugged off his suit jacket while toeing off his shoes. The fine cotton of his shirt stretched across his broad shoulders and chest, scarcely containing him. When he reached for his tie, I brushed his hands away and undid it but kept hold of the ends. With a tug, I urged him down and met his lips with mine. My saltiness flavored his lips; I licked and sucked until he opened his mouth. Slipping my tongue in, I tasted him. Tasted me again and ran my tongue along the perfect line of his teeth before returning to kiss him until we were both breathless and straining together.

I released my grip on one end of the tie but only to draw it off his neck as he undid his buttons and ripped off his shirt, baring the expanse of his chest. Powerful muscles heaved as he sucked in rough breaths and fought for control. Easing onto my knees, I leaned forward to drape the tie around his neck once more and urge him near so I could kiss the tight nubs of his dark, masculine nipples.

He dragged in a breath as I did so and reached for the hem of my dress, his hands shaky. With one swift move, he yanked the fabric upward. I released my hold on the tie only long enough for him to pull off the clinging silk dress. The second I was bare, I tugged him close until the tips of my breasts teased his smooth chest and I could suck and bite at his nipples.

His muscles trembled beneath my lips as I tasted the saltiness of his skin and trailed kisses across his powerful pecs. I moved my hands down his shoulders and across leanly sculpted abs until I reached the waistband of his pants. I hesitated there, but he laid a large hand over mine and urged it down to the long, thick bulge of his cock.

I stroked him and whispered against his lips, "I want you in me. Now."

His strangled laugh was cut off by his groan as I undid his waistband and dove my hand into his briefs to encircle him. My hand barely surrounded him, he was so thick; I ached to have him fill me.

"Bossy, aren't you?" he managed to huff out, his breathing ragged while he drew down his briefs and pants and I continued to caress him.

Arching a brow, I said, "Complaining?"

He laughed again and jerked his head in the direction of the nightstand. "Only because I have to leave you for a moment."

Reluctantly I let go, but smiled as I saw the burgundy tie still dangling around his neck. One thought pummeled me. As he fumbled in the nightstand and took out a foil packet, I moved toward the headboard of the bed and crooked a finger. "Come here."

Slightly puzzled, he hesitated, so I snagged the condom from him and grabbed both ends of the tie to urge him onto the bed. "Lie down and put your hands under your head," I said.

When he complied, I drew the silky fabric to where his hands rested beneath him and gently tied them together. As I did so, my breasts brushed his face, and he shifted upward to take a nipple into his mouth and suck on it. I let him taste, but only for a second since now it was my turn to explore.

I straddled him and let my hands roam across the thick muscles in his arms and chest, loving the leashed power over which he'd let me have dominion. My pussy was dripping again, and I was sure he could feel that wetness as I shifted down his body, massaging all that masculine strength with my hands. Tasting him and leaving a trail of love bites until I had reached his immense cock.

Encircling him with both hands, I stroked him the way my pussy soon would, running my hands up and down that thick length. Bending, I licked the tip and savored the briny precome he hadn't been able to contain. He jerked beneath me with that touch and arched his hips in unspoken request.

"Tell me what you want," I said, and ran my mouth down the sensitive underside of his erection.

"You. I want you surrounding me," he said, and shifted his hips upward again.

I couldn't restrain the smile that said I was pleased that he wanted me as much as I wanted him. Snatching the foil packet from where I had tossed it on the bedspread, I quickly tore it open and drew out the condom, but that's where anything quick ended.

With excruciating slowness I unrolled the latex down his shaft, pausing to kiss and lick each inch of skin as I sheathed him in protection. His groans and sharp jerks of his hips told me he liked it, but I had no doubt about what he'd like even more.

I cupped his balls and massaged them as I poised over him, my pussy at his tip. I moved down, hardly covering him. He moaned and strained to move his tied hands forward, but he couldn't. I'd made sure to secure him to one of the rungs of the headboard.

"Bitch," he complained, but there was a hint of a grin on his face that told a different story.

"Liar," I parried and sank down onto him, gasping as his fullness finally filled me.

I stilled then, adjusting to his size; he didn't move, waiting for me. His gaze traveled across my body and settled on my face, then dipped down for a moment, betraying what he wanted.

Leaning forward, I offered up my breasts to him and he accepted, moving his mouth from one to the other, licking and biting while my pussy clenched around him with each tug and suck of his mouth.

He arched his hips into me and I ground down, fighting the pressure building inside, wanting to hold on to the sensations of his mouth and lips, of his cock swelling even more within me and the friction of his moving in and out as we drove each other to release.

As much as I wanted his mouth on me, I needed to move. I needed to feel the power of his thrusts beneath me and the resistance of his erection along the sensitive walls of my vagina, drawing me ever higher. Pushing me toward another climax.

"Touch yourself. I want to see you touch yourself," he said, the tone of his voice jagged with need.

For that moment, I relinquished my control and cupped my

breast with one hand while I reached to my center as I rode him. I flicked my nipple with my thumb and then pinched it tightly while I fingered my clit, rubbing that sensitive nub hard as the sounds of our bodies slapping together filled my ears until he came with one powerful surge of his hips.

His hoarse shout undid me. I ground myself tight and cried out my pleasure as my climax ripped through me. Tightening my pussy, I held on to it and him as long as I could before falling onto his damp chest, our bodies still joined. Long moments passed before he softened and slipped out of me, leaving me feeling both empty and satisfied at the same time.

I sat up and leaned an elbow on his chest to explore his face. That handsome face that had so grabbed me the very first time I'd seen him. A pleased smile drifted across his lips a second before his eyes opened and his blue-eyed gaze settled on my face.

"You seem very pleased with yourself," he said, the smile broadening. Laughter reached up into his eyes, which were now a blue as bright as a sun-kissed sky.

"I am. Very much so," I said and reached behind to release him from my mischievous bondage.

As soon as he was free, he rolled over and trapped me beneath him. His touch was tender, almost reverent as he cupped my face with his hands. "Happy anniversary, Katie."

I laid my hand across the sandpapery stubble of his evening beard and stroked the planes of his face. A familiar face that never failed to stir me even after nearly ten years together. "Happy anniversary, Jesse. I hope this doesn't mean our little game is over for the night," I said, and faked a pout.

"Babe, we're just getting started," he said, grabbing hold of both of my hands in one of his and pinning me to the mattress. In a blur of action, he'd whipped the tie from around his neck and wrapped it around my wrists.

At my questioning gaze, he chuckled. "Seems only fair, don't you think?"

"I'd rather not be thinking about anything if you want to know the truth," I said, and looped my bound hands around his neck to haul him close since he hadn't tied me to the headboard.

"I think I can arrange that."

# THE KING'S RETURN

**CD Reiss**

My husband leaned over the table and picked up my fork. I kept my hands in my lap because they were twisting around each other, tensing and releasing. I glanced around the restaurant. No one was looking back. Two Michelin stars meant the staff watched without watching.

"We sailed at six," he said, spearing a cube of meat. "From Skiathos." Corban pronounced it perfectly, like the native he was, with a twist to his tongue and throat that sounded alien and brutal.

"So?" I said. "You always wanted to leave early."

"We were out at sea overnight." He lifted the fork to my face. "Open, my love."

Since he'd returned, he'd been hard to resist. He'd changed in so many ways. He'd dropped all guile and pretense. He was either open and honest or he'd become a better liar since I'd left him behind.

I opened my mouth and he fed me.

"In the morning, I swam," he said. I chewed but tasted nothing. "And you pulled anchor and left."

Eyes on my plate, he moved my food around, looking for the perfect piece. He'd kept a short beard since he came back from the dead. It added a roughness that wasn't reflected in his personality anymore. I'd always believed the lies of a clean-shaven man. I'd learned to distrust a husband with a perfectly straight part in his hair and impeccable grooming. The man who returned wore the same suits, but with an ease he'd never had before.

"I left you the life raft."

"Of course." He held up the fork again. "Half a nautical mile away."

"I'm not the same person," I said, letting the food hover. "You tell me another lie or try to convince me I'm crazy and I'll kill you again."

"I have no doubt of it."

My escape from his manipulations and lies had been clean. I had a new life alone. I couldn't do it again.

I took the fork and fed myself.

"Like I said . . ." I washed the tasteless morsel down with a gulp of four-hundred-dollar wine. "I left you a raft. When I didn't hear from you, I thought the sharks got you."

"The shark was you." He smiled. There wasn't humor in his grin, but pride. "But I don't want to get hung up on the trivial."

"What do you want?" I met his gaze across the table, the flicker of candlelight sharpening the hard angles of his cheeks and jaw. His black eyebrows arched over thick lashes and hazel irises.

The waiter refilled our water glasses. He didn't ask a question or interrupt, or if he did, we didn't hear him.

"I want you," he said.

A short laugh escaped my throat. "You'll never own me. Men like you don't change."

"I believe that's true." He swirled his wine.

"Then we understand each other."

"Not fully." He took a sip and placed his glass in front of him, sucking his lips in before he continued. "I'm going to ask you to believe something different. I'm asking you to believe something extraordinary."

Three days before, he'd just shown up in the New York office of the company he owned and taken the intern's desk. In the five years between his death and that moment, I'd gotten rid of everyone who had known him. His family was far away in Greece. To everyone at the company, he was a handsome stranger in a suit whose appearance made me, the president of a multinational conglomerate, choke on her salad.

"You've heard of the term 'gaslighting'?"

"Have I been different since I've been back?"

He'd left me alone for three days. I had no idea where he was staying, and I told myself I didn't care. He sent a card through interoffice mail. Just a phone number. I called it when I'd stopped shaking.

"There's always a honeymoon phase with you guys."

"Has it been? A honeymoon?"

It hadn't been. Not by the usual standards. No romantic talk. No roses. No promises to change. Nothing.

"I'm asking you to believe that the man who broke you down wasn't who I really was. If you can believe that, I'll believe you weren't trying to murder me."

"I don't care what you believe."

He picked up the wine bottle and offered to top my glass.

"No," I said. I didn't want my judgment clouded. He'd always had a way of making me want him, even when he was in the middle of a lie.

"What I believe is secondary." He poured himself more wine. My husband never took a drop more than a single glass. All the better to control me. "What would the authorities believe?"

"You're blackmailing me?"

"Harsh words."

"What else would you call it?"

He turned his glass absently, lost in thought. My husband pierced space and time with his attention, a trait I loved when I met him and distrusted later on. I met a thoughtful man, but after our wedding day his decision-making got so fast I made poor choices just to keep up.

"I'd call it . . ." He directed his green eyes back to me, piercing again. Still, he seemed honest, and that in itself was dangerous. I could be lulled into a false sense of safety. "I'd call it a test. A deal. For me, it's a second chance. For you? It may start as a way to understand what happened between us."

"I understand it too well. I had the empty bank account to prove it. And don't apologize. Your apologies meant nothing then and they'll mean nothing now."

He took a sip of his wine. I could never read him, but as he lowered his glass he became clearer to me. The drink was a pause to both soothe a hurt and realign his strategy.

Had he changed, or had I?

*They never change. Don't forget it.*

"What's the deal, then?" I said, curiosity taking the wheel. "I want to hear it."

Putting his glass down, he leaned his elbows on the table and folded his hands like a schoolboy.

"I won't touch you. Not a hand on your body. I haven't earned that."

I took a sip of wine, nodding into the glass. *Damn straight.*

"Do you remember when we were first together?" he asked. "You were so young, and you'd do whatever I wanted?"

We'd met when I was seventeen and he was twenty-five. He wouldn't lay a hand on me until my eighteenth birthday, but that didn't keep us from enjoying each other. Back then, he'd been commanding and dominant but gentle and sweet. His tender humiliations had driven me wild with lust. I felt a pulse of wetness between my legs just remembering them.

"A case of misplaced trust," I said, crossing my legs.

"You're wet. I can tell. You're squeezing your legs together to tamp it down, but it's only making it worse."

I swallowed. It had been too long since I'd felt that damp throb. He'd been my first and my last. A man unlike any other. Devil and saint.

"My beautiful pet," he whispered in the voice of the man he was before we were married. "Uncross your legs."

I thought I'd forgotten that voice, but my body remembered it all too well. I straightened my legs and pressed my knees together. His nod was the slightest affirmation, but it was enough to swell my building lust.

"Apart," he said. "To the width of your shoulders."

My body obliged, overruling my judgment. I pushed my wine-glass away.

"What do you want?" I asked.

"Eden." He unwove his hands and laid them flat on the table-cloth. "You brought me the only happiness I've ever had, and I betrayed you. I took everything from you and convinced you it was a gift. You believed in me. You trusted me when no one else would. I want us to start over. I want you to misplace your trust again."

"Or you'll accuse me of murder?"

"For every stick, there's a carrot."

"Which is?"

"The chance to find what we lost."

What had been lost was the one warm thing in my life. A trusted lover. An unparalleled intimate. A place where I could lose myself in someone's care. I'd missed it when he changed but had forgotten to miss it since. Not until he reminded me of it.

I was insane, and I knew it. But I had my own carrot, and it wasn't regaining the most beautiful thing in my life. It wasn't the magnetism of his gaze or the sharp cut of his jaw under the soft blades of his beard.

He wanted something, and it wasn't just the love he'd thrown away. I'd never know what it was unless I stepped into his trap.

I could get out. Once I knew how he'd lived, why he'd stayed away, and what he'd come back for—I could get out.

"Not my house," I said. "You won't step foot in my house, and I'm not staying in yours."

"Agreed."

"Hotel. On my card."

"Anything you want, pet."

"You're buying dinner."

He smiled and got out his wallet. I realized my legs were still open.

We fell into it. I was seventeen again, and he was the gorgeous older guy who found me irresistible. He didn't touch me, and I kept my hands folded away from him the whole elevator ride up to the penthouse. Alone in that little room, I could smell the cologne he used to wear. It smelled of fresh sea air and crisp citrus.

"You wore that to remind me," I said. "The cologne."

"I did."

"You won't get into my head, Corban."

"Once these doors open, it's Sir."

"Until then, you can fuck yourself."

His next breath was a laugh. "You're not going to be as compliant as you were. I can see that."

The elevator stopped.

He was right about that. Things were going to be different.

The doors slid open.

The suite had two bedrooms, a living room, and windows over-looking Fifth Avenue. The curtains were wide open to the city.

I expected him to bring me to the bedroom; instead he indicated the couch.

"Sit." I set my jaw and sat with my knees pressed together. He pushed the coffee table away with his foot and moved a chair to face me. "Do you remember the rules?"

"Yes." I stared right at him. He could have my body, but not my will. "I do what you tell me. You don't touch me."

"What do you call me?"

"Sir."

"And when do you come?"

"When you say." With no more than words, my clit throbbed against the fabric of my panties.

"Good." He looked me up and down. His gaze had a physical presence. It pushed my clothes aside and left me naked. "I won't touch you without consent. Until then, you'll just do what I say. If you tell me no, I may find your request reasonable, but if I don't, I'll punish you. Got it?"

"Yes."

"Stand up."

I did.

"Pick your skirt up around your waist."

I took a long blink. This was it. It was really happening. He leaned back and jerked his chin to me as if to say, *Get on with it.*

I half stood and pulled my skirt over my stockings and around my waist, exposing my upper thighs and underwear.

"Pull your underwear down to just above your knees." Commanding and casual at the same time.

I expected this but still found myself shocked. The air crackled when it hit my skin, lighting the places between the fabric and my body as I pulled them down. I stood before him, eyes still unwavering on his so he'd look at my challenge, not my state of half-nudity.

He bent forward with his elbows on his knees as if to catch the scent of my naked pussy. "Take the underwear all the way down."

I slid them down and stepped out of them.

"Leave your shoes on."

I was naked from the waist down, but my legs were closed. My tenderest parts were throbbing but hidden. This was where he'd always made me crazy.

"How do you feel?"

"Bored, Sir."

He laughed and leaned back, looking up at me. "When did you start lying?"

I didn't answer, but I smiled involuntarily.

"Let's see what we can do about that," he said. "Sit down and open your legs."

My gaze couldn't hold him as I sat. He watched as I spread my knees a few inches.

"More."

I gave him a few more.

"I can see your cunt, but I want you to offer it."

"You know I won't."

"Lie back."

I did, facing the ceiling; the hotel chandelier was off, the crystals lit only by the moonlight through the windows.

"Legs up. Bend your knees up and out. Don't be shy, pet. It's unbecoming."

Once I did that, he'd see everything. That was what he wanted.

I didn't have to make it any fun for him. I jerked my knees up and spread them apart.

He leaned his head down between my legs, not touching but breathing me in.

"I can smell you. I can see how slick you are. I could bury my cock in you in one stroke."

I closed my eyes against what his words did to me.

"With your hands," he said, breath inside my thighs, "spread yourself apart."

Just do it.

Get it over with.

I wiggled my hands down and spread my labia.

"Asshole too. Let me see your tight little asshole."

I opened my fingers and pulled my cheeks apart too.

"Wider."

I stretched until I could feel my ass open, clench, stretch again.

"You want me to fuck you."

"No, I don't."

"Your body wants it. Your cunt is salivating, your ass is hungry for it. The day I fuck your ass it's going to feel like coming home."

"I'll never let you."

"Say the words, 'Fuck me in the ass.'"

"No."

"Why?"

"I don't want you to."

"I won't. But I want to hear you to say it the way you used to. When you used to trust me enough to beg. Remember how you used to beg? You'd say if I'd only fuck you in the ass you could stay a virgin."

"And you wouldn't." My anus clenched for it, and he saw because I was spread wide for his eyes.

"Say it, Eden. Say it for me the way you used to."

He didn't plead, he commanded, but with a nostalgia that brought it all back.

"Fuck me in the ass, Sir. I promise you'll like it. I'll be such a good girl for you if you just put your cock . . ." I stopped with the memory of it. The pain as he stretched me with his girth. The pleasure that came later.

"Put your finger in your mouth."

Even knowing what that meant, I puckered my lips around my first finger and wet it as much as I could.

"Good, my beauty." His words were barely a breath. "Put it inside you. Let me see you yield."

I paused. What else could he make me do without touching me? How far would he go?

Pressing my pointer finger to my pussy, I teased it open easily and worked one finger in. I didn't need my spit as a lubricant. My body made all the fluid I needed.

"Another finger."

I had to hitch my hips higher to get two fingers down that far, and every inch felt so good I had to resist groaning.

"Keep your labia open with your other hand. I want to see how hard and wet you are."

"Yes, Sir."

"Move your finger out and back in." I could hear his breath quicken as I did it. His arousal was a physical thing pressing against me. "Does your finger remind you of getting fucked?"

"You're so much bigger," I said, fully in the moment. "You stretch me more."

"I will again, pet. If you consent, I will again."

"I—"

*No. Don't tell him you want it.*

"Play with your clit."

With my other hand, I circled the hard, wet knob.

"Do it hard."

When I did, my fingers slipped out.

"All the way in, little bird. Move in and out. Show me how you want me to fuck it."

I shoved them in then out while rubbing my clit.

"My cock isn't going to be as gentle as your fingers. It's been a long time. You're going to cry when I stretch you. When I get so deep you feel it and when your body opens for me, it's going to break. You're going to beg so hard for me to stop. Then . . ." I was close to orgasm. He knew it. "You're going to beg me to do it harder."

"Fuck you," I gasped.

"Three fingers."

I wedged another finger inside, and another wave of pleasure came with it.

"Offer me your body."

I wanted to. I wanted his cock.

"Fuck me."

"There's a girl. Again."

"Rip me apart with your cock. Sir."

"When I permit it, you will give me your orgasm." He stated a fact. I would come for him.

"Please."

He stood over me, erection stretching his pants. The cruel rod was a threat of painful pleasure.

"You are as beautiful as ever, pet."

"Please," I whispered.

"You're mine. We're connected in ways we don't have words to understand."

"I can't—"

"You'll last as long as you need to. You have no choice. Your body knows it even as your mind resists."

I was down to wordless grunts and moans. I told myself it was okay to come. It didn't matter. I tried to let go, but I couldn't have come even if I'd wanted to. Tears of frustration streamed down my face as he watched with his club of a cock ready. I'd let him fuck me. I'd let him ram it in every hole in my body and he knew it.

"Give me my orgasm," he said.

I exploded almost immediately. My body clenched and unclenched around my fingers as I writhed under his cool gaze. I rubbed myself until I was sore because he didn't tell me to stop. He sat next to me, folded his hands between his spread knees, watching me twist.

"Give me another, my greedy little bird."

Flicking with my fingertips, I came again, crying from the intensity, gritting my teeth against the overstimulation and a growing rawness between my legs.

"You may stop."

I couldn't speak. I gulped breaths as I took my hand from between my legs and let my fingers slide out.

He handed me a handkerchief.

"Thank you."

"We're not finished." He stood.

"I can't." I straightened my legs and put my feet on the floor, steady enough to sit up but not to come again.

"I'm going to run a bath. I still can't touch you, but I can care for you."

Looking up at him was too much like seeing the man I married. The object of my devotion. The lover I learned to worship and trust. Not the husband I learned to fear.

Fear brought me back to earth.

"This isn't going to work," I said. "I'm not going to love you again."

"Maybe, Eden." He stepped back in the direction of the bathroom. "Maybe."

Maybe.

# ONE LAST GANG BANG

Joanna Angel

*for Bill Bailey*

I might be addicted to pornography.

I love everything about it: the engineered plotlines meeting the obvious sexual enthusiasm of the performers, my own pervy voyeurism as I shout, "Fuck her harder!" at the screen while vigorously rubbing my clit. I mean, I'm not a person who has stacks of XXX DVDs lying around in the open or spends all my time on a sticky air mattress or anything like that. My mattress actually boasts Tempur-Pedic foam, thank you very much . . . but it is just as sticky. I feed off the element of sexual fantasy. I much prefer basking in the joy of loud orgasms that happen from anal over feigning a connection at an awkward Tinder-date dinner followed by a disappointing four to seven minutes of missionary (if I'm lucky enough to even make *that* happen). I'd always had an urge to explore myself sexually but never knew how to find the right partner to go exploring with. Being a porn star solved that issue quite perfectly.

I've been producing and performing in porn for over fifteen years now. In my very first scene, I had anal sex on a rooftop surrounded by strangers. Not strangers working on the production set, mind you, but the actual people who lived in the building who'd heard that a porno was being shot in the place where they lived. The curious little buggers just had to come see the dirty girl who'd agreed to get railed on a rooftop. I had never had public sex before, but watching those unknown eyes meet mine as my ass was mercilessly pounded by a stranger I hired for the day, knowing their minds were empty save for feelings of lust for my body and jealousy of the dick inside me, was thrilling.

Being a sexual performer turns me from a mundane, quasi-normal person into a bona fide superhero. Call me Pussygirl; I'll stop crime by fucking every cock in sight until those evildoers are drained.

By thirty-six, I'd made almost every type of scene imaginable: solo masturbation sequences where I would slowly rub my vulva and penetrate myself with dildos of various sizes, talking directly to the camera lens as if I were imagining that I wanted it to come to life to make swift, yet tender love to me; threesomes and foursomes and orgies and double-penetration sex scenes. I'd role-played as everything from a maid to a schoolgirl; a teacher, a zombie, a vampire, and every other monster imaginable.

You could say I've pretty much done it all. I've fucked on desks in a fitted blazer and pleated pants that I drenched in my own squirt; I've fucked on circular beds (they exist) in bikinis made of nothing but Swarovski crystals. I've fucked on couches in striped kneesocks, on love seats in lingerie, on sectionals with a pin-up pompadour in my hair and bright red lips. I've poured oil all over myself inside inflatable pools in the middle of living rooms; I've gotten down and dirty outside, underneath a bridge that overlooked the Eiffel Tower and on a rock off the coast of Spain. I love every aspect of this sexual fantasy world I've deliberately and literally inserted myself into; I'm like a john hiring all the top-tier escorts in Vegas, making my wildest sexual fantasies come to life, only I'm the sex worker and the john in one, sitting in a director's chair with a dick in my ass.

But my favorite scenes to shoot were always gang bangs.

Gang bangs are absurdly hot; there's really no other way to describe them. It's not at all a natural human sex act, though it feels like a testament to the human spirit when a bunch of dudes who really have no business shoving their dicks into the same pussy *at the same time* can do so in a serious and unbelievably sexy way. I get such a rush thinking about the many-on-one scenario. For what seems like a few spectacular moments, I am the center of these men's worlds, their only goal to ravish my body and make me quake with intense, cinematic orgasms. I am known to be a bit of a brat, and this is the only true way I am the literal center of attention. Plus, I love the challenge of it, like how at times during the act I feel like I am going to drown in a sea of dick, as if there are alternating waves of dicks and pulsating pleasure constantly crashing over me until I can't even manage a breath. I love being taken for a ride, the feeling of losing complete control of my limbs and my senses. My reward is being showered in an ocean of come, then going home and eating a very large pizza, filling me even more, and feeling like such a good whore.

Which is why, for my thirty-seventh birthday, I decided to organize the greatest gang bang ever filmed. I'd shot two gang bangs previously, and this one was to be my highest achievement: The last gang bang I ever wanted to film. I wanted to create the be-all-end-all of bang scenes, an event that wouldn't just leave me sore for a few days but would also give me such an intense, pleasurable association of flesh that just touching certain spots of my body to the memory would invoke an instant physical response. I wanted a gang bang that would make my previous scenes look like low-budget, soft-core nudie flicks on late-night cable. I wanted to be made into a screen warrior queen, crowned with semen atop a throne of cocks, the monarchy clearly stable under my reign.

So I got to work getting my maximal gang bang together. I picked a day far enough in advance to make sure there was ample time to coordinate all the pieces of the penis puzzle together. See, a great gang bang is like a symphony: Everything (and everyone) must work together in harmony. One wrong minor chord could damage the flow and draw the line between seeing a person getting beautifully pounded by five large cocks and watching five men stressfully and unsuccessfully jerk off.

It's like a rock band, but in your pussy. There's a front man leading the way and doing all the showy stuff; there's a lead guitarist doing all the solos, riffs, and fills; a second guitarist supporting the lead providing a rhythmic drive; a bass player who acts as the nice, non-egomaniacal glue to hold everyone together and keep things moving without stealing the spotlight; and a drummer anchoring everything down, getting the least amount of credit for what is actually the most important job in the act. A lot of women make the mistake of thinking that the perfect gang bang is a mix of five men you really want to fuck. In actuality, the perfect gang bang is a mix of five men who can comfortably have their sweat dripping all over one another, their balls touching, their dicks comfortably coexisting in the same wet space while still focusing on the main objective of the day, which is to fuck the person in the center in the most animalistic way possible.

The first man I picked for my epic night of pleasure was Simon Holtz, a fellow industry veteran and a virtuoso of vagina stimulation. A bearded silver fox of Romanian-German descent, Simon is the kind of guy Generation X housewives fantasize about while blowing their average-looking husbands. His hair shimmers in the light, and though he does have a little more weight on him than your typical performer, he's still extremely slim. His hips are especially inviting, ones you want pressing against your pelvis as he thrusts himself into you. He's not only gorgeous, he's got a truly Zen personality to boot—nothing matters to him but pleasure, his and his partner's. When I called him up to ask if he'd be interested in participating, he crooned, "My darling Joanna, I would be simply honored to fuck every inch of your body." I just about lost it.

Of course, for every calm and silver, you need fiery and gold, which is where Mica comes in. Mica's the flair man: everything he does with his body carries a sheen of intensity with it. He's a Latino mutt, a perfect combination of Spanish gravitas and Colombian hip movements. Not only is his body chiseled to perfection—iron abs, gleaming tan skin, and triceps that could crack a walnut—his vibe is all energy, all the time. I'd fucked him before, and when I say this guy won't stop until the job is *done,* I mean it. I knew he would tire me out in the best way during this scene.

Next on deck was Nick, a kindhearted guy from Canada and another performer whom I'd been working with on and off for a good ten years. I call him the "boyfriend" of the group. He's just such a sweetie! Blond hair, dimples on both his face and ass. He's like if a boy band member grew up and actually stayed hot. It feels oddly pure every time we fuck. He's sensual, like he'll hold my head up in place when I'm getting face-fucked too hard. Or he'll grab a pillow for my knees if they're being dragged across the ground. It's the little things!

Then there's Beau. A good Southern boy and the only American in my multicultural manwich. And yes, he has the delicious Southern drawl that makes even East Coast girls fling their thongs. The first time I hired him, he showed up on set saying, "Mornin', gorgeous." I thought he was a flirty neighbor of the house I was shooting in who'd stumbled into the wrong place. Until I saw his massive, nine-inch dick; then I knew he was very much in the right place. He is a solid, fun fuck—not too much of an ego that he can't follow along and be the second or third person in line to fuck my asshole, but possessive enough where he'll take me for himself for at least a minute.

Last, but not at all least, was Johnny. Johnny's a sex soldier: tall, solidly built, with a long, stoic face dappled with gray. He very clearly and deliberately follows orders. If I tell him to suck my clit, he will. If I tell him to get behind me and rapidly fill a hole, there will be no hesitation. Not that he's incapable of improvisation, but he's got a cock like a rifle, ready to shoot off when his commanding officer tells him to. Oddly enough, his personality is fairly soft-spoken; he mostly communicates with a series of grunts and moans, which is fine with me. I could already hear his low growl in my ear, the one he saves just for the person he's fucking doggy-style, a sign to his partner that he is enraptured.

With the five guys ready and willing, I just needed a location. My first gang bang was filmed in an alleyway on the "wrong side of town." In that scenario, I played a schoolgirl who um . . . er . . . got lost on her way home. My second gang bang was in a brightly lit living room. I wore neon lingerie, without any real context to the scene other than the fact that I was horny and . . . there. So for my third and final gang bang, I chose a dungeon, something seedy enough for my dark and depraved side, but with a large selection of clean and comfortable bondage furniture, running electricity, and a shower. It's basically as if a clean living room and a dirty alleyway had a baby. The perfect place for a horny almost-thirty-seven-year-old to get her rocks off.

It was decided. I had a solid working group of five stallions booked for the appropriate date to fuck every hole in my body. I had two camera guys, a photographer, a makeup artist, and a dungeon set up to my wildest specifications.

The night before the event though, I panicked. What the hell had I gotten myself into? What if I wasn't as good of a gang banger anymore? What if no one showed up?

What if . . . I was too old?

Was I past my prime? Would I be able to perform like I had in my twenties? What if my butthole sealed shut in the middle of the night and never opened again? What if I failed to not only orgasm, but also to entertain the people I was filming this for?

My anxieties plus the betrayal of my insanely horny body made it difficult to sleep, so I touched myself while thinking about the coming event (double punitration intended). All these studs who had so readily agreed to fuck me senseless tomorrow—why wouldn't they love me? I fantasized about what would happen, directing scenes in my head that I would certainly make reality in the morning. As I climaxed, I finally relaxed. I worked hard in life and I deserved this gang bang.

I arrived at the dungeon three hours before the shoot start to get my makeup in order. As I sat in the chair, the lighting crew picked the perfect mix of eerie blues and reds to set the ambiance for the event. The lights had to be moody enough because, you know, we were in a dungeon, but still bright enough to see all the appropriate penetration going on. It's a balance. Experienced lighting guys in the porn industry understand this challenge; I'd love to see the second key grip on whatever set in Hollywood light a dungeon and a butthole at the same time and see how well they do.

The guys arrived one by one, the two older men arriving first, genially shaking hands and getting ready to do some last-minute bush trims, while the younger ones came in with their personalities already dominating the air around them. Johnny spritzed himself with cologne, Beau made some small talk about the pork ribs he'd been smoking overnight, and Mica was doing stretches. It was a mix of men preparing for battle and a romantic date mixed in one. After a few grueling hours of sitting patiently in a chair not having sex, it was time to make my Cinderella-esque entrance to the stage. As gracefully as I could in a skintight red latex dress (nothing says "I'm ready for filthy sex" more than an outfit that started off as a piece of plastic) and black fuck-me pumps, I stood and made my grand entrance to the set to enthusiastic applause. My dress hugged every one of my curves. Of course, there was a zipper down the back of the dress so everything was easily removable, since the goal was for me to be completely naked as soon as possible. The outfit worked immediately; besides the stark, male gazes I could literally feel resting upon my body, I was very quickly greeted with five towering erections. Maybe there were more, but I wasn't paying attention to what was underneath the camera guys' pants because that would simply have been unprofessional.

I walked up to the center of the dungeon and called everyone over.

"Thank you so much for being here with me today." I gave a quick rundown of the shots I wanted because I couldn't wait any longer. I had the honor of marking the sound on the clapboard, and then I loudly shouted, "*Action!*"

The scene began with me masturbating in the middle of the stage surrounded by lit torches and a wall full of hooks and other penetrative devices. This was my idea—the dungeon and the lights and the literal fire were supposed to resemble my own version of hell. But when people tell me to "go to hell," I don't take it offensively because, well, I love to travel and hell very much seems like a place I'd enjoy. I was a prisoner, set to be tortured by my demon captors unless I gave them the information they wanted.

But I was too clever for them, as their torture would become my pleasure. I am fully aware of the fact that 99.99 percent of the population fast-forwards through the "plot" of porn, but this scenario truly turned me on so I took a little extra time with it. I threw myself into it and really believed it was happening. I felt panicked and scared and my pussy was wet. I was trapped in hell and had no choice but to fuck and suck my way out.

I sat in the center of the stage, hiking up the bottom of my dress so my vulva was in full view. I started to touch myself, slowly running my fingers over my labia, my clit, my pussy. My senses were on overload. I was sweating from the fire, liquid dripping down my face into the valley between my breasts. My hands were slick from my pussy, and every part of me was already drenched.

I rubbed my clit and fingered myself furiously. One finger, two fingers, three fingers, stabbing my own insides like I was trying to murder my own pussy. I was breathing and moaning and grunting and transforming into a succubus, waiting for Lucifer to give me my treat, only today I had five devils all to myself. *What did I do to be so lucky?* I stuck finger number four inside myself and *thwack*—Mica smacked my arm away from my own body.

"You don't get to come from your hand today," he said. His accent was so sexy. And he was right. I didn't sit in rush hour traffic then go through hours of hair, makeup, and wardrobe to come from my own body part. I could do that on my own time. My orgasm was destined to be achieved through multiple penetration. *So let's get on with it!*

Mica covered my face with an executioner's hood, walking me over to where the men were waiting for me, toward a torture chamber with chains on the walls and a massive assortment of furniture for them to use at their pleasure. I heard Nick touching himself as we walked, whispering to his rugged penis like he was calming a wild tiger. I could feel the men's eyes on me, eager to start the scene and get the satisfaction they were promised. One of the men, I think it was Johnny, grabbed me away from Mica and forcefully guided me to the center of the stage. He pressed on my shoulders and made me kneel on the ground.

"Slut," I heard Mica shout in a commanding voice. "You will be fucked in every way we want unless you give us the information we need." He slapped his cock against the side of the black hood. "Will you tell us what we wish to know?"

"Never!" I shouted back as loud as I could, my voice breathy from my horniness and muffled slightly from the covering on my head.

"Then we have no choice. All right, men, fuck her!"

Mica removed the hood, and I was suddenly faced with a tidal wave of male organs, each man clamoring for some sort of penetration or stroking privilege. I felt Simon's cock first, sliding swiftly into my mouth, not even giving me a chance to breathe, his hand weaving into my hair with fierce control. He slid himself expertly down my throat; I moaned on his dick to give him positive feedback. "My god, yes!" he shouted, pounding my mouth harder. Beau had somehow slid underneath me and was fingering my ass, grabbing lube from a carefully placed prop chalice and slathering my hole with it.

Meanwhile, Nick was looking on, jerking himself to the sight of Johnny sticking the tip of his dick in my pussy, fucking my entrance just enough to tease me before he thrust himself fully inside, his huge member hitting my best spots. His penetration was so fulfilling, I almost choked on Simon as I let out a sigh of pleasure, and I surely heard him letting out a line of signature grunts. Mica stood over my chest and rubbed his unbelievably hard cock against my breasts. I could tell he was eager, but he knew that once he got going, nothing would pull him away from the hole he was going to fuck. So he contentedly looked on for the time being, but when we made eye contact, he mouthed to me, "I will be the one to make you come. You will come for me."

My pussy was pulsating, and stopping for lube was no longer necessary. Beau's cock went into my asshole immediately. Simon stopped fucking my mouth long enough for me to be flipped into the doggy position. I closed my eyes, savoring my ass being filled by Beau's sizable cock. Another dick teased my lips open and I submitted, then that one left and another came in. All the while I was reveling in the thrill of having no idea who I was sucking on. I tried to guess. I opened my eyes. I guessed wrong. I loved it.

I was suddenly thrown on my back and cocks were stuffed into my hands. I looked up to see Johnny and Simon staring down at me, their eyes confirming that they were in complete control of my hands. I jerked them off as my ass was pounded by Nick, the sweet boy finally finding his filthy side and never looking back. Beau stood off to the side, edging himself, moaning, "Fuck, oh fuck," under his breath.

I was savoring the smooth motions of getting ass-fucked and hand-fucked at the same time, when Mica finally took his place on top of me. He ran his hands over my hot chest and stomach, lying down and guiding his cock to my aching pussy, waiting until I was fully occupied with the two dicks I was rubbing to slam himself inside me and start hammering away. The steady force of Mica's fucking flung Nick out of my ass, which served as a slowing point for him as well, and he went to go join Beau on the sidelines. But, boys being boys, their cocks couldn't stay put for long. I watched them lock eyes and in an instant agreement come together in a scissor postition and massage each other's dick. I could see Beau especially loved it.

But my ass wasn't done yet—Simon and Johnny both saw the opening and left my hands to become stability tools. Johnny positioned himself underneath me and slowly but easily slid into my anus. I heard Simon say, "Make room," which Johnny did gladly. Then I unexpectedly felt a second cock enter my behind. Yes.

This was double anal. I was a completely stuffed glove filled with seasoned, professional cock.

My body felt like it was doing everything it could possibly do; it was literally and figuratively stretched to capacity. I couldn't believe my own ass. I was so proud of it. Cheerleaders were doing an epic victory dance inside of me. How long could I keep two cocks inside me? I had no idea. I wanted to keep going, and I did. I got more and more turned on, and my insides welcomed the two cocks until I didn't even feel stretched anymore, like they were just supposed to be there. Would one cock even be enough for me after this?

The two cocks in my ass fucked me deliberately, each moving in opposite patterns to keep me filled at all times, while Mica still worked my pussy, the head of his cock rubbing the walls and igniting nerves that sent wonderful tingles throughout my entire being. I felt myself become more rigid, my holes grasping on to these cocks for dear life. Then there was a thrust from all three cocks in unison, and I was coming for the second time that day, spasms crashing over me, my mind blanking out.

But the scene wasn't over, oh no. I was fucked and fucked and fucked some more. These men were like a roller coaster that I had all to myself. What did I do right in life to deserve this festival of cocks? I was so lucky.

I could feel the guys in my ass getting close to their own climaxes, the balls slapping against my asscheeks moving higher, the skin around their dicks becoming tauter. Beau and Nick must have noticed too, as they both rejoined our group, ready to achieve their final sexual feat of the day and make me once again the center of fucking attention. Nick guided my right hand to his still rock-hard dick, Beau going around to my front to tease my mouth and ask for my tongue on him. I happily obliged. Five cocks were in me, all ready to shower me with their hot jizz.

I felt Simon go first; he moaned loudly as he slammed himself deep into my ass, filling me with a hot, steady stream. That made it very easy for Johnny to follow right along, taking over my slick ass and adding his own fluids. They pulled out of me, then stood up and assumed their position to give me all the icing on my gang-bang cake.

Beau opened my mouth and let himself fuck my face. I stuck my tongue out to give him easier access to the back of my throat, and suddenly he was yelling, "Oh lord, I'm coming!" A mineral-tasting torrent filled my mouth. I licked the tip of him clean and swallowed like a good girl.

I didn't have too long to bask in that glow though, as Nick was right there and ready, holding my head still with one hand as he made himself come on my face with the other, his breathing heavy and so manly. That just left Mica, still vigorously fucking my pussy, and I sat up on him and guided his hands onto my hips so he could more easily fuck himself with my insides. He used me like the toy I was, slamming my pussy over him until his eyes rolled back in his head and he unleashed a huge load into me, once again sending me over the edge as I relished these sexy guys' come in every orifice of my body.

Everyone clapped. I'd never felt so free.

And well . . . it didn't wind up being my last gang bang, after all. I did another one six months later. I told you, I have an addiction. In that one, I played a teacher who fucked all my students. I've officially been in porn long enough to have come full circle, graduating from schoolgirl to teacher. Somewhere down the line I can be a superintendent, and maybe after I die I'll have a hallway named after me or something.

My thirty-eighth birthday is around the corner. What kind of last gang bang should I do next?

# SPIN

## Lauren Emily

Fixing a dot of glue to the rhinestone, you place the jewel at the corner of your eye.

Such a simple move, one I've seen many times since we started performing together at the end of circus school. Tonight I'm trying not to stare—my vision blurs and I need to sit down. Tights woefully inadequate, I shriek at the unrelenting freeze of the metal folding chair.

"You okay, partner?"

Your voice is warm and gravelly like you smoke a pack a day even though you've never lit up in your life. (I'm the one with the shameful habit, cancer sticks always deep in the recesses of my gym bag, where everyone else keeps green juice and roll-on arnica.) Your ice-blue eyes, glittering with four jewels perfectly in place, fix on me. A casual observer might find you cold, but I know how you care for me—every torn muscle and insecure thought and, now, chilly ass.

"Want me to do you now?"

And you had to use those words.

I nod, teeth finding my lip, remembering in the nick of time the bright red craft glitter I've spackled on over the Revlon. As you saunter toward me, shoulders wide and strong, muscles shifting under your iridescent two-piece leotard that matches mine, I tear my eyes away from your tits, small and round like two scoops of ice cream, nipples hardening in the drafty basement of this reno-vated Catholic church that's now our artistic home. I concentrate on the jewels around your eyes that seem to wink at me, the mask of contouring, fringy-fake eyelashes, and thick, black liner.

Circus stage makeup is no fucking joke.

"Get over here," you crack, even though I'm the one sitting, before—my god—straddling my lap, thighs crisscrossing with mine. And why wouldn't you? We've been inseparable since we met in circus school two years ago—twelve months of all-day conditioning and training Monday through Friday, weekends bartending (you) and waiting tables (me) to make rent, slinging vodka tonics and jalapeño poppers while trying to ignore our screaming hamstrings. Since we started rehearsing our duo for tonight's show, at certain moments I can't distinguish your limbs from mine.

Or so I tell myself when you stand over me, a cocoon of fabric shielding us from various contortionists and hand-balancers sharing the communal training space, your eyes glowing until I have to remind myself what move comes next.

"Look up." You tap a short, manicured finger on top of my head like you've done a thousand times while sticking on my eye ornamentation. Around us people mill about, miming choreog-raphy with their hands, lying on the floor pulling their legs until knees touch forehead—all in various stages of undress. We've all seen everything at this point, but right now even Lady Gaga could walk by in the buff and I'd be oblivious, too busy inhaling your scent of sweat and daisies, listening to the sweetness of your breath, savoring the sensation of your thin fingers on my most delicate skin.

Well, second most.

"Ready for squishy trapeze?" My rhinestones glued to your satisfaction, you bounce up and down on my lap and giggle with glee.

"It's called sling, moron." I finally find my voice and poke you in the arm. You flex and I roll my eyes. "For the millionth time."

"So boring." You flounce off me, and I want to pull you back down immediately. Trail my fingers down your contoured cheek and bring your lips to mine. Finally find out what you taste like: the strawberry-vanilla of your smoothie, with a dash of minty toothpaste and an element that's just uniquely you? Who cares if I also get a mouthful of glitter?

But I stay seated. To make a move now would ruin everything: our partnership in a field almost no one's crazy enough to go into, our dumb inside jokes about Therabands, our shared post-training laughter, sputtering bottled water or shoveling down trail mix before teaching beginning contortion. You're my best friend and I can't fuck that up—or worse, see you struggle to be kind as you explain, like you've done to hundreds before me, *the energy's just not there, love.*

I'm a biracial woman in a mostly white industry. You lovingly call my body "curvaceous" but I know what most producers say. Bottom line, I don't get many chances and I can't afford to blow a single one.

And yet you disarm me, goddammit.

Who's the real moron here?

"Soraya? Chloe?" Our stage manager, Kit, pink hair artfully spiked in honor of the big show, waves her arm over at my chair. "You're on deck."

Suddenly, you're by my side again. You look me in the eyes and thread your fingers through mine, squeezing until I can feel every bone. I can't tell whether my bouncing nerves are due to unrequited lust, pure terror, or a combo platter, but I could probably levitate off the ground right now, no squishy trapeze necessary.

You bump my shoulder and our eyes lock. "Soon we'll be thirty feet in the air," you whisper.

Even standing, the warmth of your legs lingers on my thighs.

Damn tights.

There's our music cue: the tinkling piano and romantic violins of Philip Glass, a safe choice for our very first professional act. When choosing the music, I wanted Hawthorne Heights, dark metal with a persistent undercurrent of longing. You'd winked at me and promised, "Next time."

Now you gaze at me, every feature chiseled in the reds and blues of the stage lights. All around us, where congregations held Mass for over a hundred years, the audience sits in folding chairs. Soon their eyes will follow us up to the rafters, faces in and out of focus as we spin.

You mouth, *Squishy trapeze,* and I smile, the tension broken. Almost.

Standing on either side of the sling, a loop of purple fabric that is strong enough to hold four people twice our size, we each stretch our right leg into the bottom, toes pointing out of our footless tights.

No going back.

Finding "your" apparatus is much like finding the one you want to fuck. Not just a one-night stand, but over and over until you know their favorite takeout place and the one gesture—a flick of the tongue or finger traveling up their thigh—that *always* gets them going. Maybe not a soul mate, but someone whose sheets you'd like to tangle for a long, long time.

Whether you're into the hard bar and tough rope of the static trapeze, the unrelenting metal circle that is the lyra hoop, or the coiled tightwire suspended between two platforms, you have to ask yourself the tough questions. Where can you get hurt and still keep going? What burns and bruises can you endure, learn to enjoy? Most importantly, what brings you the satisfaction of a thousand orgasms, the endorphins you can't get from the most potent of drugs?

In circus school, we had a year to figure it out, but like last call, the minutes flew by.

It took some convincing to get you into sling.

"I can't *do* anything with it," you whined to me that first day. Just like in life, you're polyamorous in circus: excelling at actual trapeze, at stilts, even at the pole we all struggled to master. There was no apparatus, no human, you couldn't seduce, bend to your will, climb on top of and make your bitch.

For me, there's only sling.

There's only you.

The long loop of fabric suspended from the ceiling is the best of all worlds. Like silks, a sling is soft and yielding (though fabric burns hurt like hell). Like lyra and trapeze, sling has a bottom—a place to land, to lean back on, even to get caught in when things get especially hairy. And best of all, sling is where I first learned to spin.

You, on the other hand, are the reason I realized I'm bi. Or maybe I like guys and just you. Either way, I'm forever down with dick, but the second you sauntered into the first day of circus school, red hair disheveled and babbling in French, I was a goner. Several girls have eaten my pussy since—two rather well—but in my fantasies, it's always you.

Our music hits its first crescendo. Your toes brush mine as we touch our left feet to each other, balancing on each side of the sling, a simple but lovely warm-up move that also photographs nicely.

Wait, are you staring at my tits?

No matter—the cue is here and we need to pull the sling around us.

Except you don't do that.

With a wicked grin, you reach for my hand, lacing our fingers together just like you did backstage. Only knowing our music and not our choreo, Kit starts cranking up the sling, launching us high into the air as we spin faster and faster. Your jeweled eyes never leave my boobs, and I arch my back, proud, urging you to take it in. It's then I read the instructions on your sparkling lips: *Follow me.*

We've worked together and shared a squishy trapeze long enough I can anticipate your every move. With that delicate balance of trust and *What the hell, I guess we're doing this,* I can surmise, from a simple incline of your head, that I should delicately turn around, the rosin I rubbed on the feet of my tights keeping me from slipping off completely. Entwining my right leg around the rich purple material—"like a sexy lover," as my first coach, Julie, taught me—I extend one arm out to the side for balance and slide the other up the fabric, twisting my hand in flamenco grip. I point my toe hard. Normally this action sets my arch on fire. Not tonight.

Not when your breath is sweet and hot on my neck as you slide an arm around my waist. I focus on the fabric in my fingers, try not to look down, try even harder not to come at this touch, the first of its kind from you.

"*Oui?*" you murmur in my ear the French way, not "wee" but "weh," which sounds infinitely more desirable. Glass's notes twinkle, then shatter.

"Weh," I whisper, and your hand slides down, fingers fluttering, to where it counts.

Spinning is tricky business. Some aerialists can't handle it at all, motion sickness leaving them heaving into the rosin bucket, sipping water or frantically chewing ginger candy to settle their stomachs. You're always going faster than it looks to your audience, and when you're suspended up above with only one mat on the ground that'll hardly cushion the blow if you fall, the stakes are high and they are scary.

Me, I loved spinning from day one. I get off on the risk, the looming crash of brain and body. If I don't concentrate on the fabric, take deep breaths, just plain enjoy the ride? I'm toast, as I've learned the hard way after wiping out, slamming my shoulder into hard ground one too many times, or staggering out of the fabric begging for mercy.

But when I catch the moment, spin just right, find that sweet spot of chaos and control? There's no greater high.

You shift forward just slightly, and your ice-cream tits sink into my back. I grip the fabric above me even harder, my arch starting to cramp, but I'm intoxicated from your lips brushing the nape of my neck, where an errant strand has escaped from my shellacked topknot. I know from the way the sling pulls, the audience's *ooh*s, the unobtrusive flash of the camera down below, that you're extending your leg behind you, a flawless *arabesque* like you learned in Parisian ballet conservatory with Monsieur Reynard years and years before we met.

Better to distract everyone from your fingers playing lower and lower as my clit hardens, ignoring three layers of thong, thick tights, and iridescent dance trunks. I bite my lip at the hedonism of it all.

"You like?" you whisper as the tenor vocalist on the Glass track sounds a round *oh* in harmony with my own. When you nip my earlobe, my panties become soaked, but the performer in me wants to milk this moment for all it's worth.

I grab the fabric with my extended arm and flip out, dangling above the ground with only one elbow hooked in the fabric, to the crowd's delight. We're going full-on improv, and I can already tell I'm a hair's breadth from having an orgasm in the air. Your mouth is an O of surprise, like you didn't know I had it in me.

Ha. Two can play this spin.

Our rotation slows slightly as I wrap my legs around the sling, climbing it on one side until I'm standing over you, looking down at your wicked grin.

You know just what I'm thinking as I throw my legs over my head, inverting high in the air, my legs in a flawless straddle. The audience gasps. Down below, you twist yourself into a girl-on-the-moon, sidesaddling the sling with one perfect leg crossed over the other, your hand reaching up to caress my cheek, neck muscles straining so your mouth can meet mine.

It's an upside-down kiss that would make Spider-Man jealous. I drink it in, your tongue smooth as glass as it plays with mine, our lips dancing around one another delicately, then demanding. This moment is everything I hoped it would be. The spectators cheer their approval—this is an arts crowd, no one blinks an eye at girl-on-girl—as we dive deeper, devouring each other and traveling in a gentle circle as the piano chords build.

You break away just enough to brush my lips as you whisper, "Cocoon."

"Whatever you want," I say, my voice as husky as yours.

Standing opposite each other, we touch toes—my lips trembling, my pussy wet with anticipation—as we reach behind us, gently but efficiently fanning out the taut fabric until it billows around us. Now we're more rocking than spinning, you're straddling me once again, but I have questions.

"You want me?"

"Since the first time I stuck rhinestones on your face," you rumble in my ear.

I pull back, conscious of the warm air around us and the fact that people are waiting for us to do something, *anything,* when all I want is for you to fuck me. My adrenaline is on full blast, my instincts screaming *You could fall at any moment,* but I lean into the spin, not knowing what will happen next: total disaster or utter bliss.

As I slide my hand around your neck, you pull your face into an exaggerated mock-terrified expression. "You look like this," you say, mascaraed eyes so wide they might pop out of your skull at any second, slapping your hands *Home Alone*–style, and I burst out laughing.

"But seriously," I whisper, "what do we do now?"

You arch an eyebrow, smirking, and I wonder breathlessly whether you've planned this airborne seduction all along. "Lie back."

I do just that, settling into the womblike atmosphere and knowing the fabric will hold and catch me, *us.* Scooting the fabric under my arms, I run my fingers along the edges—the most finicky part that *never* billows out when you want it to. I play lightly along them, leaning my head back and making a bit of it. I see the audience upside down and smile at the distorted view, one that circus performers all seem to share as we cast off the comforts of homes, day jobs, and steady paychecks in favor of this wild life that underpays us, coats us in sweat and sequins, and leaves us fulfilled enough for ten normal folks.

In the cocoon you rub my clit, toying with it like Glass's musicians at the piano keys. I arch my hips, moving my arms outside the sling in a way I hope is graceful, trying not to let my features go into ecstasy-twist. But the way you're touching me, like you've always known exactly what I like, combining featherlight strokes with gentle flicks, challenges my frozen smile. You've worked your hand underneath my costume without removing my bottoms (we all have strong hands), and as you glide two fingers into me, I can feel the permanent trapeze callous on your finger and somehow that turns me on even more.

I hear the audience laughing.

Fuck.

Then I realize what you're doing: poking your legs out of the other side of the cocoon, toes pointed, thighs and calves and feet articulating gorgeous patterns. Meanwhile, in the sling, you yank down my layers just enough to suck my clit as you fuck me with your fingers.

"Oh!" I cry, the world spinning upside down. The audience *definitely* heard that one, but at this point I don't care, because I'm fucking your beautiful face and your pretty lips feel so wonderful against my hardened nub as you eat me like you're starving, swirling your legs as I return one arm back in the sling to push you harder against me, stroking your smooth skull, keeping my eyes wide open and gasping out loud as the stained glass windows of the church lose focus and I'm lost in you.

I look up as you're wiping your mouth on my thigh, lips slick and shiny with me. Crawling on top of me, you murmur in my ear, "Let go," and I purr at your scratchy timbre.

I do just that, my legs wobbly and my trust cemented.

*Whomp.* The sling shifts, forming a perfect basket around my ass as you twist your legs around my waist, holding me tight. The fabric is like a swing, and we are all out there. Your ice-blue eyes shine into mine, brighter than any lumen, as the music swells its end.

I know we'll have to talk about this. The sudden shift in our relationship, the duo we'll definitely have to rechoreograph.

But for now, the audience is hooting and hollering, and you whisper in my ear, "Hey, Soraya, you have glitter on your pubes," and my thoroughly satisfied chuckle echoes off the rafters.

Up in the air, we spin.

**JOANNA ANGEL** is an award-winning adult film star, director, producer, best-selling author, entrepreneur, and CEO of the venerated adult studio Burning Angel Entertainment. She was inducted into AVN's Hall of Fame in 2016 and continues to make her mark on the adult industry and the world at large.

**LORETTA BLACK** is a connoisseur of fine and unusual erotica. She resides in the North of England with a very badly behaved cat and an overflowing trunk of impossible ideas.

Born in Brooklyn and raised in the New South, **ALEXA J. DAY** (alexajday.com) loves stories with just a touch of the inappropriate and heroines who are anything but innocent. Her literary mission is to stimulate the intellect and libido of her readers. She lives in central Virginia with her cats.

**KATHLEEN DELANEY-ADAMS** is a queer high femme performer, author, cupcake baker, and rescuer of all living creatures. She resides in Atlanta with her butch husband, several dogs, cats, a possum named Mabel, and a murder of five crows. She has been published in a dozen erotic anthologies.

**JUSTINE ELYOT** has been writing erotic fiction for over a decade. First published by Black Lace, she has also written best-selling novels and short fiction for HarperCollins Mischief, Xcite, Totally Bound, and many others. Her latest novel, *The Story of Jo,* explores a BDSM ménage dynamic and was published by Sinful Press in 2018.

**EMERALD** (TheGreenLightDistrict.org) is an erotic fiction author interested in elevating discussion of and attention to authentic sexual experience. Her first short story collection, *If . . . Then,* was released in 2014, and her second, *Safe,* was the bronze winner in the Erotica category of the 2016 Independent Publisher (IPPY) Awards.

**LAUREN EMILY** (laurenemilywrites.com) writes erotica for Bellesa.co. Her smut has been published in *BUST* and *Between the Covers: A Bookstore Erotica Anthology* (Volumes, 2018). Lauren contributes to *Playboy* and *SELF* and is the author of the YA novel *Satellite* (World Castle Publishing, 2017). She hangs in the air and contorts her body weekly.

**ANNA MIA HANSEN** (AnnaMiaHansen.com) is a writer from Australia. She draws on her mixed heritage—her mother is Japanese and her father is Danish—to craft the fantastic worlds that feature in her fiction. She holds a PhD in Old Norse literature and is working on a steamy space-opera trilogy.

**STELLA HARRIS** (stellaharris.net) is an author, intimacy educator, and sex coach who teaches everything from pleasure anatomy to communication skills to kink and BDSM. Look for her book, *Tongue Tied: Untangling Communication in Sex, Kink, and Relationships,* also from Cleis Press.

**BALLI KAUR JASWAL**'s (ballijaswal.com) latest novel is *The Unlikely Adventures of the Shergill Sisters.* Her internationally acclaimed novel, *Erotic Stories for Punjabi Widows* (Harper Collins/ William Morrow), was selected by Reese Witherspoon's Hello Sunshine Book Club in 2017. Jaswal's nonfiction has appeared in the *New York Times, Harper's Bazaar India, Conde Nast Traveller India,* and Cosmopolitan.com.

**QUINN LeSTRANGE** is a fiction writer with a bachelor's degree in architecture. She considers herself a chameleon of romantic fiction, crossing boundaries between paranormal, historic, contemporary, and BDSM. She is based in the Los Angeles area, searching for the perfect cup of espresso and her next explorative inspiration.

**A. Z. LOUISE** is a civil engineer-turned-writer, whose conure keeps them company during the writing process. When not reading or writing, they can be found playing folk harp, knitting, or arguing with their sewing machine.

**ANGEL LEIGH McCOY** (angelmccoy.com) has been a professional game and fiction writer for over two decades. Her work has appeared in numerous publications—*Strange Aeons, Clockwork Chaos, Vile Things, Pseudopod, Fear of the Dark, Beast Within 2*—and includes the novelette *Charlie Darwin, or the Trine of 1809* (Nevermet Press).

**LEE MINXTON**'s erotic writing has appeared in *Forum* (UK), the Good Vibrations webzine, the Blowfish catalog e-newsletter, and the anthologies *Best Gay Erotica of the Year, Volume 3; Big Man on Campus; Surprise;* and *Naughty Stories From A To Z, Volume 4.*

**CARIDAD PIÑEIRO** (caridad.com) is a transplanted Long Island girl who has fallen in love with the Jersey Shore. When Caridad isn't taking long strolls along the boardwalk, she's also a *New York Times* and *USA Today* best-selling author with over a million romance novels sold worldwide.

**CD REISS** (cdreiss.com) is a *New York Times* best-selling author, which inflated her ego for about a minute. She promised her husband they'd only move to Los Angeles for three years while she got her master's degree in screenwriting from USC. A decade later, they're still there.

**JAYNE RENAULT** (jaynerenault.co) is a long-winded smutty wordsmith who likes to fill her pages with bisexual babes, scandal and infidelity, smug masturbation, and a little magic. A good metaphor turns her on more than a pretty face ever could, and she is the resident Smut Queen at Bellesa.

**ANGORA SHADE** (angorashade.blogspot.com) is an American erotic romance author living in Europe. She enjoys creating stories that surprise, amuse, or tease the reader, providing an alternative outlook to the monotony of someone's usual day.

**SIERRA SIMONE** (thesierrasimone.com) is a *USA Today* best-selling former librarian (who spent too much time reading romance novels at the information desk). She lives with her husband and family in Kansas City.

**SABRINA SOL** (sabrinasol.com) is the *chica* who loves love. She writes sexy romance stories featuring Latina heroines in search of their Happily Ever Afters. Sabrina and her books have been featured *in Entertainment Weekly,* PopSugar, and on Book Riot's list of "100 Must Read Romantic Comedies."

By day, words by **A. ZIMMERMAN** are found in ads, instructions in technical manuals, and on menus describing decadent desserts. By night, she lets her words take a decided turn for the erotic, crafting short stories full of adult pleasures that may be found in numerous magazines and anthologies.

# ABOUT THE EDITOR

**RACHEL KRAMER BUSSEL** (rachelkramerbussel.com) is a New Jersey–based author, editor, blogger, and writing instructor. She has edited over sixty books of erotica, including *Best Women's Erotica of the Year, Volumes 1, 2, 3,* and *4; Best Bondage Erotica of the Year, Volume 1; Dirty Dates; Come Again: Sex Toy Erotica; The Big Book of Orgasms; The Big Book of Submission Volumes 1* and *2; Lust in Latex; Anything for You; Baby Got Back: Anal Erotica; Suite Encounters; Gotta Have It; Women in Lust; Surrender; Orgasmic; Cheeky Spanking Stories; Bottoms Up; Spanked; Fast Girls; Going Down; Tasting Him; Tasting Her; Please, Sir; Please, Ma'am; He's on Top; She's on Top;* and *Crossdressing.* Her anthologies have won eight IPPY (Independent Publisher) Awards, and *Surrender* and *Dirty Dates* won the National Leather Association Samois Anthology Award.

Rachel has written for *AVN, Bust,* Cleansheets.com, *Cosmopolitan, Curve,* The Daily Beast, Elle.com, Fortune.com, *Glamour,* Gothamist, *Harper's Bazaar,* Huffington Post, *Inked, InStyle.com, Marie Claire, Newsday, New York Post, New York Observer, The*

*New York Times, O: The Oprah Magazine, Penthouse, The Philadelphia Inquirer,* Refinery29, RollingStone.com, The Root, Salon, *San Francisco Chronicle,* Slate, Time.com, Time Out New York, and Zink, among others. She has appeared on "The Gayle King Show," "The Martha Stewart Show," "The Berman and Berman Show," NY1, and Showtime's "Family Business." She hosted the popular In the Flesh Erotic Reading Series, featuring readers from Susie Bright to Zane, speaks at conferences and does readings and teaches erotic writing workshops around the world and online. She blogs at lustylady.blogspot.com and consults about erotica at eroticawriting101.com. Follow her @raquelita on Twitter.